Praise for S
pours in from read...

A WINDOW TO THI
(One of the Top Ten Christian Novels of 2005: *Booklist* magazine)

A high school teacher in Minnesota says, "It was amazing! I could hardly put it down and snuck it to school to finish the last couple chapters because I just couldn't wait...Thank you for writing one of the most entertaining and thought-provoking books I have ever read."

Sara Mills, at www.christianfictionreviewer.com, says, "POWERFUL... When I finished the last page, all I could think was, WOW...I highly recommend this book, and applaud Susan Meissner for writing so eloquently what is almost impossible to put into words."

THE REMEDY FOR REGRET
Kelli Standish, at focusonfiction.net, says, "Meissner's incredible gift with words has never shone truer...A must for any discerning reader's library."

Publisher's Weekly says, "The novel is readable if not deeply involving, and it refrains from the high melodrama present in many contemporary Christian novels for women."

IN ALL DEEP PLACES
Author Mary DeMuth *(Ordinary Mom, Extraordinary God* and the novel *Watching the Tree Limbs)* says, "LOVED the book. Couldn't put it down...Lyrically written, sensitively wrought.... captivated me from page one."

ArmchairInterviews.com writes, "Susan Meissner has once again skillfully examined the basic truth of what it is to be alive in the world, with all the good and all the bad that is there. But she doesn't leave it at that. She gently reminds us that it is God's grace and love that will see us through the night...Meissner's books are must-reads."

A SEAHORSE IN THE THAMES

Michelle at edgyinspirationalauthor.blogspot.com writes, "For me, *A Seahorse in the Thames* was a completely riveting and thoroughly engrossing novel unlike any I've read this past year…This book was truly hard to put down…Meissner also tucks a wealth of life-changing spiritual material seamlessly into the pages of this novel. In many ways the message she delivers is subtle, yet it rings with such a profound and universal truth that for the believer the lesson goes straight to the heart of the matter."

Reviewer and blogger Paula Moldenhauer writes, "I was on vacation and looking forward to reading in the car. I picked up several different books, but they just didn't draw me in. I needed something to capture me—either with the beauty of the writing or the brilliance of the story. I kept trying to read the other books I took, sighing, and putting them down. Then I opened the first page of *A Seahorse in the Thames*. I was immediately drawn into the beautiful writing and intrigued by the story. I'd never read anything by Susan before, but I found a new favorite in Christian authors. *A Seahorse in the Thames* is a beautiful love story combined with a very real voyage through family crisis, broken relationships, buried lies, and haunting questions."

For a complete list of Susan Meissner's books, including her riveting suspense series The Rachael Flynn Mysteries, please see page 282.

Blue Heart

Blessed

Susan Meissner

HARVEST HOUSE PUBLISHERS

EUGENE, OREGON

Cover by Left Coast Design, Portland, Oregon

Cover photos © Deborah Jaffe / Digital Vision / Getty Images; Steve Cole / Photodisc / Getty Images

Susan Meissner is published in association with the literary agency of Alive Communications, Inc., 7680 Goddard Street, Ste #200, Colorado Springs, CO 80920. www.alivecommunications.com.

BLUE HEART BLESSED
Copyright © 2008 by Susan Meissner
Published by Harvest House Publishers
Eugene, Oregon 97402
www.harvesthousepublishers.com

Library of Congress Cataloging-in-Publication Data
 Meissner, Susan, 1961-
 Blue heart blessed / Susan Meissner.
       p. cm.
 ISBN-13: 978-0-7369-1917-3
 ISBN-10: 0-7369-1917-1
 1. Single women—Fiction. 2. Priests—Fiction. 3. Fathers and sons—Fiction. 4. Friendship—Fiction. I. Title.
 PS3613.E435B58 2007
 813.'6—dc22

                                                                                    2007019255

Printed in the United States of America

            08 09 10 11 12 13 14 15 16 / LB-NI / 10 9 8 7 6 5 4 3 2 1

For Stephanie
because she loves a love story…

There are three things that are too amazing for me,
four that I do not understand:

> the way of an eagle in the sky,
> the way of a snake on a rock,
> the way of a ship on the high seas,
> and the way of a man with a maiden.

Proverbs 30:18-19
New International Version

ONE

She is absolutely stunning, the woman standing in front of me wearing my wedding dress.

Her name is Vanessa and she is drop-dead gorgeous like all Vanessas are. Shining hair, copper skin, and mocha-brown eyes. Teeth to put dentists out on the street. Soothing voice. A well-placed mole on one cheek.

The dress made for me hangs on her like art. Like it was painted on her perfectly formed body by a master of the canvas.

To make matters worse, I'm certain she knows it. Posing before the three-paneled mirror in my boutique, Vanessa is amazed at what she sees in the glass. She looks like Cinderella seconds after a fairy godmother's wand has waved away the stained muslin, and the mistreated heroine realizes there will never be another dress like this one, this one that will change her life.

Vanessa's mother, Lucille Something, stands next to her daughter, smirking. She's the one who yanked my dress off its mannequin at the back of my shop after Vanessa had walked right past it. She insisted that her daughter try it on. The MOTB now opens her mouth. "Oooh, Vanessa!" she gushes. "It's lovely. Just perfect."

Of course it's perfect. I curl my lips into a thin line. Words are forming in my head. Words of protest.

The bride-to-be begins to giggle and flashes us her Miss America smile. She swishes my dress and it still whispers my name.

Daisy. Daisy.

It's one of the many things I loved about that dress, the way the tulle and chiffon became a duet that spoke my name when rustled.

"Oh, Mom! It is gorgeous, isn't it?" Vanessa twirls to face her mother.

Daisy.

I feel a surge of adrenaline shoot through my body and in my mind I tell my beautiful dress to please, please stop saying that. I can't think straight.

Daisy.

"You know, Vanessa, I really didn't think you'd find anything in a used wedding dress shop. I mean, *really.*" Lucille speaks as if the owner of this sorry establishment—that would be me—is deaf or gone or Vulcan. "I was going to try and talk you out of coming here. But just look at you. You look divine. Who would've guessed?"

"See? I told you this was a one-of-a-kind place." Vanessa catches my eye in the reflection of me as she turns back to face the mirrors. She smiles a conciliatory grin that says, *Pay no attention to my mother. She can be rude sometimes.* Vanessa's eyes fall back on the dress. "It really is perfect, isn't it?"

This is usually when I say something like, "That's the dress for you, Vanessa." Emily. Kate. Tasha. Whomever. "Shall we see if there's a veil you like?"

But that's not what comes out of my mouth.

"Well, I don't know," I mumble instead.

Three heads swivel in my direction. Vanessa's. Lucille's. And my mother's. Out of the corner of my eye I can see my mom at the cash register, shaking her head ever so slightly. She thinks I can't see her.

No, she probably knows I can.

"What do you mean, 'I don't know'?" Lucille replies. The little laugh in her throat suggests she can take a joke.

"The thing is, I don't know that I can actually sell you that dress." I inject a modicum of lament into my tone. Like, *Golly, I wish I could sell you that dress, but I just can't.*

"Oh, no!" Vanessa's perfect face droops with disappointment. "Is it being held for someone else?"

"You could say that," my mother mumbles.

I toss my mother a look across the store, but she's marking a new shipment of earrings. Her head is down and all I see of her is her silvery-gray hair and a lime-green neck scarf.

"Why didn't you say so before she tried it on?" Lucille says to me. Like her daughter, Lucille's facial expression has also morphed. But I wouldn't say it's oozing disappointment. She is mad.

"I, uh, I'm sorry. I was only paying attention to what Vanessa was taking into the dressing room. I didn't realize this one had been taken off its mannequin."

I sense that my mother has lifted her head again.

A mother always knows when her child is lying.

"Well, for heaven's sake! Why is it out here with the rest of the gowns?" Lucille growls. She places a manicured hand on her hip for emphasis. Just in case I wasn't getting the idea that she's ticked. "It's not marked that it's being held!"

A new thought occurs to me. "It's actually not marked at all."

The gray head at the front of the store goes back down. I'm not lying about that. There is no price tag on my dress.

Lucille purses her lips but says nothing.

"Is the other person sure she wants it?" Vanessa's voice is so hopeful. I study her face for a few moments just to be able to drink in the look and taste of that kind of expectation.

"Not entirely." My voice sounds funny. Lucille is too mad to notice. Vanessa, too disappointed. My mother has surely picked up on it but she says nothing.

"Well, can you let me know the minute she decides she doesn't want it?" Vanessa has turned back to the glass, to the image of herself in the perfect wedding gown.

"Of course I can. And I've lots of other dresses for you to try on. That first one you picked out was worn by a woman who married a classmate from kindergarten. They hadn't seen each other in over twenty years, and then one day they met up again at a grocery store."

Vanessa just stares at my dress on her body.

I try again. "One of the others you have was worn by a woman who waited four years for her fiancé to awaken from a coma. They were married last spring in Rome."

Vanessa sighs. "What's the story on this dress?" She strokes my dress longingly, practically pouting.

I stiffen just a tad. "It's not that great a story."

Vanessa motions for her mother to tackle the zipper and as she does so, I see the tiny blue-satin heart that is blessed and sewn into the backs of all the used wedding dresses I sell at Something Blue. My little way of recommissioning these gowns of wonder. And removing any mental link to a past sometimes best forgotten.

Vanessa steps down off the mirrored platform, lifting the fairylike skirt. "Why? What happened? Did the couple get divorced?"

"No," I answer. "They didn't get married."

"Why not?"

I lick my lips. I've told this story many times over the past year, but that doesn't mean it gets any easier. I shrug as if to suggest I really don't know all the reasons why Daniel called off our wedding ten days before we were to say "I do."

"Well, the couple just decided they weren't right for each other."

"Why didn't the woman just take the dress back to the store where she bought it?" Lucille, too, has been pulled into the tale of woe. "She hadn't worn it."

Oh, Lucille. I had worn it. Many times in my bedroom in the weeks leading up to what was supposed to have been my wedding day. But I know what Lucille means. The dress Vanessa is wearing is technically a new, never-been-worn garment that's usually worth more than the truly used items in a resale shop.

"She had the dress custom-made, actually."

"Well, surely the seamstress could've found another buyer. A gown as beautiful as *that*."

I clear my throat. "Um, perhaps, but the girl kind of...held on to it for a while."

"Ah, so it was the guy who dumped *her*." Lucille nods her head. Like she understands everything.

I feel bile in my throat. After all these months I still feel it.

"That's so sad." Vanessa's beautiful features are crisscrossed with empathy.

"Better to find out those things *before* the ceremony than after." Lucille's tone is thick with matronly self-assurance.

"Do you know this girl? Is she okay?" Vanessa is too good to be true. Hopeful. Kind. Compassionate. Beautiful even when she pouts. I should let her have the dress. I should just give it to her. I hear the Voice of Reason within me, my alter ego to whom I journal every night, poking me, prodding me. *Give her the dress. Give her the dress.*

I cough. "She's all right," I toss my head slightly to shake away the words I don't want to hear. "She knows there's someone else out there who's going to sweep her off her feet. Someday."

"Well. Of course there is," Vanessa chirps, and she turns toward the dressing rooms.

"I wouldn't be so sure of that," Lucille mutters.

"But I still want this dress." Vanessa begins to walk away. "If the other gal doesn't want it, I do. I don't care about its first life. Besides, I believe in those little blue hearts you sew into the dresses. And I *don't* think it's possible for a dress to be cursed. So I want you to call me if she changes her mind. Okay?"

What else can I do but nod my head. "Certainly."

And as Vanessa walks away, the dress swishes and sways. I hear my name in every step.

TWO

When I was little I used to wonder why all little girls weren't named after flowers. It seemed the most natural thing in the world to be called Daisy, to share the name of something known across the entire planet as being cheerful and lovely. I remember feeling a sense of pity for Allison, my best friend in first grade, whose name meant nothing. Her name conjured no happy mental images. My room was wallpapered with daisies. Hers, with mermaids. Absolutely no connection whatsoever. Poor thing.

It wasn't until I was in junior high that I realized my name was not only synonymous with merry, white-petaled flowers but also with Donald Duck's love interest as well as all things bovine. It was hard to be twelve and be Daisy. The popular girls in my suburban Minnesota school tended to ignore me; the rest displayed a strange kind of compassionate pity for the girl with a name that evoked images of Holsteins. The boys? Well, most of them had watched enough reruns of *Dukes of Hazzard* to be able to properly remind me that life is not always fair. And people named Daisy often don't get much respect.

I never let on to my father that the lovely name he chose for me didn't have the same cultural appeal as Jessica, Heather, or Natalie. The fact that my parents had a baby girl *to* name was actually remarkable in and of itself. Statistically speaking, I shouldn't have been conceived at all. I was born to a historically infertile couple who'd abandoned all hope of producing a child more than a decade earlier. In resignation, they'd adopted my older brother, Kellen, from Korea after years of failed attempts to conceive.

My parents were both forty-four years old when I was born, and Kellen was in his senior year of high school. Do the math and you'll see that when I was twelve and wrestling with the merits of my name, my parents were both fifty-six years old. They were grandparents already.

It should come as no surprise then that my self-esteem suffered in those pre-teen years. I wanted to love my name. I wanted to be proud of my parents. I wanted to brag I had been an aunt since I was eight. But all of those things made me different. Not special. And being different in junior high did not seem like a good thing. Fitting in would have been nicer. And that was something I couldn't do.

There was really only one time in those awful, awkward years when I felt uniquely preferred by someone my own age. I would end up comparing every boyfriend—even Daniel—to the boy I met the summer I turned thirteen.

His name was Skip Holdeman and he and his parents and little brother were staying with a family from our church while on furlough from the mission field. Skip and his family were missionaries to Thailand. He was a year older than me, had settled into his man voice already, and was boyishly handsome. When he started hanging around me at church and talking to me at softball games and ice-cream socials, I chalked it up to him being new and not knowing any better. But the more he tagged after me, the more I came to realize Skip was fully aware that I was named Daisy, that my parents were born during the Depression, and that I was an aunt.

Maybe it was because I wasn't a flirt and he liked that. Maybe it was because I was actually interested in his life as a missionary kid. Maybe it was because he had a fondness for dimples—I have two. I don't really know why Skip took a liking to me. But I've never forgotten that he did or what it felt like. I think that's why I fell so hard for Daniel fourteen years later. To be chosen over anyone else in the world is a pretty heady feeling.

When Skip left that summer to go back to Thailand we agreed to exchange addresses, and he handed me his on half an index card. When I reached out to take it from him he seemed to lean forward a little. Like he was going to kiss me. I was scared to death he would and scared to death he wouldn't. His lovely blue eyes were tight on mine and he seemed to be at war over whether he should or shouldn't. I doubt he had ever kissed anyone before. I certainly hadn't. Nor had I ever been kissed. And I was too astonished to properly encourage him. I just stood there, transfixed by the notion that a boy wanted to kiss me.

He didn't, though.

But I took some comfort in the knowledge that he appeared to be angry with himself for having passed up the opportunity. He was moody the rest of the day.

We wrote to each other a few times after he left. At some point during that first year after I met him, Skip stopped returning my letters. My mother, who had been told nothing but had sensed everything, told me it's hard to maintain a relationship when you're young and so far away from each other.

What she said made sense, but I didn't want to talk with her about my wounded heart. And yet I wanted very much to be able to vent to someone. That's when I invented Harriet.

I decided I needed someone like Dear Abby or Ann Landers to whom I could pour my heart out and who could then write back and give me good advice. Writing to Harriet was easy. I just bought a notebook and started journaling to Dear Harriet.

Getting good advice back from her, however, meant traipsing into the territory of the absurd because in the end I wrote *myself* back. I became Harriet. I wrote all of Harriet's responses to my troubles. And to be honest, I still do. I still like to dump on my alter ego and then advise myself of what I should do. Yes, it's odd. But really, it's no more peculiar than talking things over with yourself, which we all do. Besides, when I'm in crisis I usually know what I should do, I just need affirmation. Or a kick in the pants.

Honestly, I really don't care what others might think of Harriet. I got through the distress of losing Skip by ranting to her and reading her answers back to myself, which began with *Boys are pigs* and morphed into *You barely knew him. He lives on the other side of the world. The chances of you seeing him again are pretty slim. You need to open your heart up to other people. People you can see.*

This was actually pretty good advice.

It took awhile, but I finally allowed myself the luxury of falling in love again. The second time it was with a high-school classmate named Ryan. We dated through our junior year and into our senior year, but we conveniently got bored with each other at the same time, which meant when we broke up I didn't feel like I'd been sliced in two. My journal entry to Harriet the day Ryan and I called it quits was something like this: *It's over with Ryan and me. We agreed we're just not meant for each other. I hope I haven't totally ruined my life. I hope he wasn't the one God picked out to be my life partner, 'cause I've totally messed it up if I'm supposed to marry him.* And Harriet wrote back, *Are you kidding? You've been wanting to break up with him for weeks. He's not the one and you know it. Go eat some chocolate. You'll feel better.*

I dated a few guys during my college years. No one particularly special. No one Harriet really liked, if you know what I mean. And I was kind of counting on meeting a nice Christian guy at college. When you spend the money my parents did for an education at a private Christian college, you tend to expect it. Anyone who doesn't isn't being completely truthful, as Harriet would say. Actually she would say they were lying.

But I graduated with my marketing and graphic design degree without a ring on my finger. I was a bridesmaid three times over that summer. I pretended this did not bother me, but Harriet knew better. After one of the weddings I wrote in my journal: *I feel all mixed up inside. I mean, I'm happy for Lindsey. And she looked so beautiful today. I loved her dress. But something's keeping me from being completely happy for her. It's like I wanted her to trip while walking down the aisle or wake up with pink eye this morning. I don't know what's wrong with me.*

And Harriet wrote back…*Yes, you do. You're jealous.*

Tell me I didn't already know that.

My Harriet is no different than the voice you have inside of you, telling you the truth even when it hurts.

And oh, how it does hurt. I have three whole notebooks on loving Daniel and losing him. Writing them killed me. And kept me alive.

I'm halfway through the fourth.

I will write in it tonight after my mom and I have closed up Something Blue. After she chides me for lying to Lucille about not seeing her take my dress off its mannequin. After I've watched a cheesy chick flick. After I've called my best friend, Shelby, who is also my ex-maid of honor.

I will crawl into bed with a cup of tea and I will tell Harriet I had a chance to sell my wedding dress today and blew it.

And she will write back…*So what else is new?*

THREE

I made a bride paper doll for the first time when I was nine. Her name was Elisabeth with an "s" and she was skinny, ridiculously flat-chested, and had my boring brownish-blonde hair—a shade produced by combining burnt sienna and maize Crayola crayons in thick, waxy layers. Elisabeth was cut from white tagboard I bought at the drugstore with my own money.

My limited drawing capabilities produced her scrawny arms that stuck out at forty-five-degree angles. She looked like an informant being frisked. The open arms made it difficult for Elisabeth to hold the many varieties of bridal bouquets I made, but honestly, the attempts to give her arms bent at the elbow were laughable. I nearly ran out of tagboard and patience before I realized I had set the bar way too high for myself.

I made Elisabeth's wedding gown before any other article of clothing, cutting it from wedding wrapping paper and gluing swirls of glitter onto its massive, lampshade-shaped skirt. Unskilled at that age in spatial relationships, it never occurred to me that the copious amounts of fold-over tabs I included on the skirt would never be anywhere near Elisabeth's body. The dress had to hang onto Elisabeth with tiny, baby-tooth-sized tabs at the shoulders and waist, and so it was forever falling off her. The veil, bedecked with daisies—what else?—sprouted from Elisabeth's head like a geyser, but I remember being fairly pleased with the end result and showing Elisabeth to my mother when the ensemble was finished.

Mom had oohed and aahed over the dress as well as over Elisabeth, who I held stone-still in my hand so the dress wouldn't fall off.

"You should make her a trousseau," Mom had said.

I had responded by asking what a "true sew" was. I distinctly recall picturing those words in my head just like that. Mom went on to tell me a bride's trousseau was the collection of new clothes she took on her honeymoon.

Well, that seemed like a pretty good idea to me. I set to work on a fascinating wardrobe of checked skirts and tops, evening gowns with ruffles and lace, and sundresses with matching hats. When I was done with all the clothes, I proudly showed them to my mother.

"How lovely!" Mom said. "Now all Elisabeth needs is a groom."

I clearly remember making a face. "Does she have to have one of those?" I said.

Mom had laughed. Sweetly, not heartlessly. "It's kind of hard to get married without one," she had replied.

Ain't that the truth.

I don't know when my fascination with everything bridal truly began. Mom has assured me that all little girls are captivated by wedding gowns and beautiful brides and the whole queen-for-a-day idea. It's the essence of fairy tale, she has always said. I don't think she ever found it odd that when I was a kid I made a new bride paper doll every six months, sometimes giving one paper doll six or seven different gowns to choose from. Nor that I never drew a groom.

As I grew older, I gave myself over to dreams of becoming a fashion designer, but the truth is, I've always had far more vision than talent. I can envision something grand and plan it, but I can't execute it. My dad, God rest him, used to tell me someone has to be the brains behind an operation. Someone has to have the vision, the big picture in mind. I remember telling him once that Michelangelo didn't just *plan* the ceiling of the Sistine Chapel. He dreamed it *and* made it happen. And my dad had asked me, How many Michelangelos can the world hold?

It's probably a good thing I majored in marketing and graphic design instead of art and fashion. I would have been a lousy designer. But I am an excellent critic. I know how something should look. It is both to my shame and my credit that I spend my evenings watching movies with wedding scenes and critiquing the dresses. It's to my shame because obviously that's a pitiful pastime for a jilted bride. But it's to my credit because I prove to myself every evening that I know what I'm talking about. That I'm no dummy when it comes to what I allow in my store.

I don't accept every gown brought to me. Nor even every gown I inquire about. I don't take yellowed gowns or hopelessly outdated gowns or gowns that are just plain ugly. And yes, there is such a thing as an ugly wedding dress.

I take gowns that have character, style, and a uniqueness about them. I buy them from people who come in off the street and from estate sales and Internet sites and thrift stores. Most of the time I know the story behind the dress. I know why a dress isn't being kept in a snug box in the attic or the spare bedroom closet. It's not always because the marriage didn't work out or that the couple needs money, although that happens occasionally. Sometimes a spouse will die and the widow, after time has passed, wants to date again but the dress she has kept holds her back. Sometimes, and this happens more often than not, a woman will bring her dress to me because she loves it and wants to share it. I had a woman tell me once, "Why should this enchanting gown be worn only once? It's a masterpiece. It's meant to be worn, not boxed up." I took her picture and her testimonial and put both on my website. Her comment is practically my motto.

And yes, there are the dresses that find their way to my boutique because the bride never got the chance to wear the gown but couldn't bring herself to take it back to the store where she bought it.

Yes, that's how my dress got here.

And yes, I really do want to sell it.

And no, I didn't already own Something Blue when Daniel broke up with me.

Something Blue was what I created for myself at my mother and Aunt L'Raine's suggestion after my world fell apart. After I had cancelled the photographer, the cake, the flowers, the reception hall, and the caterer. After I realized I needed to reinvent myself, start fresh, and get myself out of the advertising agency where I was working.

Where Daniel worked.

There is no price tag on my wedding dress at the moment. There was one when I first opened Something Blue six months ago. But I began to hyperventilate the first time someone tried on my dress. As soon as the woman in the dressing room handed the gown back to me I ripped the tag off. I put it back on again a few weeks later. And took it off. And so on and so on.

I took the tag off again on the first day of June, two days before Vanessa came to the boutique.

On the day that should have been my one-year anniversary.

FOUR

Afternoon sunlight begs to flood the floor of Something Blue but my window awnings keep it off my inventory—and off the woman in front of me, who, doused in shadow, begins to cry.

This happens sometimes.

I'm not the only one who has a hard time parting with her wedding dress.

"I'm sorry," the woman whispers.

"Don't worry about it," I whisper back. I hand her a tissue.

"You're not the first to cry coming in here," my Aunt L'Raine says. L'Raine was my mom's best friend all through high school and was married to my father's twin brother. I have known her all my life. She and my mother are my only other weekday employees. Monday through Friday it's just the three of us at Something Blue: one ditched bride and two seventy-four-year-old widows.

"And you won't be the last," my mother coos, laying an arm across the woman's shoulders.

The woman dabs at her eyes. "I told myself I was ready for this."

My mom pats her gently.

I reach out to touch the woman on her arm. "You don't have to do this, you know." My marketing professors would never approve of such a line. In theory, it totally kills the sale. But I've held a wedding dress in my arms that I absolutely love. I'll say what I want. Besides, it's my store.

"No, I do." The woman straightens her frame, inhaling deeply.

"You don't have to do it today." I keep my voice soft, reassuring.

"That's right, dear. You can come back another day," L'Raine's eyes are bright and misted over. She simply can't be around a crying person and not join them. She and I have had some wonderfully pathetic times together the last few months.

"I'll be all right. Really." The woman breathes in deeply again and raises her eyes to me. They are still glassy with pain.

"Why don't we just chat for a few minutes," I offer. "My name is Daisy Murien. This is my mom, Chloe. And my Aunt L'Raine. And you are...?"

"Darlene Talcott," she answers, and a tiny smile frames her mouth.

"Darlene, it's wonderful to meet you." I employ my lightest, yet sympathetic, tone. "Would you like some flavored water? I've got lemon, peach, and raspberry. Sorry we don't have coffee or tea but those are a bit of a hazard around white fabrics."

Darlene's smile widens. "I'm fine, thank you. Really." She unzips the garment bag in her arms and there is silence in the room except for the rustle of material. The gown is now out, exposed and glistening under my track lighting. She lays the dress on the table in front of us. It's an exquisite gown. Studded with tiny, iridescent beads and pearls. Sweetheart neckline. Empire waist. A full skirt with flounced edges. Cathedral-length train. It fills the surface of the oak table; cascades across it like a river of white foam.

"Oh, my!" My mother is enthralled. "How absolutely divine!"

"Lovely, lovely," L'Raine whispers.

Darlene is smiling but fresh tears ring her lids. She reaches up a free hand and whisks them away.

The gown looks like it's in perfect condition, but I do what I must. I lift it and inspect its zipper, check its seams, and scrutinize it for tiny tears and stains. I catch a faint whiff of perfume. I lean down to inhale. The bride wore Beautiful by Estée Lauder.

"She was going to have it professionally cleaned, but things got hectic." Darlene is apologetic. "And then she just...I ran out of time."

"She?" I raise my eyes just as Darlene lowers hers. She is staring at the dress.

"This was my sister's dress. She wore it eighteen months ago when she got married. She...she died just before Christmas this past year. Ovarian cancer."

L'Raine needs no prompting. She collapses onto a viewing sofa to our right and makes concerted but unsuccessful efforts to silence her sobs.

My mother and I are both struggling to find adequate words. There are none to be found, of course. "Darlene, I'm so sorry," I finally eke out.

"I am too." Darlene's voice takes on a childlike timbre. Mom turns and joins L'Raine on the couch, both of them covering their eyes with tissues. I could throttle them both.

"Darlene. Really." I blink madly as if I'm wearing contact lenses for the first time. "You don't have to do this *today*."

Darlene shakes her head ever so slightly. "It's not going to be any easier next month. Or even next year. I have to do this for Matthew."

"Matthew?"

"Her husband. Lacey was adamant that he marry again someday. But this has been so hard for him. Lacey found out she was sick a month after she and Matthew got married. Just a month. She hadn't even finished writing all her thank-you notes."

Fresh and only half-suppressed sobs erupt from the couch. Mom and L'Raine may as well go upstairs to their apartments and switch on a soap. They are completely useless at the moment.

"Matthew told me a few weeks ago he just can't move on knowing this dress is in his house." Darlene sighs. "He asked me to please find someone who could use it. Someone who could be as beautiful and happy as Lacey was when she wore it."

The sofa-sobbers grab two new tissues each.

"You don't think you might want to hang on to it?" I ask. "There might be someone in the family who could wear it."

"Even if there was, it would kill Matthew to see it again on someone else. We all know that. This is the best way. I'm so glad you have this shop. I drove all the way from Prairie du Chien to bring it to you."

"And I'm so glad you did." The stray tears I've held in slide free. "I assure you I'll find someone who will adore this dress." I grab a tissue myself.

For a moment there is only the sound of quiet sniffling.

"I saw from your website that you like to record the story behind each dress that you sell," Darlene says a minute later.

"Yes, I do."

"Do you think that's wise in this case? I mean, I don't want people to think for a moment that what happened to Lacey will happen to them."

"Well, we like to focus on what drew a couple together, not what, if anything, separated them," I explain. "Besides. That's why I sew in the little blue hearts in the underside of all my dresses. Each heart has been blessed by an Episcopal priest."

"That's kind of a whimsical thought, isn't it?" Darlene laughs the slightest bit. There is a faint layer of cynicism in her voice. "That a priest can bless a dress and everything will turn out just fine. That everyone will live happily ever after?"

Nothing like a spoonful of disenchantment to help the medicine go down.

"What can I say?" I shrug, feigning a laissez-faire attitude. "If you can't be whimsical at your wedding, when can you be?"

Darlene cocks her head and rewards me with another half-smile. This one, however, is genuine. "When, indeed?"

I pull out a bill of sale and begin to fill it out.

Darlene looks around the boutique floor. "You have a lovely boutique."

"Thanks."

"Been here a while?"

No. Just since I crawled out of the abyss known as rejection. This is what I am thinking. But it is not what I say.

"Just six months. We opened the first week in January."

Darlene continues to let her eyes rove over the boutique. "I take it those three dresses aren't for sale?"

I look up from my paperwork and follow her gaze. In my front window, where I usually display just two not-for-sale wedding dresses—my mother's and Aunt L'Raine's—there is now a third. Mine.

I look over at my mother and my aunt and they jump up from the sofa as if they must suddenly attend to something terribly important.

"Sometimes the one in the middle is." My answer is short and to the point.

Darlene swivels her head back to me and blinks.

I explain nothing.

FIVE

Dear Harriet:

I took in a dress today from a woman who lost her sister to cancer. It was the saddest story I'd ever heard.

Saddest in a while, anyway.

The dress is breathtakingly gorgeous. It retailed two years ago for $1500 and I bet I could still get $800 for it. I started out offering her $300. I just assumed we'd work out a price like I do with all my customers, but she didn't haggle with me. I should've guessed grieving people don't like to haggle. They've already tried bargaining and lost.

My mother and L'Raine moved my dress into the front window with theirs. Like I wouldn't notice. The three mannequins are practically tripping over each other. Arms are flailing everywhere. There isn't enough room for all three of them. You can't even see the hydrangeas and forget-me-nots at the sides.

And when I confronted L'Raine about it, all she said was, "For pity's sake, Daisy. When are you going to get us mannequins with heads! I feel like I'm the bride of Ichabod Crane." I snippily reminded her Ichabod Crane wasn't the one without a head in The Legend of Sleepy Hollow.

Mom was only slightly apologetic. "Face it, Daisy. You're not ready to sell it. Why torture yourself—and your customers?" She means lovely Vanessa, of course.

The thing that kills me is, I left the dress there.

I can't believe I'm such a coward. Mom says I'm a romantic and there's nothing wrong with that. Romantic people are fanciful, they're dreamers. They're whimsical.

The grieving sister thinks being whimsical is akin to being hopelessly unrealistic.

What do you think?

I watched the first half of Gone with the Wind tonight. It irks me to no end that we only see half of Scarlett's wedding dress when she marries Charles. Half! Would it have been that much trouble to give us one long shot showing the whole dress? It's not like they didn't spend a mint already on the rest of her wardrobe. What did Vivien Leigh wear below that lovely bodice when they shot that scene? Jeans? Would it have killed the costumers to make a whole dress?

Dear Daisy:

Scarlett surely wore a big white skirt over a big white hoop. Anyone can tell you that.

Romantic people are most assuredly more whimsical than the common-sense crowd. So what? Isn't that what you'd expect?

And shame on you for expecting a grieving woman to barter with you over the price of her dead sister's wedding dress. You should have offered her $500.

Harriet

SIX

Some people say spring in Minnesota takes its time in arriving. Winter—that lovely white season that never wants to let go—can hang around till after Easter. It can leave and then come back. There was many a time growing up when I wore a wool cap to church on Easter Sunday instead of a bonnet. I've played soccer with mittens on my hands. I've sat before a fireplace on May Day. I've put blankets on newly planted window boxes when frost was predicted. There are years when it seems like I live a mere stone's throw from the North Pole.

And just about the time you think you'll go mad, you see your first robin, and that's all anyone talks about because they've all just seen their first robin, too. The last of the snow—truly disgusting stuff that's more brown than white—finally melts away and the heads of tulips erupt from the ground like little green noses. May can begin with a lovely set of days that tease you into thinking you can put away your coat and gloves, but halfway through the month an arctic wind will have you shivering at softball games, track meets, and outdoor graduation parties.

Then one day, maybe it's Memorial Day or the first of June, a lever will be thrown somewhere in heaven, and the climate will make an abrupt shift that has you fiddling with your heater one day and your air conditioner the next. That to me is not spring taking its time. That is winter taking its time. Taking its time leaving. Spring arrives in one day in Minnesota. And leaves the next.

It is abrupt, not sluggish.

The weather will be cold and blustery one day—and then the next, warm and muggy. It can happen that fast.

Your world can change that fast.

If I had been told when I graduated from college that in less than a decade I'd not only be in business with my mother but that I'd be living in the same building with her, I would have laughed heartily and said something like, "Yes, and pigs fly south every winter."

It's not that I don't love my mother. I do. And it's not that I mind being in business with her. I don't mind it.

But my mother is not a businesswoman. She's a retired kindergarten teacher. And most new college graduates don't want to hear a prognosticator telling them that in eight years' time they will move in with their mother.

That we are in business together at all is the result of the peculiar and mysterious hand of God.

Sometimes I forget to thank him for Something Blue. The place tortures me sometimes. But most of the time, it is like balm to me.

Something Blue is really just the ground floor of an old hotel called The Finland. Most people here in Uptown still call it that, even though it hasn't been called The Finland Hotel in sixty-some years. The Finland was built around the turn of the last century by two Finnish brothers, whose first names I can never remember. I've seen pictures of what the place was like when they ran it. The lobby and first-floor restaurant, which now jointly make up the square footage of Something Blue, were paneled in rich, chocolate-brown oak and boasted punched-tin ceilings and the widest crown molding I've ever seen. The floor was tiled in alternating blue and white tiles. Those tiles are still there. How nice for me that the Finnish flag is blue and white. It's perfect for a bridal shop called Something Blue. I shudder to imagine what my floor would be like if the brothers had been from Germany.

The Finland wasn't the largest hotel in this part of Minneapolis—only thirty rooms—but it was lovely in a quaint kind of way. The brothers were excellent cooks, and their little restaurant was known all over the area as the only place to get Karelian pies and *pasha*. *Pasha* is a Finnish dessert made with *rahka* cheese, sour cream, sugar, and eggs, and flavored with almonds and raisins. It's usually served with arctic cloudberry preserves. I always get hungry when I describe *pasha*, even though I've never had it. People who remember The Finland Hotel have told me what *pasha* is like and their faces always look dreamy when they describe it. Whimsical, even.

The Finland was also the only hotel in Uptown that had a chapel for its guests. Tradition has it that the brothers were devout members of the Orthodox church and they wanted a quiet place to pray on busy weekends when they couldn't get to church. The chapel they built is a lovely little place. No one messed with it, thank God, when the hotel was remodeled to become retail space and apartments. The chapel is still at the back of what had been the lobby and is now Something Blue. Its door looks like it might lead to a cleaning closet or a bathroom. But I've left the little bronze sign the brothers made a century earlier that simply reads *kappeli*. Chapel. There are only six pews inside, one wrought-iron candelabra, and one hexagonal stained-glass window. There used to be a statue of the Virgin Mary and the Infant Jesus, but it was sold years ago. So actually, I guess the room is rather empty. But it's still the most peaceful room in the entire world, in my opinion. I love to escape there.

The Finnish brothers never married so when they died, one in 1942 and the other in 1946, the sole heir was a sister who still lived in Finland and who decided to put the building up for sale. It sat empty and unsold for a couple years and then a couple from Wisconsin named Marvin and Delores Cheek bought it. They combined their names and christened the hotel The MarDel Inn, and the place began its second life. I understand it was a happy life, but there was no more *pasha*, and as hotel chains began to spring up around the Twin Cities, there was no longer a need for hotels with tiny parking lots on busy Uptown streets.

The hotel fell into disrepair after the Cheeks sold it and none of the subsequent owners put any money into its upkeep. The lobby and restaurant were converted into retail space and the hotel rooms became those seedy kinds of places haunted by down-and-outers and cheating spouses. Architecturally, the place still oozed charm, however, and as artistic and entrepreneurial people returned to reclaim Uptown, The Finland began to attract attention. Especially when it came back on the market after a twelve-year absence. It was sold last year to a developer named Reuben Tarter.

Now here's where it gets really interesting.

Reuben Tarter once asked my mother to marry him.

This was before she and L'Raine went off to college together and met my dad and his brother. It was the summer before Mom's freshman year at St. Olaf. Reuben, who was already in college at the University of Minnesota, met her at a wedding. No kidding. Mom was a bridesmaid and Reuben was the groom's best man. He took a liking to her and asked her out the following week. And the next and the next and the next. By the end of the summer, Reuben was head over heels in love with my mother. She was only eighteen and he was only twenty, but he asked her to marry him anyway.

When my mother tells this story, she always has a hard time describing what it was like to turn poor Reuben down, and if L'Raine's around, she'll start to cry, of course. Because the awful truth is, my mother broke his heart. She wasn't in love with Reuben. She liked him. But it wasn't love.

She told him they should let their relationship mature and see where time took it, which is a pretty wise answer for an eighteen-year-old. But Mom never did fall in love with Reuben Tarter. She fell in love with Owen Murien. That first year of college, while Reuben waited patiently to see if my mother would change her mind, she met my dad. Four years later, just after graduation, my parents were married in a double ceremony with L'Raine and my dad's twin brother, Warren. They were each other's maids of honor and best men. My mom and L'Raine are the only people I know who wore wedding dresses as maids of honor.

By that time, Reuben had resigned himself to marrying someone else, which he did, and he moved away with his second-choice bride to New York and became quite wealthy. My mom and Reuben exchanged Christmas cards through the years, and my parents even had Reuben and his wife over for dinner once when the Tarters were in Minneapolis visiting family. I was three and I don't remember it.

In my mind, I didn't actually *meet* Reuben until five years ago, when my father had a massive heart attack and died. Reuben and his wife came to the funeral, much to my mother's surprise. He seemed like a nice guy. A nervous blinker. A little paunchy. Kind, though. And very rich. Then a year later, Reuben's wife passed away.

Mom didn't go to the funeral.

Reuben has been to Minneapolis several times in the past four years and he has always made a point to visit my mom. L'Raine, who was widowed two years after my mother, has told her on more than one occasion to just let Reuben woo her, for pity's sake. To enjoy the rest of her earthly days with a man who clearly loves her. But Mom has told L'Raine—every time—the same thing she said fifty years before. You can't marry someone you aren't in love with.

She's right, of course. Yet every time I think of that phrase I want to break a dish or slam a door or kick over a trash can.

So Reuben bought The Finland. He transformed the thirty hotel rooms into ten stylish apartments, and the old lobby and restaurant were remodeled to attract an *avant-garde* kind of retailer. As Providence would have it, three weeks after Daniel called off our wedding, Reuben called my mom and asked if she knew anyone who could manage the apartments and the retail space. He had someone lined up for the job, but they had quit without giving notice. He was in a bind.

And so was I.

Mom told him I was looking for a new job. She didn't mention that I was dying to get out of the building where Daniel still worked. She told him that I had a marketing degree, that I was business-savvy, and that I'd be perfect. He told her to tell me if I wanted the job I could have it.

Then my mom and L'Raine, who'd both heard me lament over what I should do with my wedding dress, and how there should be a store for people to sell used wedding gowns, and how dresses that beautiful should be worn more than once, came to me in tandem and told me I should open a boutique.

"No one knows more about wedding dresses than you," L'Raine had said. "You've been drawing pictures of wedding gowns for as long as I've known you."

I had cocked my head and said, "L'Raine, you've *always* known me."

"Just my point."

And that's how Something Blue was born.

This is my life after Daniel.

After the death of dreams.

SEVEN

Some days, when I'm in the mood to torture myself, I'll read the "Dear Harriets" from the year I met Daniel—the year we dated and were engaged—while consuming a whole box of Wheat Thins, which I slather in peanut butter and stud with raisins.

I'm continually amazed at how different I sound to myself as I describe what Daniel was like, how he asked me out for our first date, how taken I was by his impeccable taste and social prowess. I sound so naïve. That's what still gets me, a year later. Not the ache of being rejected—that is mercifully beginning to wane, thank God. But I still feel so foolish. Ashamed. Like I should've seen it coming. Only a naïve girl could've been as bamboozled as I was. For example:

Dear Harriet,

That handsome Daniel guy from IT came by my cubicle today for no reason. I mean there was obviously a reason! But it wasn't to discuss the bugs in my department's computer program. He just came over and started talking with me! I don't think he had any other reason for being on the marketing floor. Caroline heard everything he said from her cubicle. She poked her head into my cubicle when Daniel left. "He likes you," she said. Honestly, Harriet, it feels like he does. But it also feels just like high school. I feel like I'm sixteen, not twenty-six. I can't stop thinking about him...

Dear Daisy,

Keep your head. Don't go falling into a place where you can't see the bottom. Keep your hand on the rail at all times...

And this one:

Dear Harriet,

Daniel showed up at my apartment today with a dozen tulips. They are enchanting! He is so original. Leave it to Daniel to realize girls get roses all the time. But not tulips! I am going to meet his parents tonight. I hope they like me...

Dear Daisy,

What's not to like? You are who you are. That's who Daniel likes. Don't try to be someone they'll approve of. You don't know them; you don't know what they like. You are you. That's who they must like...

And this one:

Dear Harriet,

Daniel and I had our first fight. It was over the silliest thing. I can't even believe we were arguing about which movie to go see...

Dear Daisy,

It's never about the movie...

And yet another:

Dear Harriet,

I wish you had eyes and could see what is sparkling on my finger. It's the most beautiful thing, my ring. My engagement ring. I am engaged! Engaged! I can't believe I will ever be happier than I am at this moment. I'm going to be Daniel's wife. I'm going to be married. Daisy Colfax. Daniel and Daisy Colfax…

Dear Daisy,

Who says I can't see? Stop waving that thing in front of my face. You're blinding me…Congratulations, my girl. Can I be a bridesmaid?

There are more entries like these. Lots more. They are nauseating to me now. Seeing them truly makes me ill. I suppose the quantity of Wheat Thins I usually consume in the reading of them might have something to do with that. Who knows?

On days when I'm *really* in the mood to torture myself, I re-read the entries from those horrible first few days when I had to come to terms with being disengaged. Jilted.

Unwanted.

Thank goodness today is not one of those days.

Rosalina Gallardo, who lives with her husband, Mario, in one of the apartments above Something Blue, is singing in Spanish as she opens a seam on a dress that's too tight. The girl who wants this dress is nowhere near a size six. She must think Rosalina is a worker of miracles. I'll be amazed if the gal will ever be able to squeeze her body into it. Rosalina is unfazed, however, by the task at hand. I'm sure that's why she sings as she alters. I've no idea what Rosalina is saying as she snips the tiny white threads but it sounds like she is calling out to someone to come away with her. Or to come back to her.

Mario and Rosalina are originally from Ecuador, though they've lived in Minnesota the past twenty-five years. I've known them all my life. They lived across the street from me when my parents and I lived in Apple Valley—a Twin Cities suburb we moved to when I was ten. Rosalina does all the alterations for Something Blue and Mario is in charge of everything mechanical in the entire building. And I mean everything. Oh, and spiders, too.

Rosalina and I are in the alterations room at the moment, which is one of the apartments above the store I don't lease out. Rosalina's twelve-year-old niece, Maria Andrea, who's spending the summer with them, is sitting on the floor next to her aunt, taking seed pearls off a very old lace wedding dress. The dress has yellowed over the years to a lovely shade of champagne. But the pearls have gone battleship gray and must come off. Andrea sits with the gown in her lap, happily removing the blackened beads with a seam ripper. Next to her and leaning against the wall is Liam Laurent, the eleven-year-old grandson of Father Laurent, the retired Episcopal priest who also lives in one of the apartments above Something Blue. Father Laurent is my angel of God who blesses the little blue hearts before Rosalina sews them in my dresses. Liam is visiting his grandfather today. The boy has a worried look on his face.

I'm sure it's because his grandpa is holding in his careworn hands a blue satin heart, slightly padded and about the size of a quarter, and he is whispering.

"Bless and keep the young woman who will wear this gown. Keep her from harm and heartache. Keep her safe from complacency and bitterness and indifference. Envelop her with the love you have for each one of us. May she always know that love. May she always seek to give that kind of love. May she receive it from the man she will marry. For every day of their married life, for as long as they both shall live. In the name of the Father and of the Son and of the Holy Spirit. Amen."

Liam watches as Father Laurent hands the little heart back to me. I place it in a tiny Ziploc bag and pin it to a frothy white gown hanging on a metal rack. The dress had belonged to a woman who divorced her husband after twenty years of marriage—they had "gotten bored" with each other.

I turn back to Father Laurent. He has the kindest eyes of any man I've ever met. He reminds me quite a bit of my dad, actually. He's average in height and build, with cotton-white hair and wrinkles on his face from all the times in his life he has smiled

"I think Liam thinks this is nuts," I whisper to him.

Father Laurent grins. His voice is low as he leans in to me. "It only matters what *you* think. And what the lady who'll wear that dress thinks." This is why Father Laurent is practically my business partner, though I would never say such a thing to him. He understands what that little blue heart means. It's a tiny emblem of hope. Wounded people need those or we'll go mad. He winks and turns to his grandson. "Well, Liam. Shall we go to the zoo?"

Liam's worried look dissolves and is replaced by one of relief.

Father Laurent waves goodbye to Rosalina and Maria Andrea and starts to walk away.

"Goodbye, Father!" Rosalina's accent decorates her words like ribbons on a gift.

Liam follows his grandfather out of the alterations room. "What were you doing?" The boy made a polite effort to ask quietly. But I heard him, of course. Rosalina did, too. She laughs without making a sound.

"Blessing a dress." Father Laurent's voice is genial.

"Why?"

"Because the dress will be worn by someone. And everyone needs God's blessing."

Their footsteps take them to the staircase that leads to the first floor and their voices fade away.

I turn back to my next project. Assessing a collection of bridesmaids' dresses that were sent from Dallas on approval.

Max, another tenant, bursts into the room with a deck of cards in his hands. "I want to try this new trick out on you!"

He is breathless and looks like he just got up.

Max always looks like he just got up.

Max.

There is really only one reason why my old friend Max is renting one of the apartments above Something Blue.

Because my mother and L'Raine talked him into it.

Think Yenta from *Fiddler on the Roof.* Times two.

I've known Max Dacey since high school. He was in the theater group with me and we had a lot of the same friends, including my best friend Shelby Kovatch. He has never been a love interest of mine, nor have I been one of his. I like Max. But I don't have romantic feelings for him. And whenever I think of Reuben I'm glad Max has never had any for me. Max is tall, very thin, likes to keep his curly hair wild and feral-like, and he loves sleight of hand. He's been doing magic shows for five-year-olds' birthday parties since he was twelve. Max wants to be a career magician—has forever wanted to be a career magician—but his parents have always been able to talk him into staying in the family photography business. I don't think Mr. and Mrs. Dacey have ever been able to picture Max making a living changing the ace of spades into the queen of hearts. And actually Max is a very good photographer. But it's not what he loves. He loves illusion.

When I began to look for tenants for the apartments back in November, I was very selective. I wanted to have the tenants lined up before the units were even ready so I wouldn't have to advertise. There are only ten apartments, and I filled them the first week I agreed to manage the building. One apartment for me, one for alterations, one each for Mom and L'Raine, one for Rosalina and Mario—I knew with Rosalina's skill as a seamstress and Mario's as a handyman, managing the building and selling the dresses would be a breeze—and one for Reuben who wanted to have an apartment available for when he comes to the Twin Cities. My wonderful Father Laurent, who was retiring and looking for a new home, was recommended by a couple at my church, as were Wendy and Philip, who live across from Father Laurent on the third floor. About that same time, a retired violinist named Solomon Gruder, who was my dad's friend from his days with the Minnesota Orchestra, was looking to sell his house and move into something smaller. After those arrangements, then there was just the one unit left. Mom called the Daceys without asking me first and asked if Max was still looking to move out on his own. Yes, he was twenty-nine and still living at home. The Daceys were quite pleased to have Max out of the house but not out of the business and to have an "in" with future brides, who would naturally have future photography needs. Max arrived two days before Christmas with a strange collection of furniture, a thousand decks of cards—or so it seemed—and beautifully framed portraits of Dacey Photography Studio brides, which he hung on the walls of the soon-to-be-opened Something Blue.

I don't mind having Max here. But Mom and L'Raine need to look for someone else to fix Max up with. We're just friends.

Max now holds a fanned deck of cards in front of me. "Pick a card."

"Max."

"C'mon. You're not doing anything important."

I reach out and choose a card. It's the two of hearts.

"Don't let me see it, but show it to Maria Andrea and Rosalina."

I obey.

"Okay. Now put it back."

Again, I obey.

Max folds the cards into his hand and shuffles the deck. "Now I want you to concentrate on your card. Think only about your card. Picture it in your head in this deck. I'm going to read your mind."

I can't help but smile.

"You're not concentrating, are you?" He says this slyly, still shuffling the deck.

"Yes, I am." The two of hearts is now dancing inside my head.

"Is this your card?" He holds up the eight of clubs.

"No. Sorry, Max."

"Okay, okay. Wait a minute." He riffles through the deck. "Is this your card?"

The ace of diamonds.

"No. Sorry."

Max frowns. He hands the deck to me. "Guess I'm not having much luck reading your mind. You're just going to have to show the card to me."

I take the deck and look through the cards. The two of hearts isn't there. I look up at Max. "It's not in here."

Max's wild eyes are twinkling. He whips his head around to the twelve-year-old at his feet. "Andrea, did you take Daisy's card?"

The girl laughs. "No!"

"I think maybe you did."

"I did not!"

"Then what's this doing behind your ear, young lady?" And Max reaches down and seemingly pulls a card from behind Maria Andrea's ear. He shows it to us.

The two of hearts.

"Oh, *bueno!*" Rosalina exclaims. *"Bueno, bueno!"*

"How'd you do that?" Andrea's mouth falls open with amazement.

"Magic," Max whispers. He looks almost handsome when he says this. He turns to me and reaches out his hand. I hand his deck back to him.

"Pretty good, Max."

He looks triumphant. "I made it up myself."

"How'd he do it, *Tía?*" Andrea's eyes are dancing with curiosity.

"Magic!" Rosalina says, and Max grins.

I watch him leave. Skinny. Unkempt. Untamed Max. The man Mom dragged here hoping I would fall in love with him. As he walks out of the room I search my mind and heart to see if there is indeed the slightest thread of magic between him and me.

The slightest thread.

The mere semblance of what I felt when I was in love with Daniel.

But there is nothing.

EIGHT

Dear Harriet,

Max showed Maria Andrea, Rosalina, and me a new card trick today. I have to admit it was a pretty good trick. The look in Andrea's eyes was priceless. She was over-the-top impressed. It was like her opinion of him went up several significant notches between the moment he walked in (looking like a victim of electrocution, of course) and the moment he left.

It made me stop and wonder, as I've confessed to you before, if I am missing something. Is it just Mom's meddling that has Max here, living just one floor away from me? Or is Providence at work? Am I suppressing deeper feelings for Max? Feelings that, if let loose, would lead me straight to his skinny arms? It sure doesn't seem like it. There's just nothing there. Nothing beyond fondness. I like Max like I like Kellen. No, that's not true. I love Kellen. Brotherly love is not what I feel for Max. It is just simple affection. Definitely not attraction. Besides, it can't possibly be the will of God that I marry Max. I would forever be known as Daisy Dacey. That would be unthinkable, even for God.

Father Laurent had his grandson here for the day. Liam seems like a nice kid, but his mother is something else. I learned today that she divorced Father Laurent's son last summer, and that she's the one who did the leaving. I also found out today why I've never seen Liam's father. Ramsey Laurent has been in Tokyo the past four months working on some kind of contract. I feel for Liam. Really, I do. His mother never comes in when Liam visits here. Never. She just drops the boy off at the front of the building. Like she can't stand the sight of Father Laurent. I asked him about it today. I know it's none of my business. But it annoys me that Father Laurent is treated that way. "Does she think you hate her? She must not know you very well if she does," is what I said. And Father Laurent said, "No. She knows how much I still care for her. As a child of God. That's what bugs her."

Go figure.

Tonight I watched the first half of Fiddler on the Roof. Had it on my mind today. I fast-forwarded to the wedding scene. You know, the dress is just okay, and Tzietel's no beauty queen, but I love that part of the movie—up until the Russians invade and spoil everything. I love how Motel and Tzietel love each other completely. Their love seems so simple and yet deep. It's both. Simple and deep. I can't picture Motel telling Tzietel ten days before they're to marry, "Tzietel, I've been doing some serious thinking and I just don't think I want to be married to you. I'm sorry. I really am. I wish I felt differently. But I don't."

Not in a million years.

P.S.—I sent Darlene Talcott a check for an additional $200 for her sister's dress.

Dear Daisy,

The only thing that is unthinkable for God is to be untrue. He most certainly could ordain that you live out the rest of your days as Daisy Dacey. If you loved Max—and it is obvious to all, including God, that you do not—it would not matter to you what his last name was. If you are wondering if someday you will love Max, then I suggest you keep a meter on your dislike for the name Daisy Dacey. When and if it ceases to irritate you, then you will know that you were meant to love Max.

And may I remind you that you respect Father Laurent too much to poke your nose into his private affairs. His relationship with his former daughter-in-law is indeed none of your business, just as you said. Plus, you are judging a woman you have never met.

Yes, Motel and Tzietel have the same kind of love that made fairy tales famous. Don't forget, though, my whimsical friend, that this love did not come easy. It tested them.

I was going to congratulate you on sending the check to that woman but that would be like rewarding a liar for telling the truth.

But I will say it is always a good idea to do the right thing.

Harriet

NINE

I've had a revelation. It happened this morning while I sipped a mocha in the back room of Something Blue, far away from anything white. Mom was helping a young gal sort through our size fours. I couldn't see them from my vantage point behind a computer monitor, but I could hear them. The customer had just told my mother how she and her fiancé had met, and then my mom said, "And how did he propose?"

And that's when I knew.

That's when I knew I'd had a clue all along that something in my happily-ever-after plan had been seriously flawed. I'd had it all along.

Daniel hadn't proposed to me.

I had proposed to him.

In all my girlish dreams and fantasies I had never imagined that my life as a contented spouse would begin with *me* asking the Big Question. It was always going to be the guy who asked.

Harriet would say at this point, *Daisy, get a grip. You did not say to Daniel, "Will you marry me?" That's the "Big Question." And you did not ask it.*

She'd be right. I didn't actually say that.

I said, "Let's get married!"

And Daniel said, "You think?"

Before you label me a complete idiot, let me tell you that we were cuddled in his hammock on his deck with the hues of a gorgeous late

September sunset all around us. He had just told me I was the only girl for him. And it wasn't the first time he'd said that. He also said it in a kind of cute way. I can't describe it.

And I had said, "Yes! Let's get married!"

And he kissed me and said, "Okay."

I'd never really let myself believe, until this moment, that it was all my idea we get married. When we announced our engagement—and by the way, we went shopping for rings the very next day—I said to all who asked that Daniel and I had both decided we wanted to spend the rest of our lives together. Like we both came up with the same idea at the same exact moment in time. And then I thrust my ring in front of their noses to prove it.

I had totally forgotten he'd said, "You think?" before "Okay."

Until today.

I'd remembered only what I wanted to. The invigorating chill as we held each other close. The woodsy tang in the air from someone burning leaves nearby. The words he had said to me only moments before. How it felt to be within Daniel's embrace as we laughed about letting his golden retriever, Elmo, be the best man.

I should've caught on during the months leading up to our chosen date that I was running the show entirely by myself. And that *that* was why Daniel wasn't giving me any fuss about my planning every little detail and not insisting he do anything. It wasn't because he was such a compliant, genial guy but because he was only halfway into the engagement from the get-go.

But I honestly didn't see it coming. Mom said it had floored her. L'Raine told me—after she finished sobbing—that she never would've guessed Daniel was the kind of man to back out of a promise. Shelby told me she didn't see it coming either, but sometimes I think that maybe she did. I've been too afraid to ask her.

I wonder what Mom and L'Raine would've said if I had remembered how that conversation in the hammock *really* went. I wonder if they still would've thought that news of life on Mars would've surprised them less than Daniel's calling off our wedding.

You think?

I *am* a complete idiot.

Shelby hands me a plastic container of gelato and a tiny, paddle-like spoon.

"It's coconut." She is wearing a faded T-shirt and denim cutoffs that are unraveling in every direction. Her hair is pulled back with a blue bandana, haphazardly, so that her short ponytail looks like a spill of Schilling ground nutmeg at the back of her neck. June for Shelby is like one long Saturday. So is July and most of August. She teaches junior-high science at a middle school in Eden Prairie, on the west side of the metro. We are sitting on the roof of my building, in Adirondack chairs atop a sea of pea gravel.

The ice cream, smooth and creamy, melts away on my tongue like edible silk. "Why can't all ice cream be like gelato?" I murmur.

Shelby slides her own spoon out of her mouth. "Because it would cost twenty dollars a half-gallon and we'd all become destitute buying it."

"I suppose."

"Besides, if you had it all the time it wouldn't be special."

I squint my eyes against the late-afternoon sun. "You been around my mother?"

Shelby grins. "You can't have *extraordinary* every day. Whatever it is would become ordinary. It would cease to be extraordinary."

I close my eyes and swallow another heavenly spoonful. "Who says something ordinary can't be appreciated as much as something extraordinary?"

"No one has to say it. That's just how we are. Give me a taste of yours."

I hold out my cup and Shelby plunges her little spoon into it.

"Mmm. That's good." Shelby's words are thick with coconut gelato. "Want to try mine? It's orange cappuccino."

"No, thanks."

I sense that Shelby is studying me. She knows me perhaps better than anyone. She's been my best friend since ninth grade and has shared every monumental moment of mine since then. Shelby is one of the very few people who knows about Harriet and she's never chided me once for having her. In fact, sometimes when Shelby wants my advice she will say, "Ask Harriet about such-and-such and tell her to make it snappy. I need to decide what to do here." Shelby is also one of the few single friends I have left. Everyone else is married and popping out babies.

"So. You having an okay week?" Her tone is light, but I can sense the concern in her voice.

I scoop out the last of my ice cream. "On a scale of what?" I don't have to pretend anything with Shelby. So I don't.

"Well, let's say one is 'managing quite well, thank you very much,' and ten is 'my life is a total mess.'"

I toss the container on the pea gravel at my feet. "A four oughta do it."

Shelby leans back in her chair and scrapes up the remnants of her orange cappuccino gelato. "Well. That's not too bad. If you'd said eight or nine, I was going to tell you I know this great guy…"

"Please, please!" I sputter while I try to laugh. "No more blind dates."

"Ah, but this one's not blind! He's mute."

We burst into giggles. Shelby is not the one who sets me up on blind dates. It's my mom and L'Raine who excel in that department. Shelby tosses her container down by mine.

Easy silence. And then, before I can decide if I really want to know the answer, I blurt out the question that's been on my mind for nearly a year. "Shelby, were you truly shocked that Daniel backed out of the wedding? I mean, did it take you by total surprise like it did me?"

Shelby turns to look at me. "What brings this up?"

I shrug. "I just want to know. I've always wanted to know."

She looks away. "What difference does it make now, Daisy?"

"It doesn't. I just need to know."

Shelby picks at a long frayed thread on her shorts. "I wasn't completely surprised. I was completely *mad* at him. But not completely surprised. He never seemed like he really deserved you."

My mouth has dropped open. I am blushing. "Why didn't you say something?" I gasp.

"Because you were in love with him. It was my job to be absolutely thrilled for you. Besides, I thought maybe I was just jealous. I was kind of, you know. I couldn't decide if what I was feeling was envy or concern."

My mind is reeling under this new information. "So, were you, like, relieved, when he called it off?"

"Of course not!" Shelby turns back to me. "You loved him."

"But you weren't surprised."

"You said 'completely.' I wasn't *completely* surprised."

"I feel so foolish." My cheeks are still warm with embarrassment.

"Well, knock it off. You weren't being foolish. You were being vulnerable, open, and trusting. He didn't deserve you."

There is silence again. Not as easy this time. We are both looking off in no particular direction.

"I had a chance to sell my wedding dress earlier this week," I announce a few moments later.

She turns her head again to look at me. "Couldn't do it?"

"I was this close." I hold up the fingers on my right hand, making them display an inch of space.

"Liar."

"This close." I widen the gap to four inches.

Shelby stares at me, cocks an eyebrow.

No one knows me like Shelby.

"This close." I put both arms in the air and stretch them out as far as they will go.

"Daisy, why don't you just keep it? It's a great dress. One of a kind. You can wear it when you marry the guy who does deserve you."

I stare off into the distance, to the bumpy horizon of flat and pitched roofs. "There are moments when I look at that dress and I still think it's the most beautiful gown in all the world. But all the other times I just remember how devastated I was when Daniel told me he didn't want marry to me after all. It's like looking at a car wreck. With bodies strewn all over the place. And broken glass. And parts of toys and skid marks and—"

Shelby holds up a hand. "Okay, okay!"

We are both grinning.

"What does Harriet say you should do?" There is not even a hint of mockery in Shelby's voice.

Deep within me I'm certain I'll at last be at ease with the turn my life has taken when I can let that dress go. How could I not be? Let's face it. Who consents to keeping a car wreck in full view all day, every day? A person who's hanging on when they need to let go, that's who. I know what I need to do.

"Harriet says I need to get rid of it." Not a lot of vigor to my voice, but at least I'm being truthful.

"Does she?"

I nod.

"It's such a cool dress," Shelby murmurs.

Again, I nod.

Shelby tosses a hand in the air and crinkles her brow. "What does Harriet know?"

I turn my head to face her. "Harriet knows everything."

TEN

Dear Harriet,

You can now add Shelby to the list of people who weren't completely surprised that Daniel deserted me at the altar. And don't ask me, "What list?" I know there's a list. Shelby is on it. There are probably a lot of people on it.

I'm beginning to think that way down at the bottom of that list, I'm on it, too.

Shelby says I should just keep the dress. She says one day I'll look at that dress and I won't think of Daniel. Maybe so, but I will always think of me, and how that dress made me feel when Daniel was my fiancé. And then when he suddenly wasn't.

I can't imagine looking at that dress someday and feeling nothing. If I were to get to that point, I'd surely be a cold person incapable of feeling anything.

I love that dress. I want to hope that Shelby is right.

She asked me what Harriet thinks about it. I told her you'd say the dress needs to go. I'm right, aren't I?

Shelby had a date tonight with the phys-ed teacher at her school. His name is Eric. She didn't call it a date, but that's what it was. She pretended like it was just a casual thing—dinner, maybe a movie. But I could tell she likes this guy, her nervousness as she talked about him gave it all away. I could also tell she very much wanted to protect me from feeling sad that she had a date tonight with a guy who makes her *heart flutter and I didn't. So I pretended like I believed it was just a casual thing.*

She probably knows I was just pretending, but it made it easier for her to climb down off my roof to go home and get beautiful for her non-date.

I watched The Princess Bride *tonight, a lovely way to spend a Friday evening alone in your apartment. I invited Maria Andrea to watch it with me, but she was spending the night with one of her cousins. Max and Liam actually came down and watched the first half but they left after Westley killed the Rodent Of Unusual Size, retreating to Max's where he supposedly was going to teach Liam how to make a quarter emerge from his belly button.*

Princess Buttercup's wedding dress is exquisite and gets far too little camera time. Were I not so enamored of the dress I cannot sell, I'd want a dress (and a love) like hers.

Dear Daisy,

Of course there's a list. But what difference does it really make if your name is on it or not? You feel like a fool for not having a clue that Daniel wasn't ready for marriage. But who's the bigger fool? The one who can't see her fiancé is going to dump her, or the one who sees it and plans the wedding anyway?

You worry too much about what other people think you should do with that dress. It's your dress. And you have to live with it or without it. The fact of the matter is, you will live with it. And you will live without it. It is not oxygen to you. It is eight yards of expensive organza. Whatever you're feeling at this moment about Daniel and the wedding, you would probably still feel it if that dress was long gone. It's not the dress you need to get over. It's the guy.

Harriet

P.S.—If you will remember, Princess Buttercup did NOT get married in the dress you think is so exquisite. She never said, "I do."

ELEVEN

The first wedding I can remember attending is my brother Kellen's. I was five, he was twenty-three.

I was the flower girl.

I wore a dress very similar to the one worn by Laura, the bride. My satin dress was long and white, and it glistened like moonlight. I had a mini bouquet like Laura's—a bunchy knot of lilies of the valley—which was attached to a little basket of white rose petals. I don't remember very much about that day. To me, Laura has *always* been a Murien, Kellen's wife, my sister-in-law. I do remember the slippery feel of my long pearly skirt, the hot closeness of the little sanctuary where the wedding was held, and how I saw Kellen cry for the first time.

He wasn't weeping, not like L'Raine in the third pew. There was just a sparkly, misty-eyed look in his eyes that made me wonder for a moment if someone was making him marry Laura. My concern was short-lived, of course; as Laura walked the aisle toward him. That pained look gave way to a smile that made his lovely Asian eyes disappear into mere slits.

It was a huge surprise to learn that you can cry when you're happy. When you're five that just doesn't seem possible.

It's been odd to have a brother who has never pulled my hair, broken my toys, or called me names. Kellen has always been an adult. My earliest memories of him are always uncle-like.

My friends' brothers, including Shelby's, were true terrors—at least for several consecutive years. I remember being asked, "Do you have any brothers?" by sixth-grade girls whose faces crinkled into disgust as they asked. "Just one," I'd say. "His name is Kellen. He's thirty. He's married."

The conversation would end right about there. Because I had essentially told them I had no idea what it was like to have a brother.

I tried to argue the point once, with my sixth-grade history project partner. Her name was Annie and she had four brothers—two older and two younger. They were, according to her, "ruining her life." I mentioned I had a brother eighteen years older than I was and he lived in a house with his wife and daughter in White Bear Lake.

"He's old enough to be your *father*," Annie had exclaimed, half in shock and half in derision.

"That's gross!" I had said. What else was there for an eleven-year-old to say?

"So you've never lived in the same house with him?"

"No."

"You never had to share a bathroom with him?"

"No."

"Or anything else?"

No. Not really.

"You've never dodged a spitball, or been tickled until you peed your pants, or been locked in the basement, or had your Easter candy stolen?"

No, no, no, and no.

Annie had paused only a moment before telling me I didn't know anything at all about boys.

I had disagreed, naturally.

Annie, wherever you are, you were right all along.

I owe you an apology.

Liam is waiting for his mother the horn-blower—I mean no disrespect. She honks just outside the shop when she comes for him—

and he is looking at a photo I have on my desk of Kellen and Laura and their daughter, Mia. We are just inside the little office of Something Blue, a small room where The Finland Hotel bellhop kept his street clothes. Father Laurent is standing by the open front door smoking a pipe.

"He doesn't look like he's your brother." Liam's tone suggests I am kidding around.

"Well, he's Korean. My parents adopted him when he was two."

Liam studies the photo. "And that's your cousin?" He is pointing to Mia, my niece. She is twenty-one. I'm twenty-nine. An understandable mistake.

"I'm her aunt, actually."

"Oh, yeah."

He hands the picture back to me and I place it back on my desk.

"He's kinda old to be your brother," Liam looks dubious.

"I was born when he was a senior in high school."

"That's weird."

"Well, I guess God likes to surprise people sometimes. My parents didn't think they could have children of their own."

"I wish I had a brother." Liam looks away. Father Laurent has told me he has only the one grandson. I don't know why Liam's parents only had him. They've been divorced for just a year, I think. Maybe they couldn't have any more.

"Maybe someday you will."

A horn sounds from the street beyond the front door, and Father Laurent, several yards away from us, looks up. Liam doesn't, suggesting that maybe he's reluctant to go. A wicked part of me wants to keep talking to him so that Mrs. Ex-Laurent has to come inside to get him. The part of me with the little halo recognizes there may not be an available parking place in front of the building.

"So when will they be here?" Liam is speaking of my brother and his family, but now he is looking toward the front of the store and the street beyond.

"They're coming tonight after Kellen gets off work. We'll probably go out for Chinese food."

Liam turns back to me. "You said your brother is Korean."

"He is. But he loves Chinese food. So do I."

Honk, honk.

Father Laurent turns to look at us. He smiles at Liam.

"Guess that's her," Liam sighs.

"Guess so."

Liam slowly bends down to get his backpack.

"So your dad gets home next week, right?" I say, and Liam nods.

He begins to walk toward the front and I follow him. "So where does your dad live, Liam?"

"Duluth. Most of the time. He travels a lot." Liam's shuffled pace couldn't get much slower.

"Not anxious to go home?" I venture.

Liam rolls his eyes. "Not anxious for Allegra's howling."

I am picturing a little yapping chihuahua or toy poodle. The kind his honking mother could fit in her purse. The kind that some women *do* keep in their purses. Like a wardrobe accessory.

"Little dogs are so annoying," I say.

Liam stops, turns, and gives me a very strange look. "Allegra isn't a dog. She's my mom's baby. Hers and Vic's."

Oops.

He turns back around and we close the distance to the front door. I sneak a peek at Father Laurent's face to see if he heard my major faux pas. Can't tell.

Father Laurent reaches down and gives his grandson a manly, one-armed embrace. "See you next weekend, Liam. Maybe you and your dad and I can go to a Twins game. Sound like fun?"

"Sure, Grandpa. Bye." Liam turns to me. "Bye, Daisy."

"Bye!" I croak.

He opens the door just as another honk—a series of three, actually—punctuates the air around us.

I follow Liam with my eyes as he gets inside a silver Accord idling curbside. I can't see the driver's face, just a flash of sunglasses and blonde hair. He gets in, waves, and closes the car door.

The car zooms away like an arrow from a tight bow.

"So did you hear what I *said?*" I don't look at Father Laurent, but I know he's smiling.

"Yes."

Now I turn and begin to babble my excuses. "Father, Liam hadn't mentioned a baby sister, and you hadn't, so I had no idea that—"

He holds a hand up to silence my apology. "Don't worry about it, Daisy."

"I didn't know we were talking about a baby."

"Of course you didn't."

"Think he'll tell her?"

"No."

"It just didn't occur to me that…well, I mean, it just seems…a baby? So soon after the divorce?"

Father Laurent turns to me. His lovely eyes are so sad. "The baby is the reason Kristen left Ramsey. She was having an affair and found herself pregnant with the other man's child. She knew Ramsey couldn't be the father. He had been gone for eight weeks in Sydney."

The air in the room suddenly feels tight.

"And Ramsey couldn't forgive her," I whisper.

"She never asked for forgiveness. She just moved in with Vic and took Liam with her. Kristen was the one who filed for divorce and Ramsey didn't contest it. They have joint custody of Liam, but he lives with Kristen and Vic. Ramsey has him on weekends and he'll have him for the rest of the summer, when he gets back from Tokyo."

"So, how did it happen? Why did Kristen have an affair?" The question is out before I can rein it in. I shouldn't have asked. But I want to know how the relationship fell apart.

Father Laurent answers me anyway.

"I'm sure Kristen didn't plan to be unfaithful. It happened when Ramsey was gone on one of his trips. She let her guard down, and once it wasn't there, things just tumbled out of control."

"That's so sad. " My eyes travel to the street. Liam is long gone, but I look for him anyway. "Poor Liam."

"Yes. It's sad."

"And how...how did Ramsey take all of this?" It's probably obvious to Father Laurent why I would ask something so totally none of my business. He knows my story. He knows there's a wedding dress in my store I cannot seem to let go of.

"It nearly destroyed him. He didn't give up on God, and I'm thankful for that. But sometimes I think he's given up on people."

Okay. I'm done. I'm not asking any more questions. Thank heavens L'Raine is upstairs and hearing none of this.

Father Laurent takes a step toward the doorway that leads to the apartments, but then he stops and turns his head back to me. He lays his hand on my shoulder and his touch feels like a benediction on my soul. "There are worse things than having your fiancé call off your wedding, Daisy."

He turns his head back around and leaves.

TWELVE

It's a few minutes before closing time when Kellen, Laura, and Mia arrive at Something Blue. Mom is helping a customer choose from a selection of calf-length wedding gowns, when the trio appears at the entrance. L'Raine is out visiting a friend in the hospital, and I'm at the back of the store inspecting today's acquisition: a lovely tapered A-line with an overlay of Venice lace.

"Ah! Here we go!" Mom says triumphantly when she sees them step inside. "My granddaughter Mia can help us. She's your age, your size, and is a whiz at fashion. Mia! Come here, sweetheart."

My exquisitely beautiful niece smiles and hesitates. It's a sign of her accompanying inner beauty that she doesn't rush over to my mother to prove that she is, indeed, a whiz at fashion. Mia is an interior design major at the Illinois Institute of Art in Chicago and is home for the summer. She's a genius at anything that calls for taste. She's the one who picked the color for the walls in Something Blue, the fabric for the awnings and the furniture, even the light fixtures.

Kellen nudges his daughter. "Grandma needs help."

Lovely Mia strolls over to where Mom waits. She is embraced and then quickly pulled into the debate over which dress is best. Kellen and Laura make their way over to me. I drop the dress I'm fiddling with and hug my sister-in-law first and then Kellen.

At forty-seven, Kellen is just starting to sprout a few gray hairs at his temples. They make him look smarter, not older, as it seems all graying temples do for the men who have them. Kellen is a financial consultant, loves numbers like I love gelato, and thinks in equations. He's the reason I got A's in my business math classes.

Kellen was going to walk me down the aisle when I married Daniel.

I think he was the hardest one to tell that the wedding was off. And I think it's precisely because he was the one who was going to give me away.

He's not much taller than I am, but his embrace is strong and purposeful. He's always been pretty free with showing affection, but since Dad died, he's kind of taken on the role of Papa Bear. His hugs, his care for me, and his advice have all taken on a fatherly patina.

And why not? As Annie Sixth-Grader so eloquently pointed out some years ago, Kellen is practically old enough to *be* my father.

"So. How goes it?" Kellen steps back to look at me. He doesn't say it, but I know he's thinking that I would've just celebrated my first wedding anniversary a few days ago if things had turned out differently.

"I'm doing okay, Kel. How about you guys?"

"Not too bad."

"It's wonderful having Mia home for the summer," Laura chimes in.

"She looks as enchanting as ever." I look over at my niece. "She graduates in December, right?"

"Yep. She's thinking of interning for a year in Paris after she graduates."

"Wow." I often forget that I am still like Mia, still in my twenties— for a few more weeks anyway—and still have the whole world at my fingertips, too. "That's great."

"I keep telling myself that, too," Laura flashes me an achy, motherly look that reminds me I'm supposed to think like a doting aunt, not a colleague.

I excuse myself to go lock the front door, and as I'm walking, Mom shouts from her end of the store.

"Don't lock it just yet, Daisy."

I look over at her, but she has quickly turned her back to me and is deep in conversation again with the customer and Mia. I look at my watch. Two minutes after six.

The store closes at six.

Mom turns back around. "Here, Daisy, why don't you help Valerie here. You can explain the little blue heart to her. This is the dress she wants."

Mom hurries away from the customer before I have a chance to respond. My mother is perfectly capable of explaining the little blue heart. She is actually better at storytelling than I am. But she has rushed to greet Kellen and Laura, and Valerie is standing there looking at me.

I make my way over to her and tell Valerie what a lovely gown she has chosen. I'm halfway through telling her about the blessed little blue heart that will rest just under the small of her back, when the front door opens and a man steps inside. Mom walks over to him, all smiles.

Why didn't she tell me she was expecting someone?

Out of the corner of my eye I see her lead the man over to meet Kellen and Laura. Okay, so he's not a customer or Valerie's future groom or a man wanting to sell a used wedding dress.

I finish up with Valerie, placing her lovely tea-length dress in a garment bag. I walk her to the door, thank her for shopping at Something Blue, and lock the door behind her. Mia has joined her parents and the man I don't know. I walk over to them.

"Oh, and this is my daughter, Daisy," Mom pulls on my arm as I approach. "Daisy, this is Marshall Mitchell."

That's it. No explanation. Just here's a man with interchangeable first and last names.

"How do you do?" I offer my hand.

"Hello." Marshall Mitchell shakes my hand. He's of average height. A little thick around the middle. Clear, watery-blue eyes. Goatee. Suit and tie.

"Marshall is very interested in learning how to invest in the stock market, and I knew Kellen would be just the person to help him out." Mom sounds sincere but I'm having trouble understanding why on earth she'd arrange for a little financial mentoring when we're supposed to be having dinner as a family.

Kellen catches my eye. The tiniest smirk is on his lips. He nonchalantly toys with his wedding band and lets his eyes travel to Mitchell Marshall. I mean, Marshall Mitchell.

I follow his gaze to Marshall's left hand.

No wedding ring.

Marshall Mitchell is single.

I could strangle my mother.

I look back at my brother. Bridled laughter is etched across his face.

My mother is telling us how she met Marshall at the golf course last week and how they got to talking and I am only catching half of it. I'm glaring at Kellen, imploring him with my eyes to please, please get me out of this.

He gets it.

"Well, sure, Marshall. We could talk sometime. You ever come up to White Bear Lake?"

Marshall starts to answer but my darling Yenta rushes in. "Well, since you're here, Marshall, why don't you just join us for dinner? We're going to Ping's. Have you been there? It's fabulous."

"Oh, I don't want to intrude on family time—"

"Oh, it wouldn't be an intrusion at all, would it, Kellen?" Mom doesn't wait to hear Kellen's answer. "This isn't a big family to-do! We just love Chinese food. Please, you must come!"

"Well, okay," Marshall says sheepishly.

"Lovely!" Mom claps her hands.

Kellen offers me the slightest shrug of his shoulders as if to say, "Sorry! Nothing I could do!"

Well, I can do something.

"Um, Mom, I need to ask you something about that dress that you just sold. It won't take but a moment. Excuse us."

I say these three sentences with as much urgent nonchalance as I can.

Mom opens her mouth to protest but I propel her away with a touch on her elbow.

"Really, Daisy," she says as we head to the other end of the store. "Can't this wait?"

"Nope."

Seconds later we are at a far rack and I have my mother's complete attention.

"Mom, we had an agreement. No more fixing me up, remember?"

Mom produces a look of astonishment. "I'm not fixing you up. Didn't you hear what I said? Marshall came here tonight to talk to Kellen. Not you."

"We haven't seen Mia in weeks and you invite a man you just met at the golf course to have dinner with us so he can talk to Kellen?"

"What's so crazy about that? Kellen is an excellent investor. Marshall has money to invest. He's quite wealthy."

A groan escapes me. I can't rein it in. "Mom…"

"What? Your brother likes helping people!"

"Yeah, and so do you, Mom."

She looks me straight in the eye. "And there's nothing wrong with *that*."

Marshall Mitchell may be the catch of the year but I'm not interested in playing catch. Dinner now looms before me as a tedious affair.

An idea enters my mind. "So this isn't some kind of blind date you've concocted here?"

"Absolutely not."

"Okay. I'm going upstairs to put on a different blouse."

Her eyes widen just a tad and I can see that it is on the tip of her tongue to suggest which blouse I should wear. She catches it before it falls off.

I turn and make my way to the back of the building, to the stairs that lead to the apartments. I'm on the second floor in seconds. I stop quickly at my apartment and dash in to grab a lacy shawl to wear over my black silk shell.

Then I scurry up to the third floor and pound on Max's door, hoping he's home.

The door opens. Max has an iPod in one hand and a single-serving Stouffer's lasagna in the other. He's barely touched it. He's wearing jeans and a button-down shirt that no longer has any buttons.

"We're all going out to Ping's. Want to come?" I ask.

"What?" He pulls out an ear bud.

I sigh and repeat my question.

"Who's 'we'?"

"Max, does it matter? Do you really want *that* instead of Ping's?" I point to his microwaved masterpiece.

"No."

"Then come."

"Okay."

Max yanks out the other ear bud and tosses his iPod onto a little table that's littered with opened mail and loose playing cards. He hesitates for a moment and then places the Stouffer's lasagna there, too.

He steps out to join me, his open shirt flapping like a main sail.

"Max, you might want to change your shirt."

He looks down at his chest. "Oh. Yeah. Right." He reaches behind him and selects one of three shirts hanging on his doorknob. He lets the tattered one fall away and slips a striped polo over his head. "Okay."

Max closes his door behind him and we head toward the stairs.

"Max, please do me a favor and sit by me."

"You want me to sit by you?"

"My mom has invited some guy to come with us. I don't want to sit by him."

"So that's why you wanted me to come." He stops and looks at me. He's not hurt. He's amused.

"Please, Max."

He laughs. "You're gonna owe me one."

"Fine."

He begins to descend the stairs.

"Want me to pretend like I'm in love with you?" he teases.

I can play, too. "Well, aren't you?"

He doesn't answer.

Good Lord, now what have I done? A hot poker seems to have suddenly been inserted into my ears. It feels very warm in my befuddled brain.

"Max, I was just kidding." I reach out to touch his arm. He's got to understand *that* for sure.

He stops at the landing between the first and second floor. His head is dropped and I can't see his eyes.

"Max?" My voice sounds ridiculously unhinged. "Really. I was just kidding."

He looks up.

"So was I." He winks, laughs, and dashes down the last set of stairs. I have to run to keep up with him.

When we get to the bottom, he throws open the door that leads to Something Blue. The little party of five looks up.

"I ran into Max upstairs," I say as we walk toward everyone. "Thought he could join us. Max, this is a friend of my mother's, Marshall Maxwell."

"Marshall Mitchell," the man kindly corrects me.

"Oh. Sorry."

Now, *that* was an honest mistake.

Kellen is staring at me but I won't look at him. If I do, he will burst out laughing and then I will. It's not good to be laughing when no one is telling a joke.

We start to head toward the back entrance, to the little parking lot at the back of the building. Mom sidles up to me.

"Max?" she whispers.

"You said this wasn't a date you fixed for me and that it wasn't a big family to-do, so I figured no one would mind if Max joined us."

What can she say?

She says nothing.

THIRTEEN

Dear Harriet,

I'm feeling feisty tonight, so don't even think of messing with me. I don't want advice. I just want to vent.

I've decided to write a book. I'm going to title it Rules of Disengagement. *It will be a how-to book on how to survive getting dumped by your fiancé. Here's rule number one. Don't let people set you up on pity dates.*

Okay. Maybe that won't be rule number one. But it'll be up there. Four, maybe.

My mother, and you know I love her, set me up tonight on a blind date without having the courage to call it that. She met a rich, single, never-been-married, Christian man at the golf course last week and convinced him to join us for dinner tonight under the pretense of chatting stocks with Kellen. Even Kellen saw this for what it was, a chance for poor dateless Daisy to meet a decent single man. A decent, single man who drives a Jag.

She denied it of course—but you should have seen her face when I asked Max to join us. She knows there's nothing between Max and me, despite her desperate attempts to play Cupid there as well, but she was annoyed nonetheless that I invited him to join us at the last minute. And yes, I know I was using Max, but I told him I was and he came anyway.

Max was supposed to sit by me; that was my hasty plan to get out of making small talk with a rich man I'm sure I have nothing in common with. But somehow Mom got her way. Marshall Maxwell Mitchell

Melville sat by me. She finagled her way and got Kellen to sit on his other side so we could continue the ruse that the Rich Single Man had been invited to talk investments with my brother. But on Kellen's other side was my mother, which meant when she wanted to pull Kellen's attention away from the RSM, all she had to do was lay a hand on his arm and say, "Kellen, dear..."

And that's not the worst thing that happened.

The worst thing is that Max ended up sitting by Mia. And they had a great time. Laughing and talking, and her showing delight in Max's ability to make half-dollars appear out of nowhere. I seriously doubt Mom had any intention of fixing Max up with her granddaughter. No, what happened between them was that monstrous thing called natural attraction. It was appalling. Give me a break. We're talking Max and Mia. They're like polar opposites. She is elegant, sophisticated, and brainy and he is disorganized, organic, and un-cerebral. He's also eight years older than she is. He's too old. He's too Max.

To be perfectly honest, I think Marshall was embarrassed to have been snookered into Mom's little plan. He had, like, this mental list of topics to discuss with me, and when we had exhausted those, he turned to Kellen and asked him his opinion on OTC stocks. No joke. Here was his list:

1. So, you've lived in Minnesota your whole life?

2. So, you graduated from Bethel?

3. So, you go to church downtown?

4. So, you've had your boutique for six months?

5. So, your brother was born in Korea?

I was practically hyperventilating waiting for him to say, "So, you got dumped at the altar?"

Would she have told him that? Would she?

Don't answer that.

I bet what he really wanted to know was why I needed help getting a date for a Friday night.

That's what I wanted to know about him.

He seemed like a nice man. He's obviously done well for himself. He plays a gentleman's sport—golf. He was polite, kind, and tried to make small talk with me. He's probably a little older than me— thirty-two or thirty-three.

He's a polite, single Christian man with money.

Does that mean he met the right girl some time ago but she died? Or he met someone who he thought was the right girl but she dumped him? Maybe he dumped her.

Maybe he's never dated. Maybe he's never kissed anyone. Maybe he's kissed lots of girls. Maybe he's a lousy kisser. Maybe he's too picky. Maybe he wants perfection and he's never been able to find it.

Maybe that's why he only asked me five questions and then turned to Kellen. He probably thinks if he can't win someone over in five questions, there's no point in going on to number six.

And to top it off, Max and Mia were sitting across from me the whole time, joking and chatting like old friends. Or newlyweds.

I could barely eat my General Tsao's Chicken.

I feel like I've been rejected. And by a man I didn't even want to sit by.

This is sick. I wanted the RSM to want me so I could fend off his advances. And I don't want Max to want me but I don't want him to want Mia. Or anyone else. He's my Max.

Sick, sick, sick.

I have Sleepless in Seattle waiting in the DVD player and I can't seem to press play.

I wish Father Laurent didn't go to bed so early.

I wish my dad were here.

I miss Daniel. I miss having someone to love.

And having someone to love me.

Dear Daisy,

If I were going to give you advice, this is what I would say: No man worth having drops a woman minutes after meeting her on the basis of five questions. If the RSM is indeed a decent guy, he no doubt picked up on your I-really-don't-want-to-be-here signals and was politely letting you off the hook. You might want to think about who did the rejecting first.

Max is not yours. You don't love Max in a romantic way. He's nearing his thirtieth birthday just like you are, and he surely wants to spend his life with someone who finds him irresistible, just like you want to. Stand in the way of that and you will lose a good friend.

Yes, Father Laurent is sleeping at the moment, and yes, you still mourn the loss of your dad, but you are not left without a Father. Skip the movie and go down to that little chapel you are so keen about and pour out your woes to someone whose advice you will listen to, since you don't want to listen to any from me.

That's what I would say if you had wanted my advice tonight.

But you don't.

Harriet

FOURTEEN

Want to hear a love story? It's actually the story of two loves. It's my favorite love story. I never get tired thinking about it. Or imagining that sometime something like it might happen to me.

Once upon a time there were two best friends named Chloe and L'Raine. They had grown up in a farming community in southern Minnesota and spent their high school years wearing bobby socks and saddle shoes, listening to Tommy Dorsey, and dreaming about moving to the city and going to college to become teachers. Chloe was tall and had hair the color of chestnuts and L'Raine was blond and petite. They had known each other all their lives. They knew each other's deepest hopes and desires.

After high school, Chloe and L'Raine shared a dorm room at St. Olaf College near Minneapolis. They joined the choir because they both loved music. One evening, in early November of their freshman year, they had to meet up with the choir at a church north of the Twin Cities for a concert. Chloe and L'Raine had to leave later than the rest of the choir because they were volunteering at an after-school program. They didn't have a car, so they were wondering how they were going to get there, when they found out two other choir members would also be leaving later and they had room in their car. The two other choir members were juniors and music majors. They were also twin brothers. And their names were Owen and Warren Murien.

Owen and Warren had grown up on the Iron Range in northern Minnesota. Their father taught band at the local high school in the town where they were raised and their mother was the church organist. They had never thought of any career other than music. Owen and Warren were identical twins, red-haired and hazel-eyed, and sounded so much alike that Chloe and L'Raine had a very hard time distinguishing one from the other. After they met at the campus parking lot on the day of the concert, Owen said he'd wear one of Chloe's clip-on earrings for the rest of the evening so there wouldn't be any confusion. This was the 1950s, before men wore earrings, so when Owen clipped one on and said, "Let's go," Chloe and L'Raine couldn't stop laughing.

The roads were icy and slick that night, and neither Chloe nor L'Raine nor the Murien brothers had ever been to the place they were headed. They found the town where the church was located but couldn't find the church. Owen, who was driving, stopped at a jewelry store just off the town's main street to ask for directions. It was one of the few stores that still had its lights on. It was cold in the car, so Warren, Chloe, and L'Raine got out, too, and went inside with him.

They were talking loud and stomping their feet when they went inside and didn't notice at first that the store clerk had his hands up and that tiny beads of sweat shone on his forehead. An instant later, it became very clear they had stumbled in as the store was being robbed. Directly in front of the store clerk was a man in a dirty brown parka, aiming a gun.

"Go back outside!" Owen had said and he moved his body to shield the girls behind him. Warren dropped back, too, covering the girls with his body.

"No—no you don't!" the man yelled, and he stepped back a little so he could see all of them, the store clerk and the four choir members. "Get over here! Right in front of me. Get on your hands and knees!"

Owen moved his arms protectively around his back, and Warren did the same, shielding Chloe and L'Raine.

"Go back outside," Owen whispered to the two women.

"I said get over here!" the man shouted again.

"Why don't you let the girls go?" Owen said.

"Why don't you shut up and do what I tell you!"

The store clerk started to inch his way out from behind the counter. He was eyeing the door behind the college students, judging its distance. The gunman whipped his head around to face him. "I didn't tell you to go anywhere!"

"Go!" Owen whispered again.

Chloe and L'Raine took a step backward and Chloe put her hand on the doorknob.

"Get over here!" the robber screamed.

"Take it easy," Warren said and he and Owen pressed their backs against Chloe and L'Raine.

"You wanna be dead? Shut up and get over here. Girls first. On your knees. You!" He cocked his head toward the store clerk. "You empty those shelves like I told you. And the cash register. And the safe. Move!"

Chloe and L'Raine held hands and inched their way from behind the brothers and toward the man with the gun.

"Get away from that door or I'll send you both to kingdom come, I swear it," the man yelled to Owen and Warren.

As the women made their way to the empty space in front of the robber, and as the brothers edged away from the door, the store clerk chose that moment to spring free. He darted out from behind the counter and dashed toward the front door.

The robber yelled and aimed his gun for the fleeing man, who was now partially hidden by Chloe. She was technically more in the line of fire than the fleeing store clerk. Owen screamed "Get down!" and threw his body in front of her. The gun went off and Warren dove for the robber's legs, sending them both to the ground. The gun flew out of the robber's hands.

"Get it!" Warren yelled to L'Raine as he fought to contain the robber.

Chloe, who had been knocked down by Owen, scrambled to her feet to see if he was okay. He lay on his side next to her.

"Are you hurt? Are you hurt?" she yelled, searching his body with her eyes. She was afraid to touch him. Something red glistened on his forearm.

"Warren…L'Raine…" Owen said as he struggled to rise but then fell back.

Chloe glanced over her shoulder. Warren had the gun trained on the robber, who was on his knees. L'Raine was on the telephone at the cash register, dialing with shaking fingers.

"They're okay. They're all right. Warren has the gun. L'Raine is calling for the police," she said. "Are you hurt?"

Owen squinted and grimaced. "I can't believe how much it hurts."

"Oh!" Chloe said, as tears sprang to her eyes.

But then he winked and said, "How do you gals wear these things all day?"

For a second, Chloe sat speechless, dumbfounded. Then she realized Owen was not talking about a gunshot wound. He was talking about her earring.

Which he still had clipped to his right ear.

As it turned out, the bullet had grazed Owen's arm as he fell across Chloe and lodged itself in the wallboard behind them. The wound required fourteen stitches.

The four choir members never made it to the concert that night. After giving their statements and getting Owen's arm attended to, they had missed the event entirely. Instead they went to a diner and sat up half the night drinking coffee and falling in love—Owen with Chloe and Warren with L'Raine.

Four years later, after Chloe and L'Raine graduated from college, the four young people were married in a double ceremony.

L'Raine and Warren had three boys and lived in a little town on Lake Superior, where he led a high school choir. Chloe and Owen lived in Minneapolis, where Owen taught elementary band. He and Chloe tried for many years to have a child. Eventually, they adopted a little boy from Korea named Joo-Chan. They gave him the name Kellen. Many years later and to their absolute surprise, God gave Owen and Chloe a baby after all, a little girl, and Owen named her Daisy because those were the flowers he would bring to Chloe while they were dating. At night, Owen would sing "A Bicycle Built for Two" to his daughter, and she loved it. The little girl loved the line, "I'm half crazy all for the love of you."

And they were all very happy.

Ever-after seemed wildly possible.

I know it sounds a bit more like a police blotter entry than a love story, but it *is* a love story. It's love like I picture it in its truest form: My father saving my mother from the bullet; my mother dashing to the ground to see if he was okay; Warren toppling the bad guy and yelling for L'Raine to grab the gun; and L'Raine trusting him and reaching down to take hold of it.

That is a picture of love to me in its most basic form.

It's keeping the one I care for from harm, looking to this beloved's wounds, toppling evil in its tracks, bending down in trust.

I think I knew all along that Daniel didn't love me the way my dad loved my mother, the way Uncle Warren loved Aunt L'Raine.

And I suppose I didn't love Daniel the way my mother loved my father. If I did, I never would've wanted him to marry someone he didn't love absolutely.

It floors me still that when Daniel told me he was certain he'd be unhappy if we went through with the wedding, I still begged him to marry me.

As if *his* happiness meant nothing at all to me.

FIFTEEN

Saturdays at Something Blue are usually the busiest days of the week no matter what time of year it is. It's the only day I rely on additional help on the sales floor. Mom and L'Raine take Saturdays off—they'd be on their feet the whole day if they didn't—and they usually spend it golfing, shopping, and looking for eligible bachelors to fix me up with.

Three college students pretty much run the show on Saturdays. It works out great for them since they aren't in classes on Saturday and can arrange the hours so there are always at least two of them on the floor from nine a.m. to nine p.m. I give them a modest commission, too, which keeps them lively, on their toes, and not buried in a textbook behind the cash register.

This allows me a day off, too. I don't take every Saturday off, but once or twice a month I like to pretend I'm not a slave to the retail taskmaster.

And I usually begin it with a mocha on the roof. In the summer, that is.

This morning I am wearing a faded Twins T-shirt and cutoffs made from sweat pants. My brownish-blondish hair is half in and half out of a copper-colored scrunchy. No makeup yet. Maybe not at all today. The sun is warm on my legs as I sit on one of the Adirondack chairs. The two chairs are the only structures on the roof besides a couple of ventilation thingies. At least that's what I think they are. I don't know. Mario takes care of all that.

But no one else really appreciates the roof like I do.

I suppose it's because there's not much to appreciate about it. Ours is by far not the tallest of buildings in Uptown, so the view is only adequate.

But there's something about being above what normally defines my day that appeals to me. It's my way of rising above my circumstances. I like the feeling of being on top of it all—for a few moments, anyway. And only figuratively speaking, of course.

I won't stay long this morning, just long enough to finish my mocha and order my thoughts. I'm still a little unsettled about what happened at Ping's last night. And my confessions to Harriet afterward are also pinging around in my head. No pun intended.

Last night around midnight I took the advice Harriet didn't give me and I slithered down to the chapel to lay bare my pathetic soul.

The truth is, I behaved badly at the restaurant. I behaved badly before we even left for the restaurant. I dismissed Marshall as if he were subhuman. As if he were an hors d'oeuvre I wasn't even going to *try* to like. And then to get so uppity because Max and Mia were hitting it off so well.

I showed my true colors. Not a pretty picture.

Today would be a great day to sell that wedding dress. I'm feeling very unworthy of its ownership.

The hot mocha hits my tongue and stings a little.

It has just occurred to me that I have a new rule for my book, *Rules of Disengagement*. Beware of bitterness. It will creep up on you, slither inside you, and before you even know it, it will seep out of you. Be on your guard. It wants you.

I probably won't hear again from Marshall Mitchell—do I have that right?—but if I do, I will offer him an apology. I will tell him I was completely distracted by personal issues the night we met and didn't realize how rudely I had behaved until it was too late and the evening was over. He will probably say, "Oh, don't worry about it, really. Have you met my fiancée?"

Max surely has no idea about the persnickety thoughts I had

regarding his flirting with Mia, so I don't owe him an outright apology, thank goodness.

I should probably apologize to my mother, though. She means well. And she wants for me what I want for me: a love that lasts a lifetime.

Now that I know the resentment monster resides just under my skin I'm going to try and kill it every chance I get. I hope I get some chances. I hope I recognize those chances when they come.

I think I'm going to have to pay a visit to Father Laurent today to make sure I know what to look for. Surely in his career as an Episcopal priest he has pointed out opportunities to slay bitterness to people who couldn't see past their injuries.

I take another sip of the mocha.

Not so hot this time.

A voice startles me and I turn toward the sound. My mother is poking her head out of the rooftop floor. She has not taken every step to the top. Just enough to allow her to see that I am here.

"Daisy, can I talk to you for a moment?"

I sit up in my chair. "Sure, Mom. I can come inside."

"No, it's all right. I can handle the roof for a few minutes." She takes another tentative step and more of her body emerges from the building. Mom is not a big fan of heights.

"I don't mind, Mom. Really. I can come inside."

She is on the last step. "As long as I don't think about where I am, I'm fine." She steps onto the roof and propels her body forward across the pea gravel surface. "See? I just pretend I'm at the playground."

I smile and pat the chair next to me. "Okay, then. Have a seat."

Mom closes the distance and then settles into the second Adirondack chair. "It's a lovely morning."

"Sure is." The urge to apologize to her for being a spoiled brat last night is suddenly overwhelming. I say, "Mom," just as she says, "Daisy," and we both smile.

"Let me go first, Mom. I'm sorry about my attitude last night. Really. I know you meant well. I didn't mean to come off so unfriendly. I'm sure I disappointed you."

"You didn't disappoint me, Daisy. And it's me who should be apologizing. I knew perfectly well you didn't want me trying to find any more dates for you. And I went and did it anyway. Sort of."

"Sort of?" I can't help but smile.

"It really wasn't supposed to be a date. It was supposed to be a chance to meet a nice single man under relatively casual circumstances."

"Did he know that's what you were doing? Creating a causal meeting ground for him to meet your daughter?"

"I never actually said that to him. We had started talking about mutual funds while we were waiting for golf carts and I just told him I was going to be seeing my son Friday night and that he knew all about investments."

"And you didn't tell him you had an unmarried daughter?"

"Well, I did kind of mention that, yes, but it was more like a passing comment to help create interest. I knew if he could get some investment advice *and* meet a nice, single Christian girl, he'd come. And I was right."

"Except he didn't meet a nice, single Christian girl," I turn my head from her and sip my mocha.

"Oh yes, he did," Mom says quickly. "He thought you were a lovely girl. He said you seemed sad, though."

I turn back to look at her. "When did he say that?"

"After dinner. When we were all in the parking lot near the restaurant saying goodbye. You were talking to Laura."

"He said I seemed sad?"

"Yes. And no, I didn't tell him the reason you might have seemed that way. I just told him family gatherings make you think of Dad and you still miss him."

For a few seconds I am silent. Dad seemed achingly far from me last night when I was having my pity party with Harriet. "I was just thinking of Dad last night, after we got home," I say a moment later.

"So I wasn't exactly lying."

"No. But I don't want to seem sad anymore, Mom." I look away from her.

"I don't want you to either."

"This is taking longer than I thought it would."

"You were hurt, Daisy. Everyone heals at a pace of their own."

I turn my head back. "Do you suppose Reuben ever got over you?"

Mom breaks into an easy smile. "Of course he did. He married someone else."

"Yes, but did he love her like he loved you?"

Mom's answer is quick. "I should hope not. He surely loved her in a completely different way for at least one very good reason. She loved *him*."

We are quiet for a few minutes.

"I promise I won't try to fix you up again, Daisy. If that's really what you want," Mom says.

Oh, I so want to laugh. She has no idea how the thought of having my broken heart "fixed up" appeals to me. *Fix* is an amazingly complete word for having just three letters. Gotta love that "X" at the end. It sounds so final. Repaired forevermore.

"Daisy, did you hear what I said?"

I turn to her. "Maybe we should just let it happen on its own."

"If you let it, I'm sure it will."

I sigh. A breath of resignation. "I promise I will try to let it."

"That's my good girl."

Seconds of silence.

"Mom?"

"Yes?"

"Max and Mia seemed to really enjoy each other's company."

"Yes."

"Do you think they…?"

"No, I don't."

"Why not?"

Mom stands up. "Max was just being Max, Daisy. And Mia will

be in Paris this time next year. They were just having fun, sweetheart. Something I worry you've forgotten how to do."

Okay, so there's really nothing I can respond back with. My first thought is I can't decide if Mom's right or not. If she is, I'm pitiful. If she's not, it still stands to reason that I come across as someone who doesn't remember how to have fun.

Not much better.

My mother leans over to kiss me on my forehead. Her touch feels like solace. "Solomon's looking for you."

Solomon Gruder. Third-floor tenant. Retired violinist. Seventy-one-year-old widower.

"He's too old for me." I squint up at her.

See? I've not forgotten how to have fun.

Mom laughs. "He wants you to play the piano for him. He's playing at a wedding tomorrow afternoon and he says he needs to practice."

Ugh. I love Solomon. I love hearing him play the violin. But I'm a poor accompanist. Dad was light-years better than me on the piano.

"There has to be someone he knows who plays the piano better than I do."

"Daisy, you play very nicely. Besides, it's just practice. It's not like you're recording an LP."

"CD, Mom."

"Whatever."

She starts to walk away. "L'Raine and I are going golfing. And I won't even *glance* at any of the men."

"Yeah, and have you thought about how that has looked, Mom?" I call after her. "You and L'Raine ogling all the young single men on the golf course the past twelve months?"

She tosses her hand at me behind her back.

I do know how to have fun.

SIXTEEN

One of the things I miss most about my dad is listening to him play the piano. My father had the rare ability to play anything by ear, even after hearing it only once. He had perfect pitch, too, and could transpose keys mid-song. He never seemed to be impressed with this ability. To him, being able to do such feats of musical magic was as natural as breathing. No one thinks much about their ability to breathe; they just do it. It's when a person can't breathe that they suddenly realize they've been doing something truly marvelous all along. And my dad never had a moment like that—a moment when he couldn't make music. The morning of the day he died, Dad played all his Gershwin favorites. Then he had lunch. Then he had a heart attack.

He was seventy years old.

Some people whispered at the funeral that Owen Murien had had a good, long life and that it was a blessing to my mother that he went so quickly.

I wanted to yell back to them that my dad may have had a good life but it wasn't a long one. He was only seventy—and I was only twenty-five.

Didn't they know that my dad would never give me away at my wedding, that he would never hold a child of mine in his lap? That I was forever done with buying any greeting cards with the word "Dad" on them? That I would cease to address anyone with the word "Dad" forever after?

When I was dating Daniel, and especially during that memorable year when I was his fiancée, I was tremendously bothered that Daniel had never known my dad, that Daniel never had to decide if he was going to ask my dad for my hand in marriage because there was no dad to ask.

I wonder if he would've asked if he'd had the chance. I've on occasion tried to picture such a conversation.

Dad: "Daniel. Good to see you again. What's on your mind, son?"

Daniel: "Well, Daisy wants us to get married."

Dad (after a moment's reflection): "And what do you want?"

Daniel: "Um, well, I guess it makes sense."

Dad: "Does it?"

Daniel: "Doesn't it?"

Dad: "Marriage isn't about what makes sense, Daniel. It's about what completes you. If you and Daisy complete each other, then marriage is not what makes sense. Marriage is that which seals what is already whole."

Daniel: "You think?"

Solomon finds me on the stairs on my way back to my apartment. He is wearing his usual attire: twill pants, a Mr. Rogers sweater, loafers, plaid bow tie. He is holding sheet music in his hand. I see a lot of black squiggles on the paper. Lots of notes. Plenty of opportunities to really butcher a song.

"Daisy! There you are. I need you to practice this with me. I'm leaving in a little while to go watch my grandchildren play soccer so I haven't much time."

"Solomon, I'm not good enough to practice with you," I begin, but he thrusts the music in front of me.

"Of course you are. It doesn't have to be perfect."

I look down at the paper and moan.

Chopin. "This looks hard."

"Nonsense. I have all the hard notes. You'll be fine."

"Isn't there someone else you can practice with? You must have friends who play better than me."

"Yes, of course I do, but they don't live in this building. You're right here. It makes sense."

Ah, yes. It makes sense.

"Your piano or mine?" I ask.

"Have you had yours tuned?"

Now there's a reason my dad's old upright hasn't been tuned in four years. The last time he played it was the day he left Mom and me for glory. Figure it out for yourself. "No."

"Mine, then."

"Give me a minute or two, okay, Solomon? I need to run something by Father Laurent." I start to move past Solomon to head up to Father Laurent's apartment.

"He's not there," Solomon says. "He's in the chapel."

I stop, turn, and start to go back down. "I won't be long, Solomon, I promise. Ten minutes tops. Go rosin up your bow or whatever it is that you do."

I am down the stairs and sneaking into Something Blue in mere seconds. I hope no one sees me. I don't usually come onto the sales floor in cutoffs and a faded T-shirt. I open the door leading to the boutique and am relieved that Cassie, one of my student workers, hasn't even unlocked the front door. It's not quite nine o'clock yet.

"Hey!" Cassie is smiling, but an eyebrow is cocked. It's one of my rules that my workers "dress up" when they're on the sales floor.

"I won't be here but a minute," I call out to her as I head to the chapel door.

I open the door quickly but quietly and step inside, closing it behind me. Father Laurent is kneeling at the little altar with his hands folded in prayer. The morning sun is caressing the little red, blue, and yellow stained-glass window in front of him—a circle of skinny, crystal parallelograms all pointing toward the center—and the light that falls on Father Laurent hints of pink, candle flame, and watery azure.

I slip into the back pew as quiet as I can. But he has heard me. I hear him whisper "Amen." Father Laurent takes his time getting to his feet. I wonder if I should assist him. By the time I decide I will, he is up. He turns to me.

"Good morning, Daisy." He starts to walk toward me.

"Father, I didn't mean to cut your prayer time short."

"You didn't. Liam is coming early today. We're going to pick Ramsey up from the airport at ten-thirty."

He is at my pew now.

"Do you need a ride?" Father Laurent sold his car when he moved into the apartment and I can't imagine the Horn Blower taking them to the airport.

"Max is taking us."

Good ol' Max.

Father Laurent starts to walk toward the door and then stops. "Did you come in here to talk to God? 'Cause he's in a good mood today." He winks, then cocks his head and adds, "But then he's always in a good mood, isn't he?"

"Actually, Father, I came here to talk to you."

"Oh?"

"The thing is…" I have no idea what I'm trying to say.

"What is it, Daisy?"

I slump in the pew. "I don't know."

He motions for me to scoot over and he sits down beside me.

"Something's bothering you." It's not a question.

"Yes."

"You afraid I won't understand?"

My eyes fall shut. "Oh, no. I'm sure you will. It's just…I've discovered something very not nice about myself."

Father Laurent laughs. "I'm pretty sure whatever it is you have to say I've heard before. And Daisy, I've good news for you. God has heard it, too. And loves you nonetheless."

You can't help but smile when you're around Father Laurent. Even when you're confessing to harboring a monster.

"I'm bitter, Father. I'm a bitter person. I resent other people's happiness. I want men to want me so I can brush them off." I can't believe I just said that. It's true but I can't believe I've said it.

I peek at Father Laurent. He doesn't appear to be shocked. I'd say affection shines in his eyes rather than alarm.

Father Laurent takes my hand. "Daisy, when we are hurt, it's instinct to cover the wound and hold back anyone from brushing up against it. And I don't need to tell you wounds don't heal if they never see light, if they're never exposed to fresh air. If you want your wound to heal, and it sounds to me like you do, you need to stand up straight, pull your arms away, and let the light and breath of God work its cure on you."

"But how do I do that?" My voice is little more than a whisper. "I don't know how."

"You need to let go."

"Of Daniel."

"Of your unmet dream. You were not meant to have Daniel for your husband. You must trust that God was looking out for you, Daisy."

I lean my head back on the pew. Father Laurent squeezes my hand and lets go.

"If I could just sell that dress…"

"Oh, I disagree with you there. I think you should keep that dress until it no longer matters to you. The day it doesn't matter is the day you realize your wound is nothing but a scar. And the day you find you are no longer bitter."

I pull my head up to look at him. "You don't think I should sell it?"

"No. Not yet."

"You don't think having it keeps me tied to the past?"

"I think it's how you feel about that dress that keeps you tied to the past. You get rid of the dress, but not the feelings, and you'll be no better off."

I let out a monstrous sigh. "What if I can never be free of it?"

Father Laurent leans back, reaches into his pants pocket, and pulls out one of the little blue hearts we sew into Something Blue wedding dresses. He holds it out to me and I silently reach for it. When our hands meet, he drops his head in prayer.

"Father God, Lord and Master, fill your daughter Daisy with the light of your presence, the peace of your spirit, and the joy of your all-sufficient love. Help her trust you for what you have allowed to take place in her life. Silence the enemy who seeks to keep her bound to her sadness. Show her the path you wish her to take. Bless that path. Make it beautiful. In the name of the Father, the Son, and the Holy Spirit."

He opens his eyes and transfers the little blue heart to me. My fingers close around it like it is a priceless diamond.

"Keep that close to your heart. Let it remind you that today is meant to be a turning point for you."

"Thanks." Two tears escape my eyes, one on either side. I finger the tiny heart, blessed so beautifully by Father Laurent. It's so soft. And little. No bigger than a quarter. Insignificant, size-wise. "I still feel like it's going to take a miracle for me to get over this," I mumble.

Father Laurent stands up. "Well. All the more reason not to rush it, then."

The minute he says this, I begin to giggle. He stares at me. I must look insane, giggling as tears glisten on my cheeks. But I simply can't help it. I laugh louder.

"And you know what happens when you rush miracles," I say as I wipe away the tears. "You get lousy miracles."

New tears spring forth but they are tears from laughing too hard. Father Laurent continues to stare at me, half-amused and half-confused.

It's obvious he's never seen *The Princess Bride*.

SEVENTEEN

I am tripping my way across the black keys, trying very hard to play "Berceuse for Piano in D-flat Major" without making Solomon grimace in pain.

My fingers touch an unflatted A key by accident and he swivels to face me. The polished violin under his chin is already making him hunch his shoulders. Add a little facial contortion and he surely seems to have just been stabbed with a dull blade.

"Sorry!" I resist the urge to remind him he forced me to do this.

We continue and I whisper the count in my head—one-two-three, four-five-six.

I flat an F and Solomon cocks his head. "Five flats in D-flat major, Daisy. F's not one of them."

"I know, I know," I mutter, willing my hands to stay on those black keys.

Would it really have stopped the world from turning if Chopin had written this thing in D major instead of D-flat? I mean really. One tiny little half-step up.

"He should've written this in D!" I say impulsively.

And Solomon turns toward me again, his bow still caressing the strings. He doesn't miss a note. "It wouldn't have been the same."

"It would've been easier to play."

"Easier isn't necessarily better."

He sounds just like my dad. Dad would've said that changing a key does indeed change a song. There is only one way to play a piece of music, and that is the way it blossomed out of your head and heart when you wrote it. Only that one way.

And I would've said, "But you transpose songs all the time."

And he would've said, "But the transposed version is never as beautiful as the original. There is just the one way a piece of music is meant to be played. Every other way, even if it is easier, is inferior. You don't want to settle for mediocrity, Daisy."

We are nearing the end.

Solomon has eyes closed as he wraps it up. "A little ritardando here," he says, and I obey.

Ta-da.

We are finished.

I look up and see that Father Laurent and Liam have poked their heads through Solomon's open doorway. Father Laurent looks perfectly relaxed as usual. Liam looks unimpressed.

Solomon sees them, too. "Come in, Miles."

Miles is Father Laurent's first name. I can't call him that. He is "Father Laurent" to me and always will be.

"That was very nice." Father Laurent walks in and Liam follows. "Don't you think, Liam? Liam's learning the piano, too."

"Well, maybe someday you can play for me, Liam." Solomon places his violin back in its case.

"I'm sure anyone would be an improvement over me," I announce as I stand up from the bench.

"You're weren't that bad, Daisy." Solomon surely thinks it will make me feel so much better to hear I wasn't that bad.

"I thought it was beautiful." Father Laurent turns to his grandson. "Didn't you think so, Liam?"

The boy shrugs. "She hit some wrong notes."

Leave it to a kid to tell it exactly how it is.

Father Laurent smiles. "Oh, well, not very many of us can hit all the right notes all the time."

Okay, I'm ready for a second mocha and another hour on the roof. "Good luck at the wedding, Solomon, I'm sure you'll do great." I start to ease my way around the trio of men, when Father Laurent stops me.

"Actually, Daisy. I was wondering if you're still open to giving Liam and me a ride to the airport to pick up Ramsey."

"Where's Max?" I answer.

"I don't know. He's not here. I think maybe he forgot. Your aunt said she saw him leave early this morning with all his camera equipment."

Max.

"When do you need to leave?" I ask as I yank out the scrunchy in my hair. I must look like the bride of Frankenstein.

"We really should be leaving now, but as soon as you could take us would be fine."

It's not like I have a lot of things going on this morning. Sure, I can do this. "Let me change real quick." I head for the door. "I'll meet you downstairs in the parking lot in ten minutes."

"Thanks, Daisy," Father Laurent says.

I dash out, yelling a goodbye to Solomon.

He calls out after me. "Thanks, Daisy! And I meant what I said. You really weren't that bad!"

I sprint down the stairs with his words in my head. I suppose it's better than hearing, "You really weren't that good!"

In my apartment, I grab a pair of khaki capris and a pink silk T-shirt that's nearly dry from being hand-washed the night before. I slip my feet into rose-hued espadrilles and run my fingers through my hair. I stop in the bathroom long enough to put mascara on the top lashes and a dab of peach-colored blush on my cheeks. A spritz of sweet pea body spray and I am out the door.

Mom meets me on the stairs. "What's up?"

"Max forgot he was supposed to take Father Laurent and Liam to the airport this morning to pick up Liam's dad." I say this as I hurry past her.

"Oh," she says, in a kind of peculiar, thoughtful way.

But I don't have time for a conversation about Max's shortcomings.

I continue on my way and am through the door that leads to the back entrance of the building. Moments later, Father Laurent, Liam, and I are headed east toward the airport.

Baggage claim at Minneapolis-Saint Paul is one long hallway of carts, wheeled suitcases, happy people embracing each other, and bored people holding up signs inscribed with last names. It's just after ten-thirty in the morning, but the expanse of wide walkways and luggage carousels is bustling with activity. Liam and I are sitting on plastic chairs joined at the hip while Father Laurent checks the monitor for his son's flight.

I learned on the way here that Ramsey's car is at a friend's house here in Minneapolis, but that the friend and his wife are in Chicago for five days. All I have to do is take Father Laurent, his son, and his grandson to this friend's house and they will be off on their own. And I will be off on mine.

Maybe I will pop over to Shelby's and see how her date last night compares with mine. I turn to Liam sitting next to me.

"So, you must be really glad your dad's coming home." I know full well how lame that sounds. Of course he's glad.

"Yep." Liam doesn't elaborate.

"Did you hear much from him while he's been gone?"

Liam swings his head around in Father Laurent's direction. "He e-mailed me everyday. And we talked on Skype."

"Skype?"

"It's a way of talking to someone over the Internet."

"Oh."

Awkward silence.

"So what was your dad doing in Tokyo?" I venture.

"He builds gardens and stuff. He's a landscape architect."

"Wow. That sounds cool. You must have a nice yard at your house."

"Which one?"

I hesitate. Does he mean which yard or which house? "Um, where you live when you're with your dad." I hope I'm right.

"Yeah. It's pretty nice, I guess."

More silence.

"So you like playing the piano?"

"It's okay."

"Ever play any wrong notes?"

A smile creases his face. "Sure."

"Your mom make you practice?"

Liam looks up at me like I've said something very strange. "No. She never hears me play. I have a keyboard with earphones, 'cause she and Vic don't have a piano. I play on my dad's piano, though, when I visit him on weekends. He plays. He's teaching me."

"Oh. Must've been kind of hard to practice then while your dad's been gone."

Liam nods. "Yeah."

"So did you?"

He smirks. "Sometimes."

Father Laurent returns to us. "Ramsey's flight landed ten minutes early. It looks like he'll be heading for carousel fifteen."

We are sitting near carousel seven.

"I'll just stay here and let you guys reconnect," I say.

"If you're sure you'll be all right." Father Laurent's tone is kind and endearing.

"Of course."

"Okay, then. We'll be back soon, I think." He and Liam head down the busy corridor.

I spend the next ten minutes watching the flow of humanity move past me. I watch young lovers who've been separated press their lips together as if never to part again. I watch grandmothers leaning down to hug the grandchildren they probably wish they saw more of. I watch executives whiz by with tiny remote cell-phone earpieces attached to their faces, talking as if to no one.

An elderly woman takes a seat next to me and settles her belongings all around her. I smile a wordless greeting.

"I think my daughter might be running late." The woman looks over her shoulder and back around again. "At least I hope that's all it is. I hope she hasn't been in an accident or anything."

"Traffic can be a little troublesome, depending on where she lives." I don't know what else to say.

"It's just not like her to be late," the woman continues in a worried voice. She checks her watch. "I said I'd wait right by the carousels for Delta so she wouldn't have to park. But I keep watching the street outside and I don't see her."

This woman is not in the right place.

"The carousels right here are for Northwest. She might be waiting for you a few exits down." I point to the other doors that lead to the outside world.

"Oh! Oh, dear!" The woman stands and starts to collect her things. An overnight bag she'd placed on her shoulder falls to the ground. "Oh," she says again. She picks it up, grabs her purse, shopping bag, and suitcase and then drops it again.

I stand and retrieve the shoulder bag. "Here. If you place your overnight bag over the handle of your suitcase you can just pull them both along. See?"

"Thanks. Thank you so much." She begins to walk briskly away. And as she does, I see that Father Laurent and Liam are returning. And a third person is with them. Ramsey. He has Father Laurent's kind, dark eyes, but his jaw is set differently. A scattering of gray touches his temples. Ramsey Laurent is a little taller than his father, and has more hair, but the family resemblance is still strong. And yet something about him doesn't match Father Laurent at all.

Father Laurent quickly introduces me to his son. "Daisy, this is Ramsey. Ramsey, this is Daisy Murien, my landlady."

It takes a lot of effort not to laugh.

A landlady, indeed.

I'm in no position of authority over Father Laurent. The idea is absurd. He is the wise and respected one. The one I run to for direction and consolation. I simply take his rent checks and deposit them into Reuben's bank account.

"Pleasure to meet you," I say, remembering my manners and extending my hand.

"Likewise," Ramsey returns the handshake. His grip is firm, almost stern. We let go and he lets his hand fall back to rest on Liam's shoulder.

"Got all your luggage?" I say.

"Yes. Thanks. It's all here."

"Okay. Well. Shall we go?"

There is something about Ramsey that needles me as we head to the escalators and short-term parking. There is something odd about this man who looks so much like Father Laurent and yet who doesn't resemble him at all.

I decide as we enter the parking structure that Ramsey lacks the copious amounts of laugh lines that his father has. Wrinkles like that come from age, though, don't they? And Ramsey can't be much more than seven or eight years older than me.

Perhaps in twenty years he'll have them, too.

I watch him talk to Liam in low tones. I study his eyes as we continue to walk, looking for the telltale signs that creases from smiling too much are growing beneath his skin. But I don't see them.

He looks up at me.

I look away.

EIGHTEEN

Dear Harriet,

It's been a very odd day. It began all right, I guess. No...actually, it began rather pathetically. I realized while I nursed a mocha on the roof that I'm basking in bitterness, roiling with resentment. I'm an Eeyore.

This revelation is all thanks to you, since I did in fact take my woes to the chapel last night and came away from that lovely experience with the knowledge that I've all the appeal of soured milk.

I was able to make things right with my mother, though. That felt pretty good. And I guess knowing I'm a pitiful sourpuss is better than thinking I'm a pretty amiable person and what-the-heck's-wrong-with-everybody-else when it's really me who has problems.

I asked Father Laurent to help me kill the monster inside me. I found him in the chapel this morning and we talked. Then he did the most amazing thing. He pulled one of my little blue hearts out of his pocket, blessed it, and gave it to me. He told me to keep it close to my heart so I wouldn't ever forget that today was a turning point for me.

I've no idea why he had one of those hearts in his pants pocket. None at all. Maybe he misses his wife like I miss Daniel, and having it comforts him.

Actually I am learning it's not Daniel I miss. It's the euphoria of being in love that I grieve for.

Which brings me to what happened a little while after Father Laurent gave me the heart. Max was supposed to take Father Laurent and Liam to the airport to pick up Liam's dad, but he forgot and I took them instead. So I got to meet Ramsey Laurent. I knew a little about him from the conversations I've had with Father and Liam, and of course, there's that whole nasty thing the Horn Blower did to him. For some reason I pictured him looking like Father Laurent's wife, whose picture I've seen in Father's living room. But the guy looks just like his dad. But then he also doesn't look like him. It's the weirdest thing.

He sat in the front seat of my car while I drove him and Father and Liam to get his own vehicle from a friend's house. I caught him looking at me several times.

I wish I knew what Father Laurent has told him about me.

Maybe he hasn't told him anything. Maybe he's never mentioned me at all.

If you ask me, I think he spends far too much time away from home. I don't think Liam particularly likes his new stepdad. And Ramsey lives too far away for Liam to live at both houses.

And what's with that? Why did the guy relocate to Duluth when his marriage ended? Leaving his kid with no choice but to stay in Minneapolis with his mother and the man who came between his parents?

I don't get it.

Couldn't get ahold of Shelby today. She may call later tonight. Do you suppose she went out with this Eric guy two nights in a row?

I'm watching Sweet Home Alabama. The dress Reese Witherspoon wears in the almost-wedding scene is fairly understated but that's why it works. Besides, she was about to marry the wrong guy anyway.

Dear Daisy,

You are not an Eeyore. Eeyore was gloomy, not bitter. And being bitter is definitely worse than being gloomy. A gloomy person can be cheered. A bitter person can only be made un-bitter if they choose it. And there's not a whole lot anyone can do about it if they don't.

Sounds like you've made a good choice. I would imagine coming out from under bitterness might take awhile. Like losing a few pounds compares with getting a haircut. Both make you look different but one takes a lot longer than the other.

Who knows why Father Laurent had a little blue heart in his pocket? Yes, it does seem a little strange, but you may be right. Maybe he, like you, believes in the power of a symbol to soothe.

And that thing with Ramsey Laurent and his son? You don't get it because it's not yours to get. MYOB.

Of course it's possible Shelby went out with Eric again. An un-bitter person would be happy for her if she did.

Love the fit on the Sweet Home Alabama *almost-wedding dress.*

Doesn't that movie have a happily-ever-after ending?

Harriet

NINETEEN

I'm waiting on the bottom step for Mom and L'Raine. They insist on riding with me to church this morning so we can go out for brunch afterward. For once I am ready before they are.

There is hushed movement on the stairs behind me and I turn to see why my mom and L'Raine are being so quiet as they make their way down to me. But it is not my mom and aunt on the stairs. It is Father Laurent.

I smile. "Good morning, Father."

"Hello, Daisy."

I lean into the wall next to me so that he can pass. He looks a little pale this morning.

"Did you have a nice day with your son yesterday?" I ask.

"Yes, thanks. And thanks again for getting Liam and me to the airport on time."

"It was nothing."

"It was something to me. And Liam. He has missed his dad very much."

"Well, you're very welcome, then."

"He and Liam are going camping for a few days on the North Shore, starting tomorrow," Father Laurent continues in a brighter tone.

"I'm sure they'll have a great time."

"I think so, too. Well, have a lovely morning." He starts for the back door.

"You want a ride to wherever you're going, Father?" I ask.

"It's all right, I can walk."

"Well, where are you headed?"

"I'm going to visit St. Mary's today."

St. Mary's is a bit of a walk. "It's no trouble to give you a ride."

"I like walking. But thanks for offering." He smiles at me and is gone.

I hear movement again on the stairs. I turn and expect to see my mother and L'Raine. Instead Max is bounding toward me. He is wearing baggy carpenter shorts, a canary yellow dress shirt, and flip-flops.

"Hey." He is cheerful, as always.

This is the first I've seen of him since dinner at Ping's on Friday. I wonder if he even remembers that he forgot to take Father Laurent and Liam to the airport yesterday.

"Don't worry. I took care of it." I say cheerfully.

He stops on the step just ahead of me. "Huh?"

"I took care of it."

He has the puzzled face of a Labrador retriever wondering where his tennis ball has disappeared to. "Took care of what?"

"You know. Getting Father Laurent and Liam to the airport yesterday."

Realization floods over his face with alarming speed. He plops down beside me on my step. "Omigosh. I forgot."

"Yes. You did."

He looks away—at the plaster wall in front of us, at the heavy wood door that leads to the sales floor of Something Blue. "I can't believe I forgot."

I can.

He turns back to me. "So you took them? And they got there in time?"

"It's all good. Lucky for you I had a boring morning stretching ahead of me."

"So you didn't mind?"

"No, I didn't mind."

"I'll pay for your gas."

"You're not paying for my gas."

He leans forward. "I guess we're even then. You don't me owe me anymore."

"Owe you?" I can think of no reason why I should owe Max anything.

"Yeah. For going with you to Ping's on Friday. Remember?"

I throw him a look of mock contempt. "You were supposed to *sit* by me and keep me from having to make conversation with a man I didn't know. Which you didn't!"

"Well, that's not my fault. Your mother handled the seating."

"You owe *me*," I say tossing my head. "Not only did you get a free meal at my favorite restaurant, you got to sit by my gorgeous niece. You owe me for that and for filling in for you as airport shuttle service."

He rewards me with easy silence. Max could care less that he owes anybody anything. "Okay. You're right. Next time you want me to keep the blind date at bay, I'll knock over chairs to be able to sit by you. That should go over pretty good. That's probably worth two."

"There aren't going to be any more blind dates," I grumble.

"No?"

"I told Mom not to fix me up anymore. I want whatever's going to happen to happen naturally and without—"

"I totally agree," Max interrupts and I realize he's talking about himself. "I don't want anyone playing Cupid. It's just not cool."

I've been so focused on myself I haven't stopped to think that Max probably has friends and family members trying to fix him up with dates just like I have. It's one of the few things he and I have in common.

"My mother tried to get you and me together, you know," I say. "When you first moved in here."

Max is thoughtful for a moment. He doesn't seem stunned that I said this. I guess it was probably obvious to him, too, what Mom was up to. "Nah, I just think she was wondering if we *did* see each other more often, *would* we, you know, get together."

His candor surprises me, though I don't know why it should. Max is about as transparent as anyone I know. I suddenly have the urge to ask him if he's ever wished there had been more between us. I know he'll give me a truthful answer.

"Max, have you ever wanted to be more than just friends?"

He turns his head to stare at me. I force myself to not look away. "Have you?"

Not the response I was expecting.

"I asked first," I counter.

He hesitates for a moment. "When we were in high school I did."

"Really?"

"Yeah. Sure. But you were dating that Ryan dude and then when you broke up with him I could just tell I didn't have a chance with you."

"How could you tell that?" I don't recall warding off any advances by Max. How could he have known that?

"Well, did I?"

I don't answer.

"I could just tell, Daisy. And actually, when we both went away to college it seemed pretty clear we would always be just friends. And I was okay with that."

For some inexplicable reason I feel like I've just been slapped. It's a little like being abandoned all over again. Although in a different way. Deep down I want Max to have wanted me. Even though I really don't have any feelings for him beyond those of friendship. It's that monster in me rearing its ugly head again. I reach into my skirt pocket to touch the little blue heart Father Laurent gave me yesterday morning.

"But how did you *know* that?" I ask.

"Same way you did. You've always known we would only ever be good friends, haven't you? Haven't you always known?"

The little heart feels thin and weightless in my fingers. "I guess."

"It's not because we're not totally cool people, either, 'cause we are," Max offers. Guess he can tell I'm a little bruised. "It's just that there wasn't that special thing between us, that...you know..."

He stops, unable to come up with the right word. I think of *Sleepless in Seattle* and Max's flair for making coins and cards disappear.

"Magic?" I'm confident this will resonate with him.

But Max shakes his head. "No, it's not magic. Magic can all be explained. All of it. Every trick I do is really just manipulation and misdirection. I can't believe that's what true love is like."

"No, I guess it isn't."

"I think it's more like...like you suddenly find yourself a prisoner with no possibility of escape but you couldn't choose another life if you wanted to. Your whole life is wrapped up in that other person. You'll never leave. You'll never want to. I don't think there's a word for that."

I can't remember Max ever having said anything so eloquently.

"Think we'll know it when we see it?" I ask.

Max stands up. "Oh, yeah. It'll knock our socks off." He walks over to the door that leads to the parking lot, opens it, and swings it wide. "Ciao." He winks a goodbye to me.

"Bye, Max."

His surprising words are swirling about in my head as the back door closes and I hear footfalls behind me.

My mother and aunt are ready to go.

TWENTY

There's a standing invitation to everyone in the building to join Rosalina and Mario for Sunday dinner if you've no other plans and are in the mood for South American cuisine. What began as an impromptu gathering of whoever was around one Sunday evening four months ago has blossomed into something of a regular block party. Only it's not a block, it's an apartment building, and there are only nine units. Ten if you count Reuben, and he's hardly ever here.

Mom and L'Raine often come, but they don't eat anything but Rosalina's rice since they both claim to have issues with spicy food. Wendy and Philip are usually there, and so are Max and Father Laurent. I go primarily to be around people who seem to be living perfectly normal lives. Max goes for the food, and Father Laurent for the company. Solomon has been once, maybe twice. I think he has a thing about eating off a plate on his lap. It must really bug him. He usually has somewhere else he needs to be on Sunday nights.

Rosalina is as masterful at cooking as she is at alterations. Sometimes I can't pronounce the dishes she makes, but I've not tasted one yet that I didn't love, even if I did need to wash it down with plenty of ice water.

So, as I head back to The Finland after a long walk on the shore of Lake Calhoun, I'm anticipating an exquisite meal with enough eye-popping spice to chase away the boring dregs of my lousy weekend.

Shelby still hasn't called me back.

Max isn't in love with me.

I'm not in love with anyone, either.

I'm beyond gloomy; I'm bitter.

I can't sell my wedding dress.

I yank open the back door of the building and head up the stairs. The aroma of something wonderful and wild is wafting down the stairwell.

Whatever Rosalina is making smells wickedly fiery and inviting.

I turn the key in the lock and head to the kitchen to toss my empty water bottle into the sink.

My answering machine is flashing merrily. I press play.

"Hey, girlfriend. It's Shelby...come on...pick up...okay, I guess you're really not there. Sorry I missed your call yesterday. Eric invited me to meet his family. They were all getting together at Big Birch Lake for some reunion thing. So anyway, I went. But I'm home now, no plans for tonight, so call me. Okay. Catch you later."

So she met Eric's family. His family. *Think happy thoughts, Daisy.* I reach into my shorts pocket to stroke the little blue heart. *Think happy thoughts for your best friend.*

The message machine beeps as it prepares to relay the second message. It's probably Shelby telling me, "Oops, I forgot! Eric's taking me to dinner tonight so I guess I won't be home after all."

But it's not Shelby's voice I hear.

It's Daniel's.

I lean against the wall for support as soon as I hear him say my name.

My name, my name, my name...

"Daisy? It's Daniel. Um, just wondering if you have a minute or two to get together? I, uh, I understand if you don't want to. I just...I just kind of wanted to see you. Hope it's okay that I called. I'd really like to talk to you face-to-face. Um. Man, I hate leaving phone messages...I'll just try you back later. So. See ya."

Click.

Beep.

End of messages.

For a moment I do nothing. I just stand there with the wall of my kitchen holding my body erect.

Then I press play and listen to it again.

And again.

I slide down the wall, my knees coming forward so that when I rest my bottom on the kitchen floor, my bent knees are there to cradle my head.

Lord, Lord, Lord. Now what do I do?

I raise my head. "What do I do?" I yell to the ceiling where God dwells.

And I hear no answer.

Daniel called me.

Daniel wants to see me.

Daniel wants to talk to me.

Face-to-face.

He sounded contrite. He sounded hopeful.

He sounded like a man who has changed his mind.

I lay my head back on my knees.

This can't be happening. Not after everything I've been through. Not after sending back all the bridal shower gifts. Not after canceling the church, the flowers, the photographer, the caterer. Not after having to explain a million times why I wasn't getting married after all. Not after all those tears. Not after opening Something Blue and putting a sales tag on my own wedding dress and placing it on a mannequin with no head. Not after weeks and months of trying to piece my world back together.

This can't be happening.

Daniel wants to see me.

He wants to talk to me.

How long I sit like this, dazed and confused, I don't know. I just know that at some point the phone rings and I can't seem to move.

It's him. It's him calling me back. My heart is pounding madly in my chest.

I can't answer it.

It rings four times and the answering machine kicks in.

I hold my breath, waiting to hear his voice again.

"Daisy. It's Rosalina. Jus' wondering if you're coming. It's all ready and—"

I scramble to my feet as relief floods across me. I grab the phone, interrupting her message. "Rosalina, I'm here. I'm coming. I'll be right up."

"Oh, *bueno*. Can you knock on Father Laurent's door, too, and tell him?"

"Sure. Of course."

We hang up.

I'm actually not very hungry anymore. But I don't want to be home tonight. I really don't want to be home when the phone rings again.

I need time to think.

I need to pray.

I need to chat with Harriet.

No, I need to talk to Father Laurent.

I head to my bedroom and change into a clean shirt and denim shorts.

I'm out the door again in five minutes.

A few seconds later, I am tapping lightly on Father Laurent's door. From inside I hear him call out, "Come in."

I open his door and step inside. His apartment is just like mine; all the apartments at The Finland are pretty much the same. But his living room is full of bookshelves and books; comfy, fat, brown chairs; and piles of newspapers and magazines. The fragrance of fruity pipe tobacco hangs in the air. My apartment is a minimal sea of pale blue, linen white, and creamy yellow, and no knick-knacks or bookshelves or piles of magazines. I like my apartment, but Father Laurent's feels more welcoming, in spite of its clutter.

He is sitting at his computer desk by a window that looks out onto the street below. He is wearing a headset. He waves me over.

"There are actually quite a few shipwrecks up there, Liam. Even tales of ghost ships." Father Laurent is speaking into the mouthpiece of his headset and looking at his computer screen. I make my way over there and can see that he's talking to Liam using a webcam. Liam appears to be sitting at a computer desk, too. His face looks remarkably clear on the screen. "You can learn all about the *Edmund Fitzgerald* when you get up there."

Father Laurent looks up at me. "Hey, Liam. I have Daisy here with me. Want to say hi?" Without waiting a second, he hands me the headset. I fumble for it and slip it on. I lean over to catch the lens of the webcam.

"Hey, Liam. How's it going?"

"Okay."

"I hear you're going camping on Lake Superior. You'll have a great time."

"Yeah. I want to see the shipwrecks."

How like a boy to want see destruction up close and personal.

"Most of those are all under water, I think."

"My dad says there's one in Two Harbors that people can dive to. It's a schooner called the *Ely*. It sank in 1896."

"So you dive?"

The boy shakes his head. "No. But someday I want to."

Then he turns his head away from the camera to talk to someone else. Ramsey, probably.

Liam swings his head back around. "Dad's grilling and it's time to eat."

"Well, let me give you back to your grandpa, then. Bye, Liam."

I hand the mouthpiece back to Father Laurent and he says goodbye, too. He pulls the mouthpiece away from his ear and clicks off the site.

"Well. That was fun. Ramsey set me up with the little computer camera and microphone. I won't see as much of Liam now that Ramsey's back and Liam's spending the summer in Duluth. So this will help."

"Yeah. It's a great idea." My mind quickly returns to the befuddled state it was in when I knocked on his door. "Father, Rosalina wanted me to tell you dinner's ready. And—"

But he interrupts me. "You go on ahead. I think I'll just have some tomato soup tonight."

"Oh. Okay." But I really want his opinion on what I should do. "Father?"

"Yes?"

"When I got home today from my walk, there was a message from Daniel on my answering machine."

"Oh?"

"He said he'd really like to talk to me. He didn't ask me to call him back. He just said he'd try again. He wants to see me."

Father says nothing for a moment. "Did he say anything else?"

"Well, he said he'd understand if I didn't want to see him and he hoped it was okay that he called. Father, he sounded sorry. Apologetic."

Father breathes in deeply. "I see."

"Do you? Do you see? 'Cause I don't. I don't see at all." My voice sounds a little shrill in my ears.

"So what do you want to do?"

"What *should* I do?"

"Well, Daisy, there may not be a right or wrong here. I mean, I don't know if it's a matter of what you *should* do as much as what you'd *like* to do. I don't know how you left things a year ago, but if you've never forgiven him and he's asking for forgiveness, well, then I'm inclined to tell you to seize the opportunity to talk with him. Not so much for him but for you."

I really can't decide right now if I've forgiven Daniel. He actually didn't *do* anything bad to me. He just hurt me without wanting to. And I suppose I should forgive him for that. But that's not what's consuming my thoughts at the moment. "What if he wants to get back together again?"

Father Laurent blinks. "What if he does?"

"What should I do?" I know it even as I say it that no one can answer that question for me except me.

"What do you think God is telling you to do?"

I don't know. I haven't asked him. I opted for panic. "I'm not sure."

Father Laurent smiles. "In all the years I have known God, I've never known him to withhold wisdom from someone who asked for it."

"What if I don't hear God's answers very well?" I squeak.

"Well, then obviously you need to hush up and listen better."

Now I am the one who is mutely blinking. Father Laurent has never sounded more frank.

As I'm contemplating all this, Father Laurent reaches for my hand and says a quick prayer for me, interceding for me, beseeching God to lay a little wisdom on me. The prayer is over before I know it. He squeezes my hand and lets go.

"Sure you don't want to come to dinner at Rosalina's and Mario's?" I ask.

He shakes his head. "I'm a little tired tonight. Next Sunday I will, though."

"Want me to open up that can of soup and get it going for you?"

"That's very kind. But you just go on ahead."

"All right." I turn to start to walk away. "Thanks, Father."

His smile is wide as he sits there in his chair.

TWENTY-ONE

Dear Harriet,

I hardly know where to begin.

I guess I can start by telling you that I don't need to worry about becoming Daisy Dacey because it's never going to happen. Max isn't in love with me. And yes, I know I'm not in love with him, either. But I've wondered over the years if maybe he has romantic feelings for me. I can assure you he doesn't. Not since he was seventeen, anyway.

He says loving someone so much that you commit to spending the rest of your life with them is like becoming a prisoner. It's like the ultimate surrender. You cease to be your own. It sounds medieval when I write it. It didn't sound like a life sentence you'd want to get out of when Max said it. It sounded like a life sentence you hope will never end.

I don't know why I told you about that first. That is not the most unsettling thing that happened to me today.

Daniel called me. He left a message saying he wants to see me. Can you believe it? He actually sounded like he's sorry for what he did to me. Yeah, I know he apologized back then, but today he sounded like he truly regretted what he did. That's different. Before he was just sorry he had hurt me. Now he sounds like he wishes he could take it all back. Like he wishes he hadn't broken off our engagement.

He said he would try calling me again later.

I went to Rosalina's and Mario's hoping he'd call while I was gone but he didn't. So when I came back from dinner I was a mess waiting for the phone to ring, which it didn't. Finally, at nine-thirty, I called Shelby

*and we talked for an hour and I kept waiting to hear that "call-waiting"
sound but I didn't hear it.*

*Shelby thinks I shouldn't give him a second chance. I asked her, What
if he's changed? What if he's a different guy? And she said Daniel needs
to prove it first. Shelby asked me if I still loved him and I told her I've
been trying so hard this past year to convince myself I don't love him
that I really don't know what I feel. I can tell she wants me to keep my
distance with Daniel. Easy for her to say. She's got this great new boyfriend who's already taken her to meet his family and who buys her
flowers all the time and who puts little notes in her desk in her class-
room.*

Father Laurent says I should wait on God for direction.

Max says I should I wait until my socks get knocked off.

Shelby says I should wait for someone who deserves me.

*And I just see myself as an old woman sitting on the curb with ugly
socks on her feet waiting for something to happen.*

What does Harriet say?

I'm trying to watch The Sound of Music. *But I keep listening for the
stupid phone to ring, even though it's after eleven. Did you know when
Fräulein Maria is walking down the aisle in that beautiful Salzburg
cathedral with a mile-long train on her wedding dress and that beautiful
stately music that gives me goose bumps, the nuns are singing, "How do
you solve a problem like Maria?" I mean, the score sounds as lovely as
Pachelbel's Canon and she looks radiant in that wedding dress and the
nuns are singing about what a problem she is.*

But no one is listening to the words.

*It's all about the beautiful dress, the cathedral, her march down the aisle,
the music that accompanies her, and the look on Maria's smiling, veiled
face.*

No one is thinking what a problem she is.

Dear Daisy,

Regarding your current dilemma: Max is a good friend. Someone you can trust to be perfectly honest with you. Shelby is a good friend, too. She is not being cautious because she's happily in love and you're not. She's cautious because she cares about you. And Father Laurent is the consummate friend—perceptive and compassionate.

And then of course there's me. Your Voice of Reason. I tell you what deep down you already know.

You're really very lucky to have four such devoted comrades at your side.

You know what I will tell you.

I'll tell you that if Daniel calls back and you refuse to see him, you will always wonder what it was he would've said. Always.

I know you well enough to know you won't want to live with that hanging over you. Especially while you wander about the planet waiting for your socks to be blown off.

Should you start seeing him again?

My dear, he hasn't asked you yet.

You are always trying to hop your way across bridges before you get to them. Wait until you come to the point when you have to choose. And even then, you don't have to make up your mind until you're ready to take a step forward.

Yes, no one is paying much attention to the words when Maria walks down the aisle. It's indeed the music we hear. The way the notes are being played. In that one perfect way they were meant to be played.

Harriet

TWENTY-TWO

Mom, L'Raine, and I are standing in front of a dress form bearing my latest acquisition: a 1920s gown I bought on approval from a woman on the East Coast who phoned me and told me about it.

The three of us are trying to decide if we like it.

Actually, it's Mom and L'Raine who are contemplating its virtues. I am half in and half out of the conversation. More out than in.

I didn't sleep well last night.

I kept hearing "The Lonely Goatherd" song in my head, a mind-numbing effect from watching *The Sound of Music* late at night when I should've been in bed.

And then of course, I couldn't get Daniel's call out of my mind. I even got up once and listened to the phone message again, just to hear his voice. Not just the sound of his voice, but the sound of regret in his voice.

He sounds remorseful.

Okay, so why didn't he call back then?

He said he'd call back later. Doesn't that usually mean the same day?

Maybe he's afraid I really don't want to see him and he's putting off calling me back because he really had to work up the courage to call me the first time. It's possible he might think I don't want to see him. We parted on kind of a harsh note.

I don't know if "harsh" is the right word.

Less-than-amicable terms?

See, the trouble with breaking an engagement ten days before the wedding is you have to conduct so much of the breakup together. Laugh if you will, but it's true. You have to break up together. You have to coordinate who's going to cancel what. Who's going to give back what. It's like a divorce with no lawyers, no court, no papers, no façade to hide behind. All you have is the evidence of your shared dream now shattered. And you have to jointly sweep up the shards. I hated it.

I'm going to put that in my *Rules of Disengagement*. That's going in the first chapter. That there's more to calling off a wedding than just not showing up at the church. Canceling a wedding just days before it's supposed to happen is as labor-intensive as deciding to throw one together at the last minute. And it takes an emotional toll you wouldn't believe, especially if you're the one who was walked out on.

So, yes, I was a bit unstable around Daniel during the days of our highly orchestrated breakup. And then I went out of my way to avoid him at the place where we both worked until I got out of there and into The Finland and Something Blue. Oh, and I did cry like a child on his mother's shoulder when she came over to my apartment to "say goodbye."

The one time he called me afterward, to see how I was doing, I could barely speak to him. Not because I was angry but because I was so taken by emotion. He surely thought I was being curt with him because I was mad. I wasn't being curt. I was just mute with throat-closing numbness—the kind you get when words simply fail you.

So, I guess I can see why Daniel might wonder if I really don't want to see him.

Still, he should've called me back last night.

You don't set out to win someone back by saying you're going to call back later and then not call back—

"Daisy!"

I yank myself out of my mental somersaults. Mom is staring at me. So is L'Raine. "What?"

"You haven't heard a word I've said, have you?" Mom's eyes are locked on mine.

"Yes. No. I don't know. What did you say?"

"I said, maybe Rosalina could add some champagne-colored lace to make it truly an off-white dress. We're never going to be able to convince anyone this is white."

"Sure."

"Daisy, what's the matter?"

For a second I just stand there, looking at the dress but not really looking at it. Then I open my mouth and a flood of words spills out. "Daniel called me last night. He wants to see me. And I don't know what I want to do. I didn't actually talk to him. I was out when he called and he left a message. He said he'd call back. And he hasn't."

"Oh my!" L'Raine whispers.

"What does he want to see you about?" Mom's eyes are wide with speculation and concern.

"I don't know. He didn't say. He sounded...he sounded apologetic."

"Oh my, oh my." L'Raine is shaking her head.

Mom's brow is creased with consternation. "Daisy, I don't know."

"You suppose he's had a change of heart?" L'Raine's eyes are glassy with ready tears.

Mom shoots her a look of caution. "Well, he shouldn't expect just like that that Daisy wants him back. He ought to have to fight for her."

Mom turns her head back to me. "Make him fight for you. Play hard to get."

"Mom!"

"I'm serious. You make him woo you back. He has to make up for all the trouble and heartache he's caused you!"

"I knew of a man who once sent the woman he loved and had hurt a dozen roses every day until she agreed to marry him," L'Raine says dreamily.

"L'Raine." Mom's voice is stern. "Flowers don't compensate for wrongs suffered."

L'Raine shrugs. "They don't hurt, either."

I should've kept my mouth shut about the whole thing. "Let me just take this one step at a time, okay?"

"Just be careful, Daisy."

"I will, Mom, I promise."

I leave them to haggle over the color of the vintage dress and Daniel's true intentions. A customer has walked in the door. I can tell she's a woman engaged to be married and is looking for the perfect dress. I can see it in her eyes.

The morning passes slowly, as Monday mornings do, and as the afternoon begins its lazy crawl the phone rings. I'm in the little office in the back of Something Blue and I pick it up.

"Daisy? It's Daniel."

Heart, stop fluttering like a hummingbird on caffeine. Voice, please continue to keep working.

"Hello, Daniel." Nicely delivered. Soft. Under control. Not a trace of fear, feistiness, or phlegm.

"Did I call at a bad time?" He sounds very accommodating. Polite.

"No. It's not too busy at the moment."

"I tried calling you yesterday. I guess you got my message?"

"Yes."

"So. So, would it be okay if I came over?"

Heart isn't paying attention to instructions. Voice, do not fail me.

"Come over? You mean here? To the store?"

Three dumb questions in a row. Voice is also a traitor.

"Would that be okay?" He sounds insistent, but nicely so.

"Well, when?"

"I'm taking today off, so I was hoping to come by today. Like now, if that's okay."

My stomach has now joined the mutinous company of other

bodily organs. It is twisting madly inside me. I sense movement in the doorway of my office and I look up. Mom is peeking her head in. Does she know who I'm talking to? She has a very severe look on her face.

"I'm…now wouldn't actually be the best time for me." I can hardly believe I've said this. Mom starts to smile like a Cheshire cat.

"Oh. Any chance later on would be better?"

"Well…" I feign a look at a busy calendar. "Maybe just before closing today. Like four? No, more like four-thirty."

"Sure. Okay. And thanks, Daisy. I'll come by your place at four-thirty."

I suddenly do not want Daniel to step into a sea of used wedding dresses with mine bobbing helplessly in the mix. "I'd rather just meet somewhere, Daniel." Mom's grin widens. She thinks I'm being coy. I'm a coward—that's what I am.

"Oh. Okay. That ice cream place you like?"

Daniel remembers I like gelato…"Sure, that'd be fine."

"Okay. Well. See you then."

"Bye, Daniel."

As I hang up, Mom walks away whispering, "Well done, Daisy."

The afternoon slogs by like cold ketchup at a March picnic. I try not to watch the clock, but I do. I try not to practice in my head the lines I might try on Daniel—like, "I think we should take it slow this time, Daniel"—but I do. I resist the urge to go upstairs to my apartment to put something else on. I'm already wearing a very fashionable celery green suit with an ecru silk top underneath.

But green isn't Daniel's favorite color on me. Pink is.

I end up spending the hours tossing away these thoughts every twenty minutes, all the while trying to absorb Mom's and L'Raine's well-intentioned advice, which also besets me every twenty minutes.

Don't take him back all at once.

Don't hurt his feelings.

Smile.

Don't cry.

Ask how he's been.

Tell him you need to pray about getting back together.

Don't fidget.

Don't eat anything colored.

Don't hug him hello. Don't hug him goodbye, either.

By four-ten, I'm a walking basket case. Max comes into Something Blue as I'm trying to fluff up my curls in one of the floor-length mirrors.

He says hello and starts to walk past me to the door to the stairs, when Mom decides he needs to know where I'm going.

"Daniel called and wants to meet her," she announces to Max as he walks past us. "Can you believe it?"

Max stops, turns, and stares at me. "He does?"

"Don't look so surprised, Max," I yank a lipstick tube out of my purse and begin to apply a thin coat.

"I'm not surprised he called you, I'm just surprised you're going."

I turn away from the mirror. "Why is that?"

He blinks. "Because." And he says nothing else. He doesn't mention our conversation on the back stairs yesterday. But I'm sure he's thinking about it.

"She's being smart this time," Mom says in my defense. Max just shrugs.

I've got to get out of here. It's early yet, but I'll walk slowly.

"I'm leaving." I grab my purse and walk away before anyone can give me any more advice about anything.

TWENTY-THREE

I use the three blocks between Lorenzo's Gelateria and Something
Blue to have a little conversation with God.

I tell him that I'm not in the mood for a relationship with someone
if he's not going to bless it. So, if Daniel is not the man for me, I want
God to make me brave and help me tell Daniel we're not getting back
together again.

Make me brave. Make me brave.

I come within view of Lorenzo's glass-topped sidewalk tables and
their red striped umbrellas. Daniel is seated at one. He sees me and
stands. Smiles.

He looks great.

His sandy blonde hair is sun-streaked. He's got on canvas shorts,
sandals, and a tropical camp shirt. I've outdressed him.

But he looks like he's happy to see me, like he's admiring the way
I am walking toward him.

I command the butterflies in my stomach to curl up and die.

When I reach him, he leans forward, takes my hands in his, and
kisses me on the cheek just below my right earlobe. I catch a whiff of
Acqua di Gio. Intoxicating.

"Daisy, you look wonderful. Really." He steps backs and motions
toward the table. "Can I get you anything? Ice cream? Cappuccino?"

I've no appetite. None.

"No, thanks."

We sit. I lean back in my chair and he sits forward in his.

"So how have you been?" He looks genuinely interested.

I give him the answer I practiced all afternoon even though I didn't want to. "Great. And you?"

"Doing well, doing well." He cocks his head. "I can't get over how you've changed."

"Have I?"

"You look every inch like a smart professional who owns her own business."

Hmmm. What to say to that? "And how are your parents?"

He hesitates. "Oh. Great. They're both great."

"And Melissa and Kyra?" His sisters.

"Fine. Melissa just got her MBA. Kyra's got one year left at the U."

A second of silence hangs between us.

"I saw the article in the newspaper about your boutique when it opened. It was a great story." He sounds a little…over polite.

I *really* don't want to talk about Something Blue. Daniel seems impressed that I have it, but I can't move past *why* I have it. "Thanks."

Another awkward moment of dead air follows.

I wish he'd just get to whatever it is that's on his mind. We really don't need to waste any time with small talk. We were almost married, for heaven's sake.

"Daisy, I'm really glad to see that you're doing so well. I still feel bad about what happened. I really do."

I recognize the apologetic tone from his phone message. It unnerves me. I pull out the practiced line. "I know you didn't intend to hurt me."

"I didn't! Honestly, I didn't. I shouldn't have done that to you. You're an amazing person. I never really got it. And I'm sorry I didn't."

My throat is tightening despite my mental commands to calm down. "It's okay, Daniel. I don't hold it against you. Really, I don't."

He sits back in his chair and smiles wide, like I've just made his day. "I'm so glad to hear that."

I can hear my mom chiding me. *Don't let him weasel his way back into your heart, Daisy. Make him woo his way back in.*

"That makes what I need to tell you that much easier."

Mom's voice disappears from my head. What did he just say?

"See, the thing is, Daisy, I'm...I'm getting married."

A sensation of stifling weight envelops me in an instant. It feels like the ugly, heavy apron I wear when I get my teeth x-rayed has just been thrown on top of my body with alarming force. The air around me is at once oppressive.

I can't speak.

Harriet comes to the rescue. I can feel her crawling her way out of my inner self to take over for me.

"You're getting married?" My voice is calm. But it is not my voice.

"I know it probably seems kind of quick, but I met Dana in January and, well, we just...we just hit it off. It seems like I've known her all my life."

"You're getting married?"

"I don't want you worrying about a lot of our mutual friends coming to the wedding. We're actually getting married in the Virgin Islands over the Fourth of July. So it's just going to be family and a few friends."

He's studying me, searching my face for evidence that I'm going to have a fit right here at Lorenzo's.

"Wow. I guess I should say congratulations," I say instead.

I can tell he's amazed how nicely things are turning out for him. "Daisy, I wanted you to hear this from me. I didn't want you hearing it from anyone else."

"Thanks. I appreciate that." Wise, polite Harriet.

"So, are you okay with all this? I don't want to leave anything undone."

"Sure, Daniel. I'm happy for you. I wish you all the best."

Now he is practically dancing with joy. He gets the girl he loves and the absolution he craves. "Thanks, Daisy. For understanding. You really are amazing. Are you seeing anyone? 'Cause whoever he is, he's the luckiest guy in the world. Next to me, of course!"

"Of course." I totally ignore his question.

He doesn't seem to know what to say next and Harriet certainly isn't going to make it any easier for him.

"It's been great seeing you." His voice has the edge of finality to it. "Can I walk you back to your boutique?"

"No. It's such a nice afternoon. I think I'll just sit here for a little while and enjoy it."

"Okay, then." He stands, hesitates, and then leans over to give me a peck on the other cheek. "See you around."

I smile. The demure grin of a calm, collected soul. "See you."

He smiles, and then turns and walks away. His sandals make a slapping sound on the pavement.

He's wearing no socks.

TWENTY-FOUR

Dear Harriet,

Thanks for stepping in to save the day. I would've been lost without you today.

I don't know how to explain what I'm feeling at this moment. There are probably words for this, but I don't know what they are. I feel kind of numb actually. Shelby says Daniel is an absolute toad. Mom says he just happens to be nothing like Dad and that's who I should wait for—a guy like Dad. L'Raine says you can't help whom you love. And whom you don't.

Max heard everything I told Mom and L'Raine and he just said, "Well, Daisy, that's that. Want to go to Cody's tonight and watch the Twins game?"

I went.

They lost.

Dear Daisy,

Was happy to be of assistance.

L'Raine is probably right. Mom surely is.

By the way, the Twins play again on Friday. And the day after that. And the day after that.

Harriet

TWENTY-FIVE

I was tying ribbons around tiny bags of Jordan almonds the moment Daniel chose to tell me he couldn't marry me.

When he told me he *wouldn't* marry me.

It was on a Wednesday evening. I was sampling the nuts as I tied bag after bag and was on a bit of a sugar high when he dropped by my apartment. My old apartment. I had the Home and Garden Channel on and I had just finished a bean-and-cheese burrito. A little heel of wrapped tortilla was still warm on a paper plate next to me, when the doorbell rang and I went to answer it.

I was surprised to see him. He hadn't called first. The clueless romantic in me thought it was just peachy that my fiancé had come over to my apartment unannounced. That meant he missed me. I hadn't seen him at work much that day or the day before that. His department was busy doing a huge networking redesign for the executive suite, so I was under the impression he was being worked too hard.

So there he was, standing there on my doorstep, ten days before our wedding, looking needy.

"Daniel!" I cooed. "Hey! Come on in." I was bouncy, excited, with sugar and love running through my veins. He came inside and I barely noticed his mood did not match mine. I led him over to my living-room couch and proudly showed him my handiwork. I was halfway done creating three-hundred-fifty satin-and-tulle bundles of pastel-hued almonds. Each one had a little vellum streamer with the words "Daniel and Daisy" embossed in silver ink.

"Want to try one?" I handed him a pale pink almond and he hesitated before taking it.

"It's okay," I assured him. "We have more than we need. Guess I went a little overboard on the estimate."

Daniel took the almond, but he didn't eat it. He just stood there fingering its smoothness. I mistook his reticence for having had a bad day at the office.

"Something happen at work today?" I asked.

He looked at me, then at the almond in his hand, and then at the coffee table overflowing with cloudlike bundles of white netting and ribbons.

When he turned his eyes back to me I knew my life was about to change. Honestly, I did. He opened his mouth.

"We need to talk."

Do you know how much power exists in those four little words, strung together just like that? The tide of sugar in my body swirled, stopped. The room seemed to sway for a moment. When someone says to you, "We need to talk," it means something bad has happened. Or is about to happen.

I think I might have said, "What?"

"Can we sit down?" He didn't wait for me to answer. He just sat down on my couch and waited for me to do the same.

It was probably a full thirty seconds before I sat down next to him. Our knees weren't even touching. I wanted so much to be able to say, "What is it, darling?" But fear—cold and sure—kept my mouth shut.

Daniel didn't say anything at first; he just sat there with the almond in his fingers, breathing in and out. I know now he was summoning strength to tell me he wanted out.

"Daisy." He began with saying my name. I wish he hadn't. It made it so personal. Maybe that sounds ridiculous. But I was to spend many weeks after that night hearing echoes of him saying my name like that. "I don't know how to say this," he said.

I tried to concentrate on staying completely calm. I remember thinking to myself that Daniel was just there to tell me the honeymoon plans had been thwarted, that maybe the tickets to our flight to Aruba had been cancelled, or that he was going to have to go back to work right away. Or maybe his best friend, Ted, who was supposed to be his best man, had just been killed in a horrible car accident.

"Say what?" I whispered.

He took his time lifting his head to look at me. Then the words he apparently had so dreaded saying slipped off his lips like butter off a hot knife. "I don't want to get married."

When you are ten days away from getting married, when the wedding dress of your dreams is hanging in your closet and your spare bedroom is full of shower gifts and your coffee table is bubbling over with tiny bags of Jordan almonds, hearing words like that don't have any effect on you. Because your first thought is *I didn't just hear what I thought I heard.*

So my first two reactions were silence and a blank stare. I don't think Daniel was prepared for either one.

"Daisy, did you hear me?"

I don't clearly remember what I said or did next. I'm sure whatever it was, it removed any doubt in Daniel's mind about whether I had heard him or not. The next thing I do remember is standing and walking away from him. I think I may have said something like "You don't just do this, Daniel. This is not something you do! You don't just call off a wedding ten days before it's supposed to happen!"

"This is not something I'm *just* doing!" he fired back. "I've been agonizing over this for weeks."

Agonizing. Now there's a word to rip your heart from your body. Wanting to break up with me had put him in agony. Not the thought of leaving me, but the desire to do it.

"I can't believe you're doing this. I can't believe it." I was pacing the tiny living room. He still sat on the couch.

"Daisy, listen to me. I've been going over this in my mind for I don't know how long. I just don't think you'd be happy. For a little while, yes, you could be. But not for the long haul."

"Why? Why wouldn't I be?" I had stopped pacing and turned to face him.

"Because."

"How do you know I wouldn't be?"

"Because I wouldn't be." He said this rather softly. He knew it would feel like a knife in my chest. It did.

That's when I walked back over to the couch and knelt by him. The pose of supplication.

"You wouldn't be happy with me?" Tears were streaming down my cheeks.

He shook his head no.

"Why? Why not, Daniel?"

He paused for a moment. I truly believe he took no pleasure in saying what he said next.

"Because I don't love you enough."

The knife in my chest made a quarter-turn, slicing through an ache I thought couldn't get worse. A tiny sound escaped my throat. The word "What?" was wrapped up in it.

"I like you, Daisy. I really do. But you deserve someone who truly loves you with everything he's got. I'm not that guy."

This is where I began to plead with him.

"Daniel, think about what you are doing! We're supposed to be getting married in ten days!"

"I *am* thinking about it. That's all I've been doing. We'd be making a huge mistake, Daisy."

"Please don't do this, Daniel."

"It's the right thing to do."

"No, it's not!" I wailed.

He stood up. "I think I should go."

I sprang to my feet as well and reached out my hand to touch him. "Can't we talk about it this, Daniel? Please?"

He exhaled heavily. "It won't change anything, Daisy. I can't marry you. You shouldn't want me to."

But I did. Even while he stood there ready to leave the apartment and me, I still wanted him to marry me.

"Look, I'll call you tomorrow and we'll talk about how we're going to handle this."

"Daniel, *please!*"

He leaned down and placed the little Jordan almond on my coffee table next to a hundred-twenty-five poofs of white fabric and sweetness.

"I'm sorry. I'm really very sorry." He moved past me, walked to my front door, and opened it. A second later he was gone.

I felt for the bench of my father's piano behind me and sank down onto it. When I leaned back against the keys in my anguish, they made a fairylike sound.

I've never missed my father as much as I did in that moment, when I realized the man I loved didn't love me.

I knew I could—and would—call my mother and she'd be over in a flash to weep with me and hold me tight. But she wasn't the one who used to sing to me, "I'm half-crazy all for the love of you." She wasn't the one who called me her little girl. She's not the one who chose my name.

It was my dad who did all those things.

TWENTY-SIX

Weak rays of morning sunlight weave their way through the bits of colored glass in the window above the little altar, lighting the chapel with hushed hues.

I am sitting in the front pew.

Usually I come here to pray.

Today I am just here to listen.

I awoke this morning thinking of Daniel. Of how happy he looked yesterday. Of how much he clearly needed assurance that he could marry this girl Dana without any baggage from the past messing things up for him.

He said I was amazing.

Smart. Professional.

That the guy who falls for me will be the luckiest guy in the world.

Next to him.

I don't feel like any of those things are true about me. I don't feel like I am smart or professional or amazing.

Father Laurent told me once that there is someone who knows exactly what is true about me and what isn't, and that is God. He also told me on Sunday I need to shut up and listen if I want to hear what God is saying to me. About me.

Okay, he didn't say shut up.

But the implication was there.

So here I am.

It actually feels good to be sitting here and not cataloging my woes or ticking off my grocery list of things I want.

It feels really good to just sit and be silent.

I close my eyes and let the stillness fill me.

I don't notice that the door behind me opens. I am just suddenly aware that someone has taken the seat beside me. I know without opening my eyes that it is Father Laurent.

I keep my eyes closed. "Good morning, Father."

"Good morning, Daisy."

"Did you hear about my day yesterday?" I ask, eyes still closed.

"Yes."

"My mom told you?"

"She did."

I open my eyes and turn to him. He is looking at me with utter kindness.

"Are you okay?" he says.

I smile. "Daniel says I am amazing."

"Daisy."

I look down at my feet and laugh. A tiny little laugh. More like a chuckle. But I don't like the word *chuckle*. It's a word for clowns and sitcoms and folks whose only problem in life is that all the raisins fall to the bottom of their Raisin Bran. "I'm doing better than it probably looks, Father. I'm not mad at Daniel. I'm not sad for him. I'm just a little sad for me."

Father Laurent leans over to me like he is going to tell me a secret. "Maybe it isn't the best time to tell you this, but I think you should know that you've been designed for a deeper love than what you're looking for. We all have. The love you find in God and the love he gives you to give away to others is what you're really after, Daisy. It's what we all long for. And no one can keep you from having it and having it in abundance. No one but you."

I close my eyes again as I let his words—heavy, yet gentle—invade my brain. I know what he is trying to communicate to me is completely profound. I can feel it. And I don't want to miss it. But it feels like a concept just beyond my reach, just outside of what I can understand.

"Everything you hunger for, you've already been given," he continues. "You're already loved beyond your wildest dreams. You are wearing the ruby slippers, Daisy. They've been on your feet the whole time."

I open my eyes and look over at Father Laurent. He is smiling. He knows my fondness for movies that make me cry. "You make it sound so easy."

He pauses just for a second. "It's not that it's so easy, it's that it's so magnificent. And you don't have to fight for it. It's already yours."

I lean into him and rest my head on his shoulder. I hope he doesn't mind. It's on the tip of my tongue to call him Dad. Dad used to give me advice like Father Laurent is giving me right now. I miss him.

"Still have the little blue heart I gave you?" Father Laurent says.

"Yes."

"I want you to remember what I've told you today. Can you do that? Can you look at that little heart and remember this?"

"Yes, Father."

"Good girl. Don't forget."

"I won't. I don't quite understand it, but I won't forget it." I lift my head. I want to ask him something. "Father?"

"Yes?"

"How come you had that heart in your pocket the day you gave it to me?"

A look of longing seems to cross his face. "I was keeping it for someone."

He stands. Waits for a second with his left hand on the back of the pew. And then takes a step. Guess we're done talking about that.

"Thanks, Father."

He turns his head slowly back around. He looks a little pale. "C'mon. I'll make us a cup of tea."

I follow him out of the chapel. L'Raine is at the front counter of Something Blue. It's still twenty minutes to opening and she is polishing the glass case where our most expensive hair and veil decorations glisten on a swath of navy blue velvet.

"Good morning, L'Raine," I call out and she looks up with a sympathetic, puppy dog look on her face, testing my resolve to stay focused the very minute I emerge from the chapel.

Ahead of me Father Laurent pauses for a moment. Then he takes a step forward and stops again. He pitches forward a tiny bit and then grabs his left forearm.

"Father?"

He turns toward me and I see fear in his eyes. I rush toward him as he sinks to his knees. A groan escapes him and he screws his eyes shut in pain.

"L'Raine! Call 9-1-1!" I scream. I fall to my own knees as Father Laurent's legs give out. He collapses hard against me.

Please, please, please, God. Don't take Father Laurent. Don't take him. Don't take him.

I hear L'Raine sputtering to give our address. I hear her saying she doesn't know if Father Laurent is breathing.

I can feel Father Laurent's chest rising and falling but I cannot seem to turn my head and tell L'Raine this. It's like if I mention it, it will stop.

"Daisy?" Father Laurent whispers.

"Shhh, Father. Help is on the way."

"Don't forget what I told you."

TWENTY-SEVEN

The ambulance is several minutes ahead of me as I dash out of the building to get into my own car. Max is with me. When I ran up to my apartment to grab my purse and cell phone I was yelling his name over and over. Solomon appeared first on the stairs, in his bathrobe and clutching a bagel.

"Get Max!" I yelled as I dashed into my apartment to get my things.

"What's he done now?" Solomon called after me. "Hey, did I hear sirens?"

I didn't answer and Solomon did what I asked. Max was on the landing when I came out of my apartment; thankfully he was wearing more than just boxers—his usual attire at eight-forty-five in the morning.

"What's up?" Max had said, his hair traveling in every compass direction possible. "I thought I heard a siren."

"Max, you've got to come with me. It's Father Laurent. He collapsed downstairs. We need to follow the ambulance to the hospital."

Max said nothing. He just burst down the stairs ahead of me. When he and I got to the floor of Something Blue, Father Laurent was on a stretcher with an oxygen mask over his face and paramedics were wheeling him out the door. Mom had come downstairs and was standing next to L'Raine, who was crying softly. Mom's face was pale. No doubt she was thinking of my dad. So was I.

"Is he okay? What happened?" Max said this to the paramedics,

but they just turned to me and told me they were taking Father
Laurent to Methodist Hospital and that I should try and contact his
family.

His family.

It took me a second to comprehend that we—Mom and L'Raine
and Solomon and Mario and Rosalina and Wendy and Philip and
Max and me—aren't Father's family. It just feels like we are.

Now as Max and I bolt for my car I realize I must find a way to
get a hold of Ramsey.

I run back to the door and throw it open. I poke my head back
inside Something Blue. Mom and L'Raine haven't moved. "Mom!"

She turns her head to look at me. She is ashen.

"Go up to Father Laurent's apartment and go through his desk.
Look for an address book or anything that has Ramsey's telephone
number inside it. Or look for the Horn Blower's number!"

Her eyes widen.

"I mean Kristen! Look for Kristen's number. Okay?"

"All right."

"I've got my cell phone. Call me when you find a number."

I turn and dash away.

"What happened to him?" Max says a moment later as I start the
car and peel out of the parking lot.

"We were coming out of the chapel. He hesitated when he first
stood up in the pew and then he faltered as he was walking out. Then
he collapsed." Tears of fear are building in my eyes.

I turn onto busy Hennepin Avenue and my hands are shaking on
the steering wheel.

"Want me to drive?" Max's voice is kind, not patronizing.

"I'm okay. Thanks. Thanks for coming, Max."

"Sure."

We arrive at Methodist Hospital many long minutes after the
ambulance. I find a place to park and as Max and I are walking
toward the ER doors, my phone rings. It's Mom.

"Honey, I think I found a number for Ramsey. It's in a little brown phone book. There's three numbers under his name, actually. One says 'work,' though. And one starts with three threes."

"That's probably his cell phone. Give me the rest of that one, Mom. He and Liam are camping at the North Shore. I'm sure he has a cell phone with him."

Mom tells me the rest of the number. "Is…is he okay?" she adds. Her voice is weak. Like mine. I can't imagine running Something Blue without Father Laurent. I can't. Who will bless my little blue hearts? Who will bless me?

"I don't know, Mom. We just got here. I'll call you when I know."

I click the phone off and Max and I walk through the emergency room doors and toward whatever news waits inside.

It seems like a very long time before Max and I are told that Father Laurent isn't dead. I suppose it's only twenty minutes or so. I don't know. Time has no meaning in an emergency room.

Father had a heart attack, we are told. He survived it.

I keep saying this to myself over and over.

I've stepped outside twice to try to reach Ramsey. Both times I've gotten his voice mail. Both times I've left a message for him to call me.

The nurses understand that Max and I aren't Father Laurent's children, though we worry, fret, and pace like we are. They've told us we'll be able to see Father Laurent in a few minutes, before they move him upstairs.

A man in scrubs and a white coat is now walking toward us. Max and I stand in unison. The doctor stretches out his hand to me. "Hello, I'm Dr. Newell. Are you the family of Miles Laurent?"

"Kind of," I answer. "He feels like family to us."

"Does he have any family?"

"I'm trying to reach his son, Ramsey. He's on a camping trip. I've left two messages. I'm his friend. Daisy Murien. This is Max Dacey."

"Okay. Well, I understand you'd like to see Mr. Laurent before he's moved upstairs. I just want to let you know it can only be for a few minutes. He's stabilized but his heart has had a pretty rough morning, so you'll need to make the visit short. Mr. Laurent suffered a—"

"Father Laurent."

"Excuse me?"

"He's a retired priest. His name is *Father* Laurent."

"Oh…I see. Well, as you know, Father Laurent suffered a moderately severe myocardial infarction. A heart attack. He's got a significant arterial block that we need to take care of or he will likely have another one. We believe the best route for Mr.—ah, Father Laurent is to take him upstairs to our cath lab and insert a balloon into the blocked artery to get things running again. We use a catheter, so it's noninvasive surgery and we usually see great results. Father Laurent has been briefed on the risks and benefits and he's ready to go."

"There are risks?" I don't like hearing the word *risks* while standing in an emergency room.

"There are risks with almost any medical procedure, Ms. Murien. But we simply have to ease the conditions that led to this heart attack or he will have another—possibly more serious—episode."

Ramsey, Ramsey, where are you?

"Can you wait until I get ahold of his son?" I ask.

"If you manage to reach him in the next few minutes we can. Otherwise, no."

I hate this.

"How long will the procedure take? How long will Father Laurent have to stay in the hospital?" Max asks.

"He'll be under a general anesthetic and will be hospitalized for a few days while we monitor him. Many people are fully recovered within a month or so after an attack like this one and undergoing angioplasty."

"So we can see him now?" I ask.

"Sure. But just for a minute or two."

We follow Dr. Newell into a room with a wide door. Father Laurent is lying on a bed at a forty-five-degree angle. He is wearing a blue polka-dotted hospital gown. I've never seen him wear anything so juvenile. Monitors, tubing, and beeping machines are all around him. He sees us and smiles.

"Guess you're not rid of me yet." His voice is weak.

I reach for one of his hands. "Don't even joke that way, Father."

"Does Ramsey know?"

"I'm trying to reach him. I have his cell-phone number. My mom got it out of your apartment. I hope you don't mind."

"Of course not."

"I'll keep trying until I get him."

"Thanks." He turns his head slowly to Max. "She made you come?"

"I made ambulance sounds so we could get past all the traffic," Max jokes.

"That was nice of you. Thanks, Max."

"Father." I still have hold of his hand. "They're moving you upstairs soon to the cath lab. They told us we could only see you for a few minutes. But I want you to know I'm coming upstairs, too. I'll be right outside your door if you need anything."

"You don't have to stay, Daisy."

"Yes, I do."

I wish there was more I could do. He thinks staying is too much trouble, and I'm painfully aware of how insufficient it is. I feel for the little heart in my skirt pocket and withdraw it.

"Want to hold onto my little blue heart?" I whisper.

He grins. "I don't have any pockets in this thing. You keep it for now. Add my name when you pray over it."

The door behind us opens and a nurse steps in. "Okay, folks, we need to get Father Laurent ready for his transfer upstairs, so…if you don't mind?"

I lean down and kiss Father Laurent on the forehead. "Don't you even *think* of going anywhere," I tell him.

Max and I turn and leave the room. The beeping sounds of the machines match the cadence of our footfalls.

As soon as we're back in the lobby my phone rings.

It's Ramsey.

"What's this about my dad being in the hospital? Which one? Is he okay?"

Ramsey sounds agitated and afraid. I wonder if Liam is nearby listening to this.

"He had a heart attack this morning. I'm at Methodist Hospital with him. The doctor in the ER said it was a moderately severe one. They're taking him upstairs right now to insert a balloon into one of his arteries."

"Surgery? Just like that?" His voice is strident.

"The doctor said it's not invasive. They use a catheter to put it in."

"Can't they wait until I get there?"

"I asked, Ramsey. Believe me, I did. The doctor said it's not safe to wait. Your father could have another attack. And the next one could be worse."

There is silence on the other end.

"Okay," Ramsey finally sighs. "Liam and I will get there as soon as we can. We're in Grand Marais and we have to break camp. But we'll get there just as soon as we can. Methodist, you said?"

Grand Marais. That's practically in Canada. A good five-hour drive from here. "Yes. Methodist."

"Okay." Ramsey pauses. "Thank you for being there with him."

"You're welcome."

Another little pause.

"Okay. Goodbye."

"Bye, Ramsey."

I press the off button and turn to Max. "You don't have to stay, Max. You can take my car back and tell my mom and L'Raine how he is."

"How will you get home?"

"I can call you later. You going to be around?"

"I'll be at the studio most of the day, but yeah, I'll be around."

"I'll call you, then."

"Okay. Let us know if anything changes."

"Yep."

He walks away and I turn to the nurses' station to find out on which floor I can find the cath lab.

TWENTY-EIGHT

It is well after one o'clock before I'm allowed to see Father Laurent in his room on the third floor. I was told the angioplasty procedure went well and there had been no complications.

The room is dimly lit. Father Laurent is tucked snugly into a half-raised bed surrounded by humming machinery. He looks tired and pale.

"I hope they're done poking and prodding me for a while," he says good-naturedly when I step inside. His voice is weak.

I smile at him. "Your nurse tells me you're a squirmer around needles. I didn't know that about you."

His grin is immediate but faint. "Needles are for hems and haystacks. Have you heard from Ramsey?"

I pull up a chair by his bed. "He and Liam are on their way. They were in Grand Marais when I got ahold of them, so it will take awhile. They should be here soon."

"Where's Max?"

"I let him take my car back to Uptown. He's working at the studio today."

"But how are you going to get home?"

"I can call him. He said he'd come back to get me. I'm sure my mom or L'Raine could come for me, too."

He nods.

"Grand Marais," he says a moment later, frowning. "That's such a long drive...You told Ramsey I was okay, didn't you?"

"Yes. Don't worry. I'm sure Ramsey will drive safely."

"Guess I've ruined their camping trip."

"Father."

"This was going to be such a great time for them to get away together."

"Father, don't."

But Father Laurent doesn't seem to hear me. He just keeps talking, whispering, like I'm not even in the room with him. "This last year has been…been so hard on them both. They've needed this time away for months. Ramsey's been gone so much, working, trying to find his way back. It's been so hard…I used to counsel couples going through divorce. I knew it was a tough road, but I never really knew how much someone could suffer when their marriage ends until I saw someone I love go through it. And Liam was there, too, watching the whole thing. Watching his family get ripped in two."

He stops and I say nothing.

Maybe he *has* forgotten I'm in the room with him.

But then Father Laurent turns to me. "I didn't mean to unload on you, Daisy."

"I do it to you all the time." I match his soft tone.

"You do, don't you?"

I reach into my skirt pocket and pull out the little blue heart that Father blessed and gave to me. I think I know now why he had it in his pocket that morning in the chapel. "Was this for Ramsey?"

"Yes, it was."

"Want it back?"

"That one's yours. I know where to get more."

I fold my fingers around my little blue heart.

"I think I'll take a little snooze, Daisy. I believe they've got me doped up."

I reach with my free hand and pat his arm. "Sleep tight."

He closes his eyes and in seconds his breathing is slow and measured. I look over at the machines monitoring his pulse and heart rate—just to make sure he's okay. The moving lines look calm and unhurried.

I lean back in my chair and exhale for what seems like the first time in several hours. The little satin heart in my hand is warm from being in my pocket. I absently stroke its smooth contours, quietly picturing all the dresses in my boutique that have a heart like this one sewn into their backs. All blessed. All offering hope.

The quiet warmth of the room, the steady rhythm of the monitors, and the effects of two sleepless nights lull me into a stupor. I'm not aware when I drift off. I only know that one minute I have the little heart in my palm and am looking at it—and the next, a hand is on my shoulder and a man is saying my name.

"Daisy?"

I jerk my head up and my eyes fly open. Father Laurent is standing over me speaking my name.

No, it isn't Father Laurent. It's Ramsey.

I can feel blood rushing to my cheeks. Ramsey moves his hand off my shoulder.

Liam is standing next to him. They are both in shorts and khaki shirts and Ramsey is unshaven. I look over at Father Laurent, who is still sleeping.

"What time is it?" I mumble, trying to focus on my watch.

"A few minutes before three."

"I can't believe I nodded off like that. Hey, Liam."

"Hi, Daisy."

I stand and try to shake the sleep from my head. "Did you just get here?"

"Yes. I was just talking with the doctor out in the hall. We've only been here a few minutes, though. Thanks for staying, Daisy. You didn't have to do that."

"I wanted to."

Liam walks over to his grandfather and stares at the assortment of equipment at his bedside. "What's all this stuff?"

"Just different ways to show that Grandpa's doing okay," Ramsey turns back to me. "Thanks again for coming."

I feel like I'm being dismissed. It stings a little. "It wasn't any trouble." As I move to get my purse on the table behind me, Ramsey bends down to the floor. I see him close his fingers around a little blue heart resting by my feet.

"Is this yours?" He's standing now, holding it out to me.

Again, I feel my cheeks flood with color. "Yes. I guess I dropped it." I reach out my hand and take it.

From behind us I hear Liam say his grandfather's name.

We turn toward the bed and I can see that Father's eyes are open. He turns his head toward Ramsey. "Sorry about messing up your camping trip." His voice sounds a little groggy.

"Don't be silly, Dad." Ramsey moves toward his father.

"I'm not being silly. I really feel bad about it."

"Liam and I have the whole summer to go on a camping trip. We'll just go another time."

Father Laurent turns his head back toward Liam, who's still scrutinizing the machinery. "Well, I'll try to find a way to make it up to you both."

"We'll be fine, Dad. You have everything you need? Are they treating you all right?"

"Like a celebrity."

"Okay. I'm just going to go out in the hallway for a minute and make some hotel reservations. I'll be right back."

"Hotel reservations?" Father asks.

"So I can stay here in Minneapolis while you're in the hospital."

"You don't have to stay in a hotel, Ramsey. Just stay at my place. Liam knows where everything is. Daisy, you can give him an extra key, right?"

"Sure."

Ramsey looks deep in thought. "Well, I suppose I could. You don't want to go back to your mom's for a few days, do you, Liam?"

"No," Liam answers quickly.

"All right, then. I guess that will work."

"Good. Why don't you go and get cleaned up and settled in. You look a little organic, Ramsey. Besides," Father turns his head toward me. "This lovely young lady needs a ride home."

The drive to The Finland is blissfully short, thank goodness, because I don't know how to fill the silence other than by asking Liam a million little questions about the camping trip he and his dad almost went on. Out of the corner of my eye, I see Ramsey glancing at me. I can't tell if he's wishing I would just shut up or if he's wondering if he's allowed to answer any of the questions.

When we arrive, I take the pair through Something Blue to meet my mother and L'Raine and to let them know that Ramsey and Liam will be staying at Father Laurent's place. I step inside my office to find the spare keys to the apartments and when I come out with them, Ramsey is standing at the front counter, looking at one of the brochures for my store. He's reading about the little blue heart. My trademark. Liam is standing next to him looking bored.

Ramsey looks up at me as I walk toward him. "You really sew a heart into each dress?" His tone almost hints at mockery. Almost.

"Yes."

"For luck?"

"For something better than luck."

"And my dad is the one who blesses them?"

Apparently Father Laurent has told his son what he does in his spare time. I wonder what else he has told Ramsey. "Yes, he is."

Ramsey folds the brochure back into place and lays it on the counter with the others.

"He doesn't mind doing it, you know."

"I'm sure he doesn't." Ramsey leans down to pick up a duffel bag at his feet and Liam does the same. "Is that why you had one at the hospital today?" Ramsey's tone reveals nothing. I can't tell if he finds that notion mercenary or quirky. "So my father could bless it?"

I stiffen just a tad. I hope he doesn't notice. "No."

"No?"

I start to walk away and he and Liam follow. "No. Your father has already blessed that one."

We take the stairs to the third floor in silence.

TWENTY-NINE

Dear Harriet,

Father Laurent nearly died in my arms today.

Well, maybe he didn't see that great white light and all, but he did have a heart attack on the floor of the store this morning and I really did think he was gone—that as he lay there against me, struggling to breathe, he was slipping away to heaven.

I was scared to death, no pun intended. And he thought he was dying, too. He kept whispering to me not to forget what he had told me this morning. He had found me in the chapel waiting for wisdom from on high and he'd told me something I probably should've known all along. He used what might have been his last breath to remind me of a rather amazing thing, that it's the love of God in me and for me and through me that is my gravity, my oxygen. My light in a dark place. I don't know that I've ever really considered that it's the love I give away—not the love I receive—that truly defines me. I'm still not quite sure what to make of it.

The whole time I was waiting at the hospital I kept thinking how different this was from Dad's heart attack. I never had the chance to say goodbye to Dad. I had no opportunity to get used to the idea that he was leaving me. One moment Dad was mowing the lawn and the next he was in heaven. And he did it alone. No one held his hand when he went, or kissed his brow or begged him to stay. I think that's why I still miss him so much, because he left without saying goodbye.

I don't think Father Laurent is in danger tonight—meaning I don't think he's going to leave this world. I confess I fretted all day about what I would do if Father Laurent disappeared from my life. Ramsey made some comment today that made me consider whether the only reason I dread life without Father Laurent is because no one would bless my little blue hearts. That sounds so selfish. It looks even worse when I actually write it on paper. But I can't escape the fact that it's true. From the beginning of this journey those little blue hearts have been emblems of hope to me. Every time I sew one inside a dress I think of the words Father Laurent has prayed over it. The words are a little different for each one, but the hope is the same. Without the blessing, those hearts are just bits of blue fabric. It's the expectation I attach to them that gives them meaning. To me and to everyone else.

And yes, I need hope in my life right now. And yes, I have indeed made Father Laurent my personification of hope, just as you are my personification of reason. So argue with me on this at your own peril.

Dear Daisy,

Don't worry; I'm in no mood for arguments tonight. Am too busy contemplating Father Laurent's whispered words of wisdom. The Voice of Reason doesn't often get a chance to ponder the all-encompassing, übermysterious love of God.

Harriet

THIRTY

The knock at the door is light and tentative. I grab my coffee mug for one last swig before heading downstairs to the boutique. I swing my door open and Wendy is standing there looking flustered.

"Daisy, I'm hearing that funny noise again in the bathroom. It's coming through the heating vent. It's like, I don't know, a scratching, grating sound. I don't know what it is. Philip doesn't either. Should I tell Mario?"

She looks like she's in a hurry. "I'll tell him, Wendy," I offer.

"Maybe you should go up there and listen to it yourself. It's the weirdest sound. Mario didn't hear anything last time I called him about it. It had stopped when he got there. I'd take you up right now but I'm late for work already."

I grab my keys from the hook by the front door. "I can go check it out. I'm just on my way downstairs anyway."

"Okay. Philip's long gone so you don't need to worry about walking in on him in the buff or anything." Wendy turns and heads toward the stairs. "If you don't hear anything, just flush the toilet or run the sink. Sometimes that's when I hear it."

As I make my way to the third floor I'm grateful Mom and L'Raine are punctual people. They are both likely already downstairs at Something Blue and likely for twenty minutes already. It's not often I have to handle building concerns. Mario is as capable as they come. But this shouldn't take long. I will either hear Wendy's strange noise or I won't. And I won't be able to do a thing about it if I do. I'm wearing a linen suit and pumps—I'm not exactly dressed for bath-room trouble.

When I reach the third floor, I see that Liam and Maria Andrea are sitting outside Max's open door. Liam has a deck of cards spread out before Andrea.

"Is that your card?" Liam turns over a two of spades.

"No."

"Yes, it is."

"No, it's not."

"Are you sure?"

"I'm sure. That's not my card."

Liam looks up at me.

"One of Max's tricks?" I ask.

"It doesn't work."

"Maybe you didn't do it right," Andrea says.

"Maybe it doesn't work." Liam again.

As I start to walk past them to Wendy and Philip's apartment, Max emerges from his open doorway. A camera bag is slung over his shoulder. He hands a tripod to Liam.

"You guys ready?"

Liam slides the cards into a pile and Andrea rises to her feet.

"Where are you guys off to?" It appears the three of them are going somewhere together.

"Max is taking pictures of tigers. He said we could come." Liam is now on his feet, too.

"The zoo?"

Max shakes his head. "Nope. A big cat sanctuary south of here. On the way to Iowa. They've got lions, too."

"I'm sure they're in cages?" It doesn't surprise me that Max is taking pictures of un-zooed tigers, but his inviting Liam and Maria Andrea to come along unnerves me just a bit. I can just see him asking Liam to make a lot of noise so the tiger will look at him…

"Uh, yeah. Sure."

A Max answer to the T.

Father Laurent's door opens and Ramsey steps out. His eyes linger on me for just a second. Then he turns to his son.

"Hey, Liam, don't forget to call me at the hospital when you get back and I'll come back for you."

Before I can stop myself and think it through, I open my mouth. "I can bring him down to the hospital when he gets back."

Ramsey swivels his head to look at me.

"Cool," Max says, as if that's that. "Let's go then. Andrea, better get your screams out now, before we get there." Max starts to walk away.

"I'm not scared," Andrea replies and follows him.

"Bye, Dad." Liam stuffs the playing cards in his pocket and takes off after them.

For a second Ramsey and I just stand there watching them go, listening as Max tells Liam and Maria Andrea that a tiger's stripes are like a human's fingerprints. No two tigers have the same pattern.

Then Ramsey turns to me. "So you have a car? I thought maybe you didn't."

What an odd thing to say. "I have a car. It's no trouble to bring Liam down. Really."

"I just thought…because yesterday at the hospital you needed a ride home I thought maybe you didn't have a car."

Of course I have a car. What amazing, smart professional who owns her own business doesn't have a car? "Max came with me to the hospital in my car. I let him take it after we knew your dad was going to be okay. He had to work."

Ramsey looks past me to Max's front door. His gaze then settles back on me. "You don't have to bring Liam down to the hospital if you have better things to do. I don't mind coming back for him."

"But I don't."

He stares at me.

"I mean I don't have better things to do. I'd like to see Father Laurent today. If that's okay."

He blinks. "Ah, sure. That'd be fine."

"Okay."

Silence.

"Did you find everything you need in the apartment? Can I get you anything?" I ask.

"Everything's fine. Unless you have access to a fax machine?"

"I have one in the office downstairs. Feel free to use it anytime."

"Okay. Thanks. I should only need to send a few pages. Something I should've taken care of before the camping trip. May as well do it now."

Does he mean at this precise moment? "Now?"

"What?"

"Now? You want to do it now?"

"I guess I could. Just a sec."

He disappears back inside Father Laurent's apartment. He didn't mean now in the literal sense. He meant it in the general sense. I'm a dope. A second later he is back with papers in his hand. "Okay," he says.

He shuts the door behind him and we begin to walk toward the stairs. It seems very quiet in the hallway. Too quiet.

"So, Liam tells me you're a landscape architect."

His eyebrows arch the tiniest bit. I know that look of surprise. I do that all the time. He is wondering what else I know about him.

"Uh. Yes, I am."

"That sounds like a lovely way to spend your day—making yards beautiful."

Ramsey stares at his feet as we descend the first set of stairs. "I guess it is."

His answer surprises me. "Isn't it?"

"Well, what I've been doing lately is designing green roofs. They're an aesthetic feature, but they're more functional than anything else."

"What's a 'green roof'?"

"It's a roof covered with vegetative material. Green roofs keep buildings dry by conveying water away from the roof deck. And they reduce the volume of storm water in city sewer systems and absorb ambient heat."

"Sounds like a fancy way of saying you build roof gardens."

"Well, your typical roof garden is containerized. A green roof doesn't use containers. The roof *is* the garden."

I think that sounds absolutely heavenly. I tell him so. Ramsey seems unimpressed with what he does for a living.

"So, how do you do it? Do you put topsoil on the roof and just plant grass and stuff?" I ask. We are near the entrance to the boutique.

"It's a little more complicated than that. The growing compound is pretty specialized."

"But the stuff that grows is ordinary, right? Like grass and shrubs and vines."

"Pretty much."

I place my hand on the door to Something Blue. "Sounds like a lovely roof garden to me. I bet it looks like one, too."

He shrugs. He doesn't correct me.

It's on the tip of my tongue to say it's too bad he has to go all the way to Tokyo for four months to be a part of something so lovely and functional but Harriet within me insists I keep my meddling mouth shut.

It's not until Ramsey has faxed his papers and left for the hospital that I realize I never made it to Wendy and Philip's.

THIRTY-ONE

Max, Liam, and Maria Andrea return from their tiger photo shoot a little after one o'clock. Max immediately heads upstairs with his equipment but Liam and Andrea stop in my office at Something Blue. Andrea shows me the tiger whisker she found outside one of the cages. It's white, curved and as thick as a guitar's low E string.

"So how was it?" I ask, handing it back to her.

"They're pretty lazy. And their poop stinks."

"Did you know tigers are bigger than lions?" Liam volunteers.

"No, I didn't know that."

"They're only successful one out of every twenty hunts. And they live and hunt alone."

Now that sounds downright depressing. "Guess I'm glad I'm not a tiger."

Liam nods. "Daisy would be a pretty lame name for a tiger."

Andrea makes a little snorting sound. "All the tigers there had stupid names. Gus, Elmo, and *Tony*. Stupid." She runs her finger across the whisker. "If those were my tigers I'd name them Captain, Orion, and Gabriel."

"But you wouldn't have tigers. You think they stink," Liam says.

Andrea begins to walk away, fingering the whisker. "Not the tigers. Just their poop."

Liam turns to me, surely about to make a comment about girls before remembering that I am also one.

"So." I change the subject. "Ready to go visit your grandfather?"

Liam and I arrive at the third floor of Methodist Hospital twenty minutes later. The door to his grandfather's room is closed. Liam is about to open it when I suggest we knock first.

From within we hear Father Laurent tell us to come in.

Liam opens the door and we step inside. Father Laurent is in his bed, but the mattress is raised to nearly a sitting position. Color has returned to his cheeks. He looks ten times better than he did yesterday. But his countenance still seems haggard, despite the flush to his cheeks. Ramsey is seated next to his father. He, too, looks a little beleaguered.

Something has happened. Something I won't like.

Ramsey's eyes communicate something to me. He has sensed I'm aware something is amiss. He offers a mere shake of his head. *Ask nothing.*

"Hi, Grandpa," Liam walks toward the bed. "I saw some tigers today. Up close. I got to touch one on the back."

Father Laurent smiles. "Well, there's something you've done that I've never done. I don't think I've ever touched a tiger before."

"You should go next time Max goes there. It was cool. They have lions, too. But they weren't out today."

The door opens behind us and a doctor walks in. I don't recognize him. He seems surprised to see Liam and me there. "I see you have company," the doctor says. "I'll just leave these for you then. We can talk later, Mr. Laurent." The doctor lays a sheaf of papers on the bedside table and walks away.

As Father Laurent thanks him, my eyes travel to the papers. A surge of panic spills over me and I inhale abruptly. I turn to Father Laurent as cold fear mingles with the panic.

He just smiles at me; a weak smile, but one that still creases his face with tiny laugh lines from happier days.

I open my mouth but before I can speak, Ramsey clears his throat.

"Liam, would you mind running down to the vending machines and getting me a Pepsi?" He stands and hands his son a five-dollar bill. "You can get yourself a drink, too, if you want."

"Can I get a candy bar?" Liam asks as he takes the money.

"Sure."

As soon as Liam is gone, the words are out of my mouth. "What is it? What has happened?"

Ramsey looks to his dad. Neither one says anything.

"What is it?" I look from one to the other.

Father Laurent turns to me. "The doctors found a tumor on my prostate gland."

"A tumor?" The only word scarier than tumor is cancer. And I say it anyway. "Like, cancer?"

"It's a very treatable form of cancer." Father Laurent's voice is void of worry.

I swallow. "So what does that mean?"

"Usually it means the doctors watch to see how quickly the tumor changes size, but mine is a little bigger than they're comfortable with. They're probably going to want to do some radiation treatments. As soon as I recover from this other little thing."

This other little thing.

I hardly know what to say.

"Many men recover from this kind of cancer, Daisy. If it's caught early."

"Did they catch it early?"

Ramsey looks away. Father Laurent hesitates for a second. "They think so."

"Did you know you had this? Were you feeling sick? I would've taken you to the doctor if you had told me."

Ramsey sits up in his chair when I say this. I think he's a bit miffed at me. I don't care. I wasn't the one planting grass on Japanese roofs for the past four months.

"I really didn't feel that sick. This is not your fault, Daisy. It's no one's fault."

We are all quiet for a few moments.

"What kind of radiation treatments?" I finally say. "Do you have to be hospitalized?"

"No. The doctor is recommending radiation seeding. They inject these seeds into the gland to shrink the tumor. It's an outpatient procedure. It's supposed to be the newest thing."

"And it's been successful?"

"Very. The oncologist I saw this morning highly recommends it."

"So you're still coming home?"

Ramsey shifts in his chair. Then the door bursts open and Liam walks in with a can of soda pop and a Snickers.

"They were out of Pepsi, Dad. I got you root beer." He is oblivious to the tension in the room. He hands Ramsey the can and then turns toward Father Laurent. "Want a bite of my Snickers, Grandpa?"

"Wish I could say yes, Liam. But the doctors probably wouldn't like it if I did."

"Why?"

"I need to be a little nicer to my heart. It doesn't like all those fat grams, I'm afraid."

"Well, that stinks."

As do quite a few other things.

I don't stay long after hearing this new development. When I get back to Something Blue, Mom and L'Raine can tell something is weighing on me and it isn't long before they coax it out of me. When I tell them that on top of having angry arteries Father Laurent also has prostate cancer, Mom goes pale and L'Raine tears up. I tell them what Father Laurent was careful to tell me, that this kind of cancer is very treatable, but they are like I am. Unable to hear the word *cancer* and not think the worst.

A customer walks in and I whisk away the horrors of what I know and what I don't and pretend that nothing matters more to me than finding the right wedding dress for this lovely girl. But as soon as I start to tell her about the little blue heart sewn into the first dress she selects, I get teary and have to excuse myself to have a make-believe coughing fit.

The rest of the afternoon is a tedious affair. When Shelby pops in a bit before four and asks if I want to go get a smoothie, I am more than ready for the diversion.

The June sun is bathing the sidewalk with ripples of heat as we head to our favorite smoothie shop.

"How goes it?" Shelby is probably expecting my latest update on the toad formerly known as Daniel.

And I begin to tell her what is really troubling me at the moment—my worries over the health of Father Laurent.

Twenty minutes later, after we've sipped our drinks to the halfway point, I come up for air.

"So is he cute?"

I surely must look like I've no familiarity at all with the English language.

"Huh?"

"This Ramsey guy. Is he cute?"

I'm struggling to comprehend my shock at her question. I *am* shocked, no doubt about it. But not shocked that she asked. More like shocked that I'm shocked that she asked. I'm sure there's someone, somewhere, who knows what I mean. "I don't see what his looks have to do with anything!"

Shelby shrugs and pushes her straw up and down in her cup to break up the clumps of melting ice. "You talk about him like he interests you."

"I do not."

"He doesn't interest you?"

What a bizarre question. "I haven't given it a moment's thought, Shelby. All I've been concerned with is Father Laurent. I hate the idea of him being sick."

"Oh. Okay. Well, Father Laurent's a great guy and all, and I know he reminds you of your dad, but Daisy, your store won't fold if Father Laurent is too sick or too busy with treatments to bless your little hearts. You could bless them yourself."

I hope she can see that I'm appalled. "That is *not* the only reason why I want him well."

"Of course it's not. But you could, you know. Bless them yourself."

"It wouldn't be the same. I'm not a priest, for Pete's sake." Shelby clearly doesn't understand the marketing genius of my little set-up. Those little blue hearts are my logo, my brand, my business identity.

"You could get someone else to do it."

"Shelby, how many pastors, retired or otherwise, would be willing to do what Father Laurent does for me? I bet your average minister would think the whole thing is nuts."

We start to walk back to the boutique, and as we stroll, Shelby concocts a plan to solicit a new heart-blesser for me on eBay.

She's nuts. I'm not going on eBay with this.

We open the door to Something Blue and step inside just as Ramsey and Liam walk in from the back of the store.

"Everything all right?" I ask.

"We just decided to let Dad rest a bit," Ramsey says. "It's been a busy day for him."

Ramsey points toward my office. "Mind if I check to see if a fax has arrived for me?"

"Not at all. I'll be right there."

Ramsey and Liam head to my little office and I turn to say goodbye to Shelby. She's smirking.

"You need to open your eyes, Daisy," she whispers. "He's quite handsome."

THIRTY-TWO

Dear Harriet,

I've spent the evening surfing the Internet, looking up all the information I can find on prostate cancer. Father Laurent was diagnosed with it today. The doctors detected a tumor during an exam at the hospital. Cancerous, of course. This, on top of everything else.

Father Laurent's doctor told him this kind of cancer is highly survivable. Like that's supposed to allay all our fears. He will undergo a new kind of radiation treatment as soon as he recovers from his heart attack. Father Laurent didn't say what the doctors will do if that doesn't work. I told Max about it and that I'm worried it won't work, and he just said it's not cool to kill your chickens before they've hatched. I asked him, "What the heck does that mean?" He said, "Don't make reservations for the worst-case scenario." Life according to Max Dacey.

Shelby says my fears are a little childish. Well, she didn't actually say that, but that's how I felt when she said it. Like a spoiled child who wants her way. She said I could just bless those hearts myself, which is a preposterous idea. Who wants to wear a wedding dress blessed by a jilted bride? Ludicrous. She also thinks finding another man of God to bless my little hearts could be as easy as posting the opening on the Internet. Can you imagine the kind of responses I'd get?

No thanks.

Shelby asked me if I thought Ramsey was good-looking. I told her Ramsey's looks are the furthest thing from my mind and how on earth could she ask such a thing. She said I spoke of him like I was interested in him. How do you speak of a man and sound like you're interested in him?

She saw him today at Something Blue and told me she thought he was very handsome. The truth is, I'm not unaware that he's attractive. And he does interest me. But not because he is nice to look at.

I think it's his sorrows that draw me. The love lost that attracts. Because I know that road. Been down it. Am traveling it still.

I saw him tonight—up on the third floor, when I remembered I'd never gone to Wendy and Philip's this morning to listen for the weird bathroom noise. I left Wendy's not having heard it, but when I was coming out of her apartment, he was opening Father Laurent's front door. And so there we both were.

Two pathetic souls.

I smiled and nodded and he did the same.

I'm watching Steel Magnolias, which is really dumb because I cry like a professional mourner when M'Lynn breaks down at the cemetery after burying her daughter, Shelby. And it's not just because my best friend is named Shelby. It's that whole "no one should have to die that young" thing. I will probably turn it off just before she dies.

I like to gauge my reaction from time to time to Shelby's wedding dress at the beginning of the movie. It's huge. Her hair is huge. Her veil, her bouquet. It's all '80s huge. Huge.

You know, it worked back then. You could wear big glasses on your face and have big hair and drive a big car and wear a big wedding dress and it was okay.

No one thought those things were big back then.

Perspective is everything.

Dear Daisy,

So you've figured out that Ramsey's handsome. So what. Console yourself with the knowledge that it's not the first thing you noticed about him. There are degrees to shallowness.

It's not a pathetic thing to be drawn to someone's sorrow. Isn't that what sympathetic *means*? Who doesn't like the idea of being sympathetic? It's only pathetic when you compare your sorrows to someone else's with the purpose of gauging whose are worse.

Fashion in the '80s was no different than fashion in any other decade. People you didn't personally know told you what looked good and what didn't. And whatever you were told, that's what you believed, regardless of how you really felt about it.

How nice for me to be the Voice of Reason who can wear whatever she wants.

Harriet

THIRTY-THREE

I am carrying a bouquet of tiger lilies and daisies as I head to Father Laurent's room, and it suddenly bothers me—just as I'm about to open the door—that there are more daisies in my arms than lilies. I stop just outside the room and contemplate the audacity of having a dozen or more bridal-white flowers in my hands, all bearing my name—albeit with a lower case "d." How uncouth.

I am considering yanking a few out, when the door opens and Ramsey appears. He made the trip back to Duluth yesterday to pick up uncamplike clothes. Today, instead of shorts and a faded Hawaiian shirt, he's wearing a tangerine Henley and cream-colored cargo pants.

"Daisy. I almost ran into you." His gaze immediately falls on my flowers. All those arrogant, pompous daisies.

"It's fine. I'm fine." I mumble, wishing I had a box of chocolates instead. Make that rice cakes. "Are you on your way out?"

"No. Was just going to get a cup of coffee. It can wait." He opens the door and holds it for me. "Dad and I were just talking about you."

I snap my head around and a little bone in my neck protests. His tone doesn't sound particularly neighborly. It doesn't sound particularly anything. "Really?"

He motions with his head toward the open door. "Want to come in?"

No, what I want is to know what he and Father Laurent were saying about me. "Sure."

"Hello, Daisy." I hear Father Laurent's voice from within the room. I step inside and am relieved to see him looking pink-cheeked again. He is sitting up in bed in his own pajamas. Ramsey follows behind me.

I walk toward Father Laurent and lean down to kiss his wrinkled cheek. "Hello, there." I nod toward my bouquet. "Is it okay to give a man flowers?"

"Of course it is. Look at that. Lilies. And daisies. They're perfect."

"Yeah. Daisies. I wasn't thinking when I bought them. All I saw were the tiger lilies."

"Well, I should think you'd want to give daisies away every chance you get."

I smile. Somehow it doesn't sound so pretentious when he suggests it. "I have to say you look wonderful today, Father."

"Ah yes, it's the spa treatments, pedicures, and protein drinks," he quips. "But they're letting me out tomorrow, so all that will come to an end."

"Well, it will be wonderful to have you home again."

He turns his head toward Ramsey. "Yes, I'm looking forward to going home myself."

"Actually, Dad and I were just talking about that." Across from me, Ramsey leans over a little to rest his hands on Father Laurent's bedrail.

"I thought you were talking about me." I wink at Father Laurent. I wonder if he knows how difficult that was for me to say and not sound ridiculous.

"Well, your name came up when we were talking about where my father should go home *to*." Ramsey's answer is quick. Guess he didn't get my little joke.

A ripple of unease begins to work its way across me. "To his home, of course."

"I'm thinking that may not be the best place for my dad to be right now."

I turn my head to face Father Laurent. Surely he doesn't want to leave The Finland. Leave Something Blue. "You don't want to come back to your apartment, Father?" It comes out rather squeakish.

"I have every intention of coming back."

"Dad." Ramsey's voice has that "we're not done discussing this" quality to it.

Father Laurent turns his head toward his son. "I really don't think you want an old man tottering around your house."

"Well, I was thinking we could find a nice facility for you in Duluth."

"Good heavens, no, Ramsey. I don't want to live in a nice *facility*. I want to go back to my apartment."

"Dad, come on. How are you going to manage all those stairs? You're not supposed to be climbing stairs. And how are you going to get back and forth to your doctor's appointments? And how are you going to keep track of all your medications? And what if those radiation treatments make you sick?"

"I'm not an invalid."

"I can help," I offer. Ramsey shifts his head to face me.

"No offense, but you've got a business to run and an apartment building to manage. There's no way I can entrust my father's care to someone that busy."

"But—" I begin, but Ramsey cuts me off.

"Dad, it just doesn't make any sense for you to return to your apartment. You had a serious heart attack and now you've been diagnosed with cancer. You can't just go back home and pretend everything's normal. Everything's *not* normal."

"I'm not pretending everything's normal," Father Laurent said. "But I don't think everything's dire, either."

"Dad, look. There's a time in every person's life when they must recognize they can't take care of themselves. Someone needs to step in for them. I can't go back to Duluth and leave you alone in that apartment!"

"But he won't be alone. I said I would help," I try again. "I don't mind."

"See?" Father Laurent says.

Ramsey stands up straight and looks at me. "Could I talk to you for a minute? Out in the hall?"

Father Laurent sits up abruptly in his bed. "This is between you and me, Ramsey!" As soon as the words are out of his mouth, he starts to cough.

"Please, Dad. Just lie back. Okay? I'll be right back." He settles his father back on his pillows and then motions toward the door. I follow him out.

As soon as the door is shut behind us he turns toward me. "Look, I appreciate everything you've done for my dad, really I do. And I know you enjoy renting to him and having him do whatever it is he does for those little hearts. But I think we need to think about what's best for *him*."

The implication is clear. He thinks all I care about is having a friendly priest around to bless my wretched little blue hearts.

"You think I don't have what's best for him in mind?" I hope I sound offended because I am.

He blinks and then answers me. "Well, let's be honest here. My father performs a helpful service to you and you—"

Okay. Now I'm really mad. I interrupt him. "You know nothing about me. And if we're being honest here, you should consider whether *you* have your father's best interests in mind. You think putting your father in a facility so you can go gallivanting around the planet without worrying about his medications or doctors' appointments or whether his radiation treatments are making him sick is looking out for his best interests? Sounds like *you're* looking out for your own."

Oh, dear. He looks very angry. I can sense Harriet within me shocked to her reasonable core. Appalled.

"I can't believe you just said that to me." Ramsey's face has gone kind of white. It's not a good color on him. "The way my father talks about you—"

"It doesn't feel very good, does it?" I shoot back. "To be accused of being self-serving? You said basically the same thing to me."

"I did not accuse you of running around the *planet* oblivious to the needs of your family."

But I can't quite concentrate on my next response. I keep hearing the words *the way my father talks about you.* Shame overwhelms me. I shouldn't have said what I did. Harriet is knocking around inside me, shouting at me to apologize.

Ramsey is staring at me. My face is aflame. I feel on the verge of passing out, that's how warm the hallway has gotten. It's obvious Ramsey doesn't know whether to storm back into his father's room or offer to get me a drink of water.

"I'm sorry." My voice sounds weak and defeated and I can't look at him. "Please. Please forgive me for saying what I did. I just...I would be very sad to lose your father's companionship. He means a great deal to me. And it's not just because of the hearts. It really is so much more than that. He..." But I cannot seem to finish the thought. I wipe away a stray tear.

I sneak a peek at Ramsey. I do believe he is thoroughly flum-moxed.

Ramsey says nothing for a moment. Then his voice softens. "I'm sorry, too. For thinking it was just the hearts you were worried about. But I don't see another way out of this. I can't leave my father to recover from a heart attack and begin treatment for cancer while I live two hours away. I won't do that to him."

"But I meant what I said. I can help."

"And run your business? And manage the building? You don't have the time to take on a patient, Daisy. And he's my father. Not yours."

I know he didn't mean for this to sting, but it does. I know I winced. I think he senses it.

"I mean I wouldn't expect you to care for him like that. I should be doing it."

"But I wouldn't mind. His friendship is very special to me. I lost my own father a few years back and I..." But there aren't adequate words to describe how much I miss my dad and how much Father Laurent's presence in my life soothes that ache.

Ramsey pauses for a moment but then shakes his head. "But I just can't leave him here. Liam and I have to be back in Duluth on Monday morning."

My mind travels back to the first day I met Father Laurent, when I was just beginning to formulate my plan for the boutique and rounding up tenants for the apartments. He was one of the first to sign a lease and the day he did, he asked about my fledgling business, which at that point was nameless. I told him I was thinking of sewing a little blue heart into every wedding dress as a "something blue" item, and also to give each used dress one new, shiny thing about it. He had said what a lovely idea it was for me to bless each dress with a little hope. I laughed and said that of all people I was the least likely to bless a secondhand wedding dress, and that he was a far more suitable bestower of such a blessing. He had said anytime I wanted him to bless my little blue hearts, all I had to do was ask.

So, really the idea came from him.

From the beginning of my woes, he has been my beacon, the physical hand of God on my needy soul. I'm not out of the woods yet. It is still a little murky on the path out of here. I'm not ready to let him go.

Ramsey is standing in front of me, looking very concerned. Tears have started to slide down my cheeks. I swipe them away. "You have to go back to Duluth?"

"I need to work on getting contracts for this month and the next. I don't have anything lined up until late August. I've got bills to pay like everyone else. And Duluth is my home."

For a moment we are both silent. Then, out of the blue, a completely crazy idea falls across me.

Crazy and wonderful.

And perhaps completely doable.

I thrust the flowers toward Ramsey. "Get these in some water. I need to check something and make a phone call. Tell Father Laurent I'll be right back."

I don't look at him, but I know Ramsey is staring as I walk away.

THIRTY-FOUR

Oddly enough, one of the things Daniel liked about me was my flair for idea-hatching. Most of our dates were orchestrated by me, and many of them were far more multifaceted than just dinner and a movie. We biked along the bluffs of the Mississippi in October, ate roasted turkey drumsticks at the Renaissance Festival, played laser tag, made our own sushi, and took salsa dancing lessons. And of course it was my idea to get married. I guess that would be the one idea he decided he didn't like after all.

I had great ideas for our wedding, too. It was going to be held in a historic church in St. Paul, the altar festooned with fountains of ivy and jasmine and peach blossoms. I had bagpipes lined up to play our processional. My bouquet of peach gerbera daisies was also going to include two white roses that Daniel and I would remove, after we lit the unity candle, and give to our mothers. My bridesmaids' dresses were made of slipper satin in a lovely multihued shade known as nectarine. Daniel and I were going to face the congregation when we weren't facing each other and have our parents join us in a circle of prayer on the altar. I was going to have individual cakes at each reception table; all would be decorated with fresh flowers and candied nuts. Instead of rice or birdseed or bubbles showcasing our exit, we were going to leave the reception in a promenade of sparklers.

And of course, I had my dress custom made just for me: a design that I hatched in my head at the age of twelve and improved on as the years went by. Yards of creamy white organza, hints of sparkle in the softly-ruched bodice, a classic neckline that was modest yet flattering, and a scooped back that was as exquisitely tailored as the front.

A scooped back that now hides a little blue heart on its underside.

Yes, I'm a master planner. A go-to gal if something needs to be planned.

So I wasn't inordinately surprised that while fighting back tears of frustration in front of Ramsey I suddenly happened upon an idea that would make everyone happy, and keep Father Laurent at The Finland.

All I really needed to do was find a certain building-maintenance repair bill from a few months back and make a call to Reuben in New York.

My part would be easy. Pitch the idea, and pray Reuben would go for it.

So that's what I did as I drove back to the building from the hospital. I prayed.

Lord, have Reuben say yes. Have him say yes. It's a good idea. Make him smart enough to see it.

When I pop into Something Blue from the back entrance, both Mom and L'Raine are surprised to see me.

"That was a short visit." Mom places a dress back on the rack.

"I'm going back. I just need to make a quick phone call."

Her eyes follow me to my little office. She no doubt wonders who I have to call from the office that I can't call from the hospital on my cell phone. But I don't have Reuben's number programmed into it. I hardly ever talk to him. I think he likes it that I run a smooth show here and don't have to bug him with every little thing.

I open a file drawer and pull out the maintenance receipts. Then I grab my address book and find Reuben's number. It's four o'clock in the afternoon on the East Coast. I'm hoping he's home.

He answers on the third ring.

"Reuben, it's Daisy."

"Well, hello there. Haven't talked to you in a while. Everything all right?"

"Yes, we're all fine here, Reuben. And you?"

"Oh, can't complain. Your mom doing well?"

He means for it to sound like casual interest. But I can tell that deep down in some little place Reuben doesn't visit very often are feelings for my mother that are decades old. It's kind of a haunting concept.

"She's very well, Reuben. I actually called to share an idea with you about The Finland. I think it's a really good one."

"Oh?"

"Well, you know we had that water damage to the building back in March from melting snow and heavy rains? And that it was over eighteen hundred dollars in repairs."

"Yes, I remember."

"I have an idea to keep that from happening again and make the building really stand out as a fixture on this street. I think it would raise the property value and please the neighboring business owners."

"Okay, I'm interested."

"One of my tenants, Father Miles Laurent, has a son who constructs green roofs. They're like gardens on rooftops but they're extremely functional. They absorb and displace water runoff in the spring and fall, and they absorb heat in the summer. Plus they look really nice. It would be an added feature that would allow you to boost your rent to any future tenants. They're very cost-effective in the long run because of the money you'll save on building maintenance and cooling costs."

I pause and allow the idea to settle. When I can sense he is still thinking I throw in another bargaining chip.

"Your building would be one of the few in Uptown to have one. It would be an innovative thing and I think it would be looked upon favorably by people who tend to turn up their noses at nonlocal property owners."

Reuben is silent and I'm not sure how to interpret this. Just as I'm fishing for another possible angle, he speaks. "You know, I have a fondness for gardens. It's a very intriguing idea. And this would be functional, too. That's very appealing."

I'm afraid he's going to ask me how much it will cost. I haven't the foggiest. I hope he doesn't. It really shouldn't matter. Reuben is a millionaire many times over.

He doesn't ask, though. "Is this something you want this fellow to do right away?"

I can barely contain my enthusiasm. "Yes, actually he has an opening in his schedule at the moment. So he'd be able to start very soon. And Reuben, his dad is recovering from a heart attack so I know it would be helpful to him if he could just stay in your apartment while he works on this and his dad recovers. If that's all right."

"Well, you've thought of everything!"

Yes, I'm the idea queen.

"So can I ask if he'll do it?" I venture.

"Yes—yes, I think you should. Let me know if the cost estimate surprises you. Otherwise I trust your judgment. This is a very interesting idea, Daisy. I must say I can't wait to see the results."

"I think it's going to be great, Reuben. Thanks for letting me run with this."

"No problem. Keep me posted, though. Let me know how much money we'll need to cover this. And I'd like to see his design as soon as he has one. Can you send me that?"

"Sure, Reuben."

"Well, good work, Daisy. We'll talk again, no doubt. Say hello to your mother for me."

"I sure will."

We hang up and I let out a little victory whoop. When I look up from my desk I see my mother standing in the doorway.

"Were you talking to Reuben?"

"Yes, I was." I stand up and grab my purse. "He says hello. I'm going to ask Ramsey to stay and build a garden on our roof. He does that for a living. Reuben says he can stay in the extra apartment."

Mom's face is awash in bewilderment. "What's this all about, Daisy?"

I really don't have the time or the desire to explain the whole thing.

I opt for the condensed version. "It's the only way I can get Ramsey to let Father Laurent stay in the apartment while he recovers from his heart attack and undergoes his radiation treatment. Ramsey's all set to move Father Laurent into some facility in Duluth."

"Oh. Oh, dear."

"Father Laurent doesn't want to go and I certainly don't want him to. Ramsey thinks we can't take care of his father, and I need to prove that we can. This will give us some time to show him. Where's Liam?"

"Well, I think he went with Max to the studio this afternoon. He was going to be photographing some skateboarders or something."

Oh, well. I'd like to have Liam's stamp of approval on this when I suggest it to Ramsey. I'm pretty sure Liam won't mind spending the better part of his summer at The Finland. He's made a fast friend in Max. I'm sure he will like this idea.

"I've got to go back to the hospital, Mom. Can you and L'Raine mind the store?"

"Of course. But we want to go see Father Laurent later today, too."

"I won't be long. I promise."

I head back out to the parking lot pretty sure I'm right about not being long. Ramsey will either love this idea or hate it.

When I arrive at the hospital, Father Laurent is alone in his room, asleep. My daisies and tiger lilies are stuck inside a water pitcher on his bedside table. There is no sign of Ramsey.

I head to the nurse's station to ask if anyone knows where Father Laurent's son is. I am directed to the family lounge at the end of the hall.

Ramsey is sitting on a sofa, reading a newspaper. ESPN is playing on a TV monitor across the room. Another man is asleep in an armchair. Ramsey looks up as I step into the room.

"You're back." He folds the paper and places it on the table in front of him. "Dad's asleep, though."

"I know. I saw him. It's actually you I wanted to talk to."

He says nothing but his eyes communicate curiosity. I take a seat beside him on the sofa. "Remember earlier when you said you didn't see any way out of taking your dad back to Duluth with you?"

"Yes."

"Well, I've found a way."

"What do you mean?"

"I've found a way for your father to stay at The Finland, and for you to be near him and for you to have a contract to work on."

He looks positively baffled.

"The owner of my building wants you to put a green roof on it."

"You can't be serious." Baffled has given way to suspicious.

"I'm very serious. We had over eighteen hundred dollars in water damage last spring. And I bet with one of your roofs that wouldn't happen anymore. And it would improve the look of the building and be an asset to the tenants. Plus, Reuben, the owner, keeps an apartment in the building that is fully furnished and unoccupied. He lives in New York and only comes to the Twin Cities a couple times a year. So you could stay right in the building while your dad gets better and while you build the garden."

He opens his mouth to say something, closes it, and then opens it again. It's like he has twenty comments to make and he doesn't know which one to deliver first.

"Are you telling me that in the past thirty minutes you made all these arrangements?"

I can't tell if he's impressed or disturbed by such a notion. "Well, it wasn't hard to convince Reuben that this is a great idea. And it's not a stretch of the imagination to think that you and Liam could stay in his empty apartment. It makes perfect sense. It's empty. And it's right next door to your Father's apartment."

"But you don't even know what I charge to build a green roof."

"I seriously doubt you would charge us something unreasonable. If the project is fair market value, Reuben will gladly pay it. He thinks it's a great idea. He loves gardens. And so do I. And you could take as much time as you needed."

"It only takes a couple weeks to build one on a roof the size of yours."

"But you could take as much time as you needed."

Ramsey stares at the table in front of him, obviously deep in thought. When he raises his head, the suspicious look is gone and in its place is unease.

"Why are you doing this?" he asks softly.

What should I tell him? That I'm slightly neurotic, recently rejected, unable to let go of the past, and fairly addicted to his father's brand of compassion? It's probably all true, but I doubt it will go over well. Truth can be told in a variety of ways. I choose different words.

"Your dad has been like a father to me." My voice is not much louder than a whisper. "This last year has been a really hard one for me. I don't know if I would've made it without your dad's friendship and counsel. My own father is dead. And I miss him terribly. To be honest, I don't want to lose your father's presence in my life."

Ramsey looks back down at the table, his gaze unfocused. I know my words have hit him in the place of our common ground—the aching heart. We've both just been through a year that brought us to the edge of despair.

"And also because your father doesn't want to leave," I add. "He deserves to be happy."

More seconds of silence.

"You should have an elevator in that place." He says this like it's his last line of defense.

"We have a service elevator at the far end of the building. No one but Mario ever uses it, and only for moving heavy things. It's the old-fashioned kind with a gate. But it works."

Ramsey runs his palm across his face.

It occurs to me that if he moves to The Finland for the rest of the summer he will be mere minutes away from his ex-wife.

I wait.

"What kind of roof is it?"

I breathe a half-sigh of relief. This is progress. But I don't know what he means. "Kind?"

"Flat, sloped, or pitched?"

"Oh. Flat. It's covered with pea gravel."

He cocks his head. "You've been up there?"

"I go up there all the time."

"What for?"

"Because it's quiet and peaceful and uncomplicated up there. There's nothing but sky and pea gravel and other rooftops."

He seems to consider this for a moment. Then he exhales, like he's letting out the last breath of his resistance.

"I'll look at the roof tonight and I'll let you know."

"So Father Laurent can stay?"

"I'll let you know."

He gets up and walks away. The man in the chair snorts himself awake, changes position, and falls back asleep.

THIRTY-FIVE

Dear Harriet,

Okay, so I blew it today when I accused Ramsey of being selfish. So let's not even discuss it. I apologized. I really do regret saying what I did, even if it might be a tiny bit true.

He looked at the roof of The Finland just before dark. I went up there with him. He kind of stared at my two Adirondack chairs for a moment, but then he walked off the square footage, peeked over the limestone rim, and inspected the tuck-pointing on the bricks closest to the top. Then he put his hands on his hips and said, "I can do this."

I don't know if he meant that he can do the roof or that he can lay his head to rest at night only a few miles away from the Horn Blower. Either way, it was the same thing as saying Father Laurent can stay. At least for now.

The fact is, Father Laurent doesn't want to move. This is his home. We should all be bending over backward to make sure he can stay here. I know I have ulterior motives. I know I could mail a box of little blue hearts to him in Duluth and he could bless them one by one and send them back. But this really isn't about those little blue hearts. It's about keeping my world spinning on its new axis. I really don't want to grapple with changes that will mess with that. Every time I think I've got my feet firmly on the ground, it starts to shift and tip. It's like little gnomes are watching me try to keep my balance and when it looks like I've got my life on an even plane, they yank the rug I'm standing on. I need for everything around me to just be still.

Even as I write this, I realize this is probably just how Ramsey feels, like a novice gymnast on a balance beam stretched across hot coals. This afternoon while I was trying to convince him to stay in Minneapolis— and thinking he was just wanting to keep his life on an even keel—it dawned on me that he fears walking the balance beam with Kristen practically watching from the sidelines. He'll be just minutes away from her for as long as he and Liam stay here. He might even run into her and the Usurper at the grocery store, or at the mall, or on a lakeshore path. Maybe he'll run into them while they're strolling with their new baby—the one Kristen was carrying when she told Ramsey she was leaving him.

Oh, to have such a thing in common. Rejection.

I wonder if he feels about Kristen the way I feel about Daniel. I don't actually love Daniel anymore, not like I did. It's hard to keep loving someone who doesn't want you. But then to have that person choose someone else? To have them choose your replacement and to see them clearly and deeply in love with that other person?

That's the strongest poison there is. That will kill love.

But it won't kill the hurt.

That you have to put to death yourself.

Maybe that should be another one of my Rules of Disengagement: Be ready to choose a method of execution. Plan to take an active role in killing the desire within you for things to be back the way they were. You must slay it with your own hands. No one can do it for you. The love you had for that person who rejected you can be stripped away in an almost passive fashion. But the wish that you could rewind the clock, change the course of time, know the moment when they began to love you less so that you could freeze that moment and massage it away, that you have to put to death—you alone. You must show no mercy. If you do not kill it, it will kill you. And you won't even know you are dying.

Dear Daisy,

I'm trying to think what your Father Laurent would say to you if you
had written these words to him and not me. I think he would say it's not
about killing the hurt as much as it's about releasing it. You can kill an
angry beast that is trapped at your feet or you can let it go. It seems to
me if you kill something, then there are remains to be dealt with. What
do we usually do with remains? We bury them. And we leave a head-
stone to mark the spot.

If you set something free—push it away and walk away—there is
nothing left to remind you of its existence except your own memories of
having had it. Which, my dear, are not all bad.

I am proud of you for apologizing to Ramsey. But I think we both know
you did it not because you shouldn't have said something so unkind,
but because you couldn't live with knowing you said something Father
Laurent would never think you capable of saying and thinking nothing of.
Ramsey clearly has an impression of you given to him by Father Laurent.
That impression matters to you.

As it should.

Harriet

THIRTY-SIX

M ax, Liam, and I decorated the outside of Father Laurent's room with balloons and streamers in preparation for his homecoming this morning. Rosalina baked a cake—low-fat, of course. Mario spruced up the service elevator, painting its walls a soft cloudy blue. And Mom and L'Raine made sure there were no spiders, cobwebs, or layers of dust in Reuben's cozy apartment. When Father Laurent arrived this morning, the whole building turned out to welcome him home. You'd think he was a war hero returning to America after years away. Liam made sure his grandfather knew he'd had a part in helping Max and me decorate the third-floor hallway. Ramsey seemed to note this with interest as well.

I am immensely glad that today is Saturday and that my fabulous college girls are downstairs manning Something Blue. Neither Mom nor I nor L'Raine wanted to miss seeing Father Laurent come home to where he belongs. The fanfare was appreciated of course, but exhausting. As soon as Father Laurent received our hugs and well-wishes, he went inside his apartment to lie down. Liam and Ramsey left shortly thereafter for Duluth to pick up more belongings, and Mom and I promised to look in on Father Laurent until they returned.

It is now late afternoon, Father Laurent is reading the newspaper and I'm attempting to clean out my fridge. I've put it off as long as I can because I hate doing it. There are containers at the back that scare me silly. I don't care that the contents are snug inside sealed, molded plastic. I'm going to throw them all out—plastic containers and all—without even peeking.

Mom knocks at my front door, opens it, and pops her head inside. "Daisy?"

"In the kitchen, Mom," I yell back.

She rounds the corner and looks down on me from the other side of the open fridge door.

"Kellen just called. He's coming to Minneapolis tonight."

"That's nice. Is he coming by?"

"Well, he'd like to."

"Does that mean he can't?"

"No, he can, but he was thinking he'd just swing by. He wants to pick you up to go out to eat."

I toss a little blue container of unknown matter into the trash can. "Don't you want to come?"

"Well, he was thinking it would be just you this time."

"What? A little brother–sister bonding?" I laugh at the thought because Kellen is more like an uncle to me than a brother.

"No. Not really. Laura will be there, too."

I look up at her. "Mom, what's this about?"

"He just…oh, for Pete's sake. Daisy, Marshall Mitchell would really like to see you again. He and Kellen have been doing some business together and your name has come up and he wondered if you'd care to see him. He asked Kellen if he thought you'd be open to that."

He asked Kellen?

"He couldn't ask *me?*"

"Well, maybe he thought you'd say no."

"So, asking Kellen is safer because why?"

"I don't know, Daisy. All I know is Kellen said he's in Minneapolis this afternoon to take care of some business. And that he and Laura are meeting Marshall later for dinner and he thought you might want to come."

I stand up and search the countertops for my cell phone. "Where's he at?"

"I don't know. I think he's already here in the metro somewhere."

I find the phone by the toaster and snatch it up. I punch in Kellen's speed dial and wait. He picks up on the fourth ring. I can tell by the background noise that he's in his car.

"What's all this about, Kellen?"

"Daisy, relax. It's just a harmless double date. He likes you. He wants to see you again."

"He likes me? He doesn't even know me!"

"Well, he'd like to get to know you."

"Why couldn't he have called me himself?"

"Well, he didn't want to scare you off."

I begin to pace the kitchen. Mom has closed the fridge door and is standing there, watching me, rapt. "Scare me off?" I reply. "What's that supposed to mean?"

"He didn't want to seem too forward. He could tell you'd been hurt before and he—"

I don't even bother to fiddle with the volume of my voice. "What do you mean he could tell I'd been hurt before? What did you tell him?" Mom's eyes bug out at my verbal explosion.

"Daisy. Calm down. He could tell. You spend any amount of time around a hurting person and you can tell. It's not that easy to hide hurt from a perceptive person."

"So Mitchell Maxwell is a perceptive person!" I sound a little like the Wicked Witch of the West.

"Marshall Mitchell. And yes, he's a very compassionate, perceptive kind of person. I think you'd like him, Daisy. Just give him a chance."

I pause for just a moment to calm the demons inside me who want to screech.

"What have you told him, Kellen?" It takes me a moment to say this.

"Daisy—"

"What have you told him?"

"After *he* told me he could tell you were hurting, I did tell him you had been engaged recently, and that your fiancé had called it off."

He can't see me, but my face floods with color nonetheless. Mom sees it. She looks away. Even she can sense Kellen has said too much.

"Kellen, I can't believe you did that," I moan.

"Why not? It's true."

"It's none of his business."

"Daisy, it's been, what, a year? When are you going to get over this? You need to start getting out and meeting other people."

I am almost speechless.

"I thought you were the one person I didn't have to worry about measuring up to, Kellen! When Mom tried to fix me up with Marshall that first night, you were on *my* side!"

"There aren't sides to this, Daisy. And that was before I knew him. He's a really nice guy."

"So is our mailman."

"Daisy."

I stop my pacing and search my brain for a wisp of common sense. *Harriet, where are you?* I wish I could run up to Father Laurent's apartment and ask him what I should do. But he just got home. He's recovering from a heart attack. I can't do it.

Lord, Lord, tell me I'm not being ridiculous about this. Lord, tell me I'm not being unreasonable.

"Daisy?"

Then from somewhere inside me I hear echoes of what Harriet "wrote" to me last night—that I need to stop looking for ways to kill my hurt and start looking for ways to let it go.

Easier said than done. It's kind of hard to let go of something that seems to be attached to you with superglue.

"Daisy, are you still there?"

"I'm still here."

"So will you come?"

"If Marshall really wants to see me, then please tell him to stop by the store sometime and maybe we'll go get a cup of coffee together. I'm not going to go out with a man I don't even know, Kellen."

"It's just one date, Daisy."

"Yeah, well, my relationship with Daniel began with just one date."

"So did mine with Laura, and look how happy we are."

"I'm not coming, Kellen. And not because I'm afraid to. I'm not shopping for a new man to love. And that's what this would feel like to me. Like a shopping trip. I'm flattered Marshall wants to see me again—surprised, actually. If he really would like to get to know me as a friend, then tell him what I told you."

Kellen is silent for a moment. "All right. Are you mad at me?"

"I'm getting over it."

"He doesn't feel sorry for you, you know."

"Excuse me?"

"It wouldn't have been a pity date."

Oh, that's comforting.

"No, but it would have been a shopping date," I tell him. "For both of us. I don't want to go shopping."

"So going out for a cup of coffee sometime isn't shopping?"

"It wouldn't be for me."

He exhales. "Okay. I'll tell him."

"You can still stop by and say hello."

"You mean just me and Laura."

"Yes."

"Okay. We'll do that."

"All right."

"So you're not mad."

"I'm not mad."

We click off and I turn toward Mom as I lay my cell phone back on the counter.

"He meant well," she says.

So did the men who built the *Titanic*.

THIRTY-SEVEN

Dear Harriet,

I think there's something seriously wrong with me.

I had the opportunity to go on a date tonight with a man who for some unknown reason is interested in me and I turned it down.

I felt like I made the right decision. For about twenty minutes.

Then I started playing with my self-doubts and found instead that I felt like I had just let go of another opportunity to sell my wedding dress. That's what assailed me as I climbed the stairs to my boring, empty apartment after Kellen and Laura left to go have dinner with Marshall Mitchell. I felt the way I do every time someone wants to buy my dress and I tell the person it's not for sale.

I saw Father Laurent this evening just for a moment, but he was with Ramsey and Liam so I couldn't unload on him and ask for his counsel. I had gone up to the third floor to see if he was alone, to see if I could borrow just a couple seconds of his wisdom. When I saw that the door to his apartment was open and that Ramsey and Liam were bringing in dinner to him, I pretended to be there only to clear the hallway of the streamers and balloons.

Max found me wadding the streamers into a wrinkled mass that refused to stay bunched. He seemed surprised I was taking them down so soon. Or maybe he was surprised I was frowning as I did it. He asked me if I wanted to go to a Bible study with him at a friend's house. They were starting a study on Ecclesiastes. It didn't take me long to decide to go. The idea of studying a book that declares everything is meaningless sounded pretty appealing.

I dropped the downed streamers into a chaotic tumble on the floor just as Ramsey appeared at the open doorway to the apartment. He saw the crumpled Welcome Home streamers and me and Max, and he just blinked and closed the door.

I felt like I had just insulted his father.

It was like icing atop a really bad cake.

Vanities of vanities. All is vanity.

I didn't get much out of the study, my fault completely, and as we walked home to The Finland, Max asked me what I thought of Bettina.

Bettina?

The girl he'd been sitting next to, of course!

I vaguely remembered the little blonde wisp of a thing with the petite butterfly wrist tattoo. Pretty. Charming. Skinny.

I told him she was lovely and he beamed.

He spent the rest of our walk home telling me how he'd met her last week at the study and how smart she is and kind and talented. And that she likes his magic tricks.

I could see it in his eyes, even in the hushed splash of streetlight, that this girl had swept him away. Tugged at his socks.

And all I could think was, Is this how you meet the person who will change your life? At a chance meeting at a friend's house when the furthest thing from your mind is finding your life partner?

I thought of Shelby, who was simply teaching thirteen-year-olds how to dissect frogs when Eric entered her world. And that my mother and L'Raine met my father and my Uncle Warren when all they were looking for was a ride to a choir concert.

I have to admit, Harriet, that concept resonates with me. That's how you would know it was real, wouldn't you? When it happened when you weren't looking. But maybe it just isn't that way for everybody. Maybe I'm one of those people who is going to have to look.

Shop, as it were.

It's not the way I dreamed it—which is why I think something is seriously wrong with me. Or maybe it's just my dreams that are flawed.

Dear Daisy,

Being an unmarried Voice of Reason, I can only suppose there are many ways to meet the person who you will share the rest of your life with. I think Father Laurent would say you will know it's "real" when you can no longer see your life independent from that other person; when your greatest desire is to offer love, not collect it. It seems to me how you meet that person doesn't really figure in.

I wouldn't say your dreams are flawed. Perhaps they are just too little. You might consider adding this to your Rules of Disengagement book: Be ready to adjust the size and shape of your dreams.

By the way, you were wise to clean up those crumpled streamers from the floor when you got home.

It would have been wiser to have just left them up since you had no intention of taking them down until after the weekend.

But what's done is done.

Harriet

THIRTY-EIGHT

The door to Rosalina and Mario's apartment is always open on Sunday afternoons. It is the easiest way to remind The Finland's tenants that there is always an open invitation to have Sunday dinner with the Gallardos. Tantalizing fragrances waft up and down the staircases beginning around three o'clock with hints of coriander and turmeric and garlic. No one is likely to forget who is making dinner.

Today, Rosalina is fixing *llapingachos rellenos*—stuffed potato patties. I only know this because on my way out the door to church this morning she asked me pick up some shallots for her at the grocery store. She told me to tell everyone her *llapingachos rellenos* aren't too spicy unless you drown them in *tamarillo* sauce, which is precisely what Mario does. This was especially for Mom and L'Raine's sake, since they both tend to shy away from anything with a kick. Solomon is actually thinking about coming—a nice surprise. Wendy and Philip will be there. Max, however, will be off wooing Bettina.

It's been relegated to me to explain Sunday afternoons to Ramsey. I don't see why he needs a special invitation. Liam knows about them. So does Father Laurent. But Rosalina thinks Ramsey Laurent is too polite to just show up without having been properly invited.

So now, at five o'clock, I am heading for the stairs to the third floor.

At the landing, the first door on my right opens and Solomon pokes his head out.

"Daisy! Just the person I'm looking for!"

"Are you coming, then?"

"Coming where?"

"To Mario's and Rosalina's, of course. I heard you were coming."

"I can't. I have to play at St. Patrick's tonight. Someone backed out at the last minute. Come play this for me."

He thrusts a sheaf of music at me.

Brahms' "How Lovely Is Thy Dwelling Place" from the *German Requiem.* Only three flats. But ten pages at least. And countless accidentals dotting every one of them. I shall fairly obliterate it the minute my fingers hit the keys.

"Solomon, you know how I play. You know how I handle the classics. You should play show tunes. Then perhaps I'd actually be able to help you."

"I only need to go through it once."

"I'm sure that's about all you'd be able to stand."

"This one's not that hard. I haven't played it in a while. I'm rusty."

It always amuses me when inordinately talented people find fault with themselves. I don't know that I've ever heard Solomon play a wrong note. I hand the music back to him.

"All right. I'll be right back. I have to go invite all the Laurents to dinner at the Gallardos.' But I'm warning you, Solomon, it won't be pretty."

"Okay. But don't dawdle. I have to be there in an hour."

He slips back into his apartment as I walk across the hall to Reuben's usually empty apartment.

I knock on the door and wait. No answer. Ramsey and Liam are either gone or next door at Father Laurent's. I turn and walk the few steps to Father's front door and knock. A moment later, Liam opens it.

"Hey, Liam."

"Hi."

"Just wanted to let you guys know dinner is at Mario and Rosalina's at six if you want to come."

Before Liam can say anything, I hear Father Laurent calling my name from within the apartment.

"Daisy, come on in."

Liam steps aside and holds the door open for me. I take a couple of tentative steps inside. Father Laurent is seated in one of his comfy leather chairs. His feet are up and a cup of something steaming is in his hands. Ramsey is on the sofa across from him with the Sunday paper strewn about the cushions. He's sipping something hot, too.

"Hey, Father Laurent." I step fully in.

"Want to join us for a cup of tea?" Father Laurent's voice is as kind as ever. Ramsey appears void of thought.

"I'm sorry, I can't. I told Solomon I'd help him with something."

"Oh."

"But you're looking like your old self, Father. That's so nice to see."

"Well, it's wonderful to be home." His voice lingers on the last word like he's trying to communicate to me that he's grateful for my part in getting him home.

"I just wanted to remind you that it's Sunday and Rosalina's cooking dinner for the building." I turn toward Ramsey. "There's a standing invitation on Sundays for everyone in the building to join the Gallardos on the second floor for supper at six. Rosalina's from Ecuador. She's a really good cook."

"She is indeed," Father Laurent chimes in. "I'm not quite up for it, but Ramsey, you and Liam should go."

"I don't want you fending for yourself for dinner, Dad." Ramsey sits up in the sofa when he says this and places his cup on the coffee table. Like he needs his hands free.

"I'll be fine. I can open a can of soup."

Ramsey shakes his head and starts to open his mouth but I jump in. "I can stay with him. You and Liam can go."

"Can we, Dad? Can we go?" Liam clearly has been bored this afternoon. "Will Max be there?"

He sounds so hopeful, but I tell him that Max has other plans. "He usually does come, though."

Liam looks downcast for a second. "Can we still go?"

"I don't know…" Ramsey says.

"I don't mind staying," I try again.

"No one needs to stay." Father Laurent sounds insistent. "I'll be perfectly fine. Really."

"I don't think it's a good idea." Ramsey sits back into the cushions.

"Why not?" I ask and I can feel Harriet within me falling off her inner chair. She hates it when I'm impertinent.

Ramsey is taken aback, I think, by my asking. And the way I asked. It was kind of snippy.

"Because my father just had a heart attack." His words are edged with equal snippiness.

"But I said I would stay with him."

"Thanks just the same."

He has that here-I-stand-I-will-do-no-other look in his eye.

"Well, can I go?" Liam says.

"Of course you can," Father Laurent answers before Ramsey can say anything. "Are you sure you can't stay for a cup of tea, Daisy?"

I turn my head back to face Father Laurent. "No, I really did promise Solomon I'd help him out. Thanks anyway. I'll come and see you tomorrow, though." I take a step toward Father Laurent and place a kiss on his forehead. Out of the corner of my eye I see Ramsey staring at me. Kind of wide-eyed. Perturbed.

Well, well, well. I do believe he's jealous I have such a great relationship with his dad.

"Good night, Father." I start to head out of the apartment practically shaking my head at the notion that Ramsey is envious of my relationship with his father. Like it's so hard to have a meaningful bond with Father Laurent and oh, how he wishes he had one. For pity's sake, it's the easiest thing in the world.

As I walk away Liam asks if he can come with me now instead of waiting another hour and I say, "Sure" in a very loud and jolly voice so Ramsey won't put the kibosh on that, too. Next thing you know he'll be jealous that his kid likes hanging out with me.

"I'm going with Daisy!" Liam yells and shuts the door behind us as rapidly as he can, thinking the same thing as me, that if he doesn't, someone will protest and he will hear it.

"I have to play something for Solomon real quick, Liam. The door is open at Rosalina's. You don't have to wait until six. And I'm sure Andrea won't mind having someone her age for company."

He gives me a peeved look that tells me it's not cool to intentionally seek out a girl's company and heads down the stairs, two at a time. I stop at Solomon's and knock. He opens his door and quickly ushers me in to his polished piano.

As I start to play, the notes from his violin do what they always do. They carry me away to a lovely place and I start to flub up my part.

"Forte there, Daisy. Give me some volume!" Solomon says with his left jowl crunched against the chin rest.

I pound out the notes as best I can and when we are done and I'm playing my last notes at the bottom of the register, he turns to me.

"That was better than last time."

"You're too kind, Solomon."

"You really should practice more."

"Well, you really should find another pianist to practice *with*." As I rise from the bench I suddenly remember that Liam told me Ramsey plays the piano. And this just strikes me as odd. I'm not sure why. Maybe because music is so beautiful. Romantic, almost.

Ramsey doesn't seem that interested in beautiful things.

"I hear Father Laurent's son plays," I continue. "He's going to be here for a little while. I'm sure he's better than me, Solomon."

"Really? Well, I didn't know that about him. I'll have to ask him. I do like the way you play, Daisy. You have a lovely touch. When you hit the right notes."

Such is my lot. A lovely touch when I hit the right notes.

THIRTY-NINE

The clouds above me are fat with substance. An errant and fore-
boding breeze sneaks through them to ruffle my loose hair as I sit
on the roof and sip from a Caribou Coffee cup. The Monday-morning
sun is hidden away and a low rumbling echoes off the horizon. The
forecast calls for rain.

I close my eyes and lean back in my chair, savoring the solitude
for as long as I can. When the rain starts I'll have to head back downstairs, where day-to-day life in all its chaos and splendor awaits me.

Shelby wants to bring Eric by this afternoon so I can meet him.
She doesn't really need my approval, but I think she wants it anyway.
They're going to a matinee and then dinner. Ah, the unhurried summer
lives of schoolteachers! Shelby asked me if I wanted to join them and
I declined. They'll just stop by Something Blue on their way to the
theater.

I am trying to imagine what her Eric looks like. Shelby has
described him to me. Medium build, brown hair, fit and trim. But
for the life of me all I can picture is the gym teacher from the movie
Runaway Bride, the guy Julia Roberts almost marries (in a perfectly
lovely dress, by the way) but doesn't. Just picturing Eric looking like
that man makes me want to laugh. I hope I don't burst into hysterics
when I meet him.

You know, there were people who thought I was the runaway bride
when my wedding was canceled. They thought I was the one who
chickened out at the last moment, that I was the one who ran like a

scared rabbit from the handsome groom. As I sip, I attempt to picture Richard Gere running, in his tuxedo, away from Julia Roberts, and jumping into the Federal Express van to get as far away from her as he can. The thought is laughably absurd. That just wouldn't happen. I giggle there on the rooftop with my coffee cup. And then I stop because that is pretty much what happened to me.

My groom ran away from me.

I chase these thoughts away and begin to hum my favorite song from the *Runaway Bride* soundtrack. It has a lovely melody line. I've seen the movie a dozen times, of course. The words to "I've Never Seen Blue Like That," start to fall off my lips while my eyes are still lazily closed. They are really quite beautiful—

And then someone clears his throat.

My eyes fly open, my coffee cup ejects itself from my hand, and I find myself gaping at Ramsey Laurent.

"Sorry!" He is as wide-eyed as I am. Ramsey bends down to retrieve my cup, which, despite its lid, is oozing its contents on the pea-gravel surface of the roof. He hands it to me. I swear his hand is shaking.

"You scared me to death," I whisper, taking my cup.

Okay, so my hand is shaking, too.

"I…I just came up here to start on the design. I can come back later." He turns.

I get up from my chair. "No—wait, Ramsey. There's rain on the way. You may as well get done what you can today before it starts. As you can see, I wasn't doing anything important."

I am shaking coffee off my wrist as he turns back around.

"Did you get burned?"

"It's not that hot. I've been up here awhile."

"Oh."

Silence.

"When you have a design ready, Reuben would like me to fax it to him." I sound oh-so-businesslike. "Is that okay?"

"Sure. Of course."

More silence.

"Well, I'll let you get to work," I start to move away. "Unless you need anything."

"Yes. No. I mean I'll be fine."

"Okay." I walk past him and he says my name. I've been around him almost a week and he really hasn't said it that much. He usually just starts talking to me when he needs to say something. For some reason, when he says my name, the sound of it pulls at me. I turn back around. "Yes?"

He hesitates, and then takes a big breath. "Look, I owe you an apology. For yesterday."

An apology? For yesterday?

"It wasn't that I didn't trust you to help my dad open a can of soup. I know you could've done that. And I know my father would have enjoyed your company. He thinks a lot of you. But I..."

He falters. I stand there and blink, surprised beyond words.

"I just didn't...I just haven't spent a lot of time in social gatherings since my divorce and I really wasn't ready to jump in just like that. It was me, not you. It's taking me a little while to feel comfortable being around other people again. That's probably something that someone like you can't understand."

His voice falls away again like he really doesn't know how to say what's on his mind. I doubt he's rehearsed this. And I'm not really sure what he means by "someone like you." But he's wrong nonetheless.

"Of course I understand."

"You do?"

I'm beginning to think he really knows nothing personal about me at all. I guess I shouldn't be so surprised. It wouldn't be like Father Laurent to talk about other people *to* other people for no other purpose than just spreading news. "Well, yes, I do. You don't owe me an apology, Ramsey."

He seems to relax a bit. "No, I do. I'm really trying to work past this. But I need to mend the fences along the way. Especially the ones I break myself."

I smile. "That sounds like wise advice your father would give someone."

He smiles back. "It is."

My smile fades a little as I consider that maybe he was told to come and ask my pardon. "Did your father send you up here to tell me you're sorry?"

Surprise floods his face. "No. Not at all. It's just been bothering me, that's all."

"Well, I don't know what kind of person you think I am, but I do understand what it's like to be hurt. You don't have to explain anything."

He looks down, like he doesn't want to make eye contact for a moment. Perhaps I shouldn't have let on that I know he was the one who was walked out on.

Omigosh. I shouldn't have.

"Ramsey, I'm sorry."

He looks up again and it's like his face has aged a little in the moments he looked away from me. "So how much do you know?"

I swallow. "We don't have to talk about this."

"Did my father tell you what happened?"

"Well, see, before you came home from Tokyo and Liam spent his weekends here, your ex-wife would just honk for him on the street, which I thought was rude, and one day Liam didn't want to go when she was coming for him and he said it was because he didn't want to hear Allegra's howling and I thought he was talking about his mother's dog or something and Liam said no, it was his baby sister. And then Liam left and I turned to your father and said how shocked I was there was a baby already and Father Laurent said the baby was—"

I shut my mouth as Ramsey turns his head away.

I'm a super dunce. I can feel my face turning a thousand shades of red. Why didn't I just shut up? Harriet, where were you? *Lord, help me make this right.* "Ramsey, please forgive me. I'm an idiot. Please?"

He turns his head slowly around to face me again. "There's nothing to forgive."

"Please don't be angry at your dad for explaining how those two could have had a baby so soon. I practically asked."

"What's to explain? It's not hard to do the math. Anyone can figure it out. Even Liam knows."

Again my face floods with hot embarrassment. His voice sounds so detached. If I didn't know any better I'd say L'Raine was nearby insisting I weep for this man—my eyes are stinging. Ramsey must see the tears rimming my eyes. The expression on his face has just now changed from vague to perplexed.

"It's none of my business," I whisper. "I didn't mean to stick my nose where it doesn't belong."

He says nothing. I shake my head and blink back the tears and he just stands there looking at me. Transfixed, almost. He's wondering why on earth I would be so affected by what happened to him. He doesn't know I live with rejection, just like he does. Every day. All day.

A drop falls on my forehead and I reach up to touch it. Another one falls.

The rain has started.

"Guess I won't get to that design this morning after all," he says.

"There's no rush."

We stand there for a moment as the rain begins in earnest. Then we silently head to the stairs that lead to third-floor roof access. By the time we are back inside, the rain has begun to pour down upon The Finland, the drumming on the roof sounding like a million tapping feet.

FORTY

Dear Harriet,

You've never said anything you've regretted, so you probably can't begin to understand how bad I feel about my diarrhea of the mouth up on the roof today. It would've been nice if you had come to my rescue and saved me from the embarrassment of reminding Ramsey that his wife left him for another man—a man whose child she was already carrying. I can't believe I just went on and on like that.

And then when I nearly started crying. You should've seen Ramsey's face. I don't think I've ever seen a man more bewildered.

Actually, I'm the bewildered one. Ramsey told me today, before I threw his misery up in his face, that his father thinks the world of me. Don't you find that odd? Father Laurent is my anchor in the raging water, my beacon in the dark. I can't understand what I could possibly be to him other than an off-and-on annoyance.

And then that he would convey such a thing to his son. How could Ramsey know his dad thinks so highly of me unless Father Laurent had said something to that effect? It floors me.

I don't think Ramsey knows Daniel left me. He surely must know I've been engaged. But I don't think he knows it was my fiancé who called off the wedding, broke the engagement, told me he didn't really love me, and sent me spiraling down to places I'd never been before.

Ramsey was certain I wouldn't understand how reluctant he is to get back into having a social life. That can only mean one thing. He thinks I called off my wedding. Or that it was a joint decision between Daniel and me.

I need to know what Father Laurent told him. And what he hasn't.

And don't ask me why I need to know. I just do.

P.S. Shelby brought Eric to the store today so that I could meet him. He's a very nice guy. Doesn't look a thing like the gym teacher on Runaway Bride. *She looked so happy standing there next to him. And I could tell he dotes on her.*

It's amazing, really, what can happen to you when you're just going about the business of explaining to junior-highers the digestive system of frogs and toads.

Dear Daisy,

There's a perfectly good reason why you blurted out what you did in front of Ramsey today. I hadn't disappeared; you just didn't stop to consult me. And I'm not one to interrupt. If you had just taken a moment to consider what you really wanted to say, it probably would've come out differently. But you live your life in the real world and thinking on the fly is how you live it. You can't pause for time in the middle of a conversation and consider your response options. Your dad would tell you to file this experience away for future reference so that the next time you are up against a tide of emotions, you won't speak before you think.

And I've no need to ask why you must know what Father Laurent told Ramsey about you.

I know perfectly well why it matters to you.

And so do you.

Harriet

FORTY-ONE

The drawing in front of me lies across my desk atop bridal magazines and eBay printouts. It is a two-dimensional schematic, or so Ramsey tells me, of what The Finland's green roof will look like. Ramsey is pointing out all the features Reuben will surely want to know about: how the vegetation will absorb rainwater and slowly discharge it as manageable runoff, how it will ease the urban "heat island" effect around the building, that it will contain a lovely collection of sedum species plus pathways for easy-access maintenance. Nested in the drawing are plant names like *Aster novae-angliae, Monarda didyma, Perovskia atriplicifolia,* and *Phlox paniculata "David."* The names are enchanting.

He pauses for a moment. "So what do you think?"

"It looks wonderful. But I'm afraid I don't know what these names mean. And what's a sedum?"

"Sedums are a diverse group of plants. They're hardy, drought-resistant, and easy to care for. And they're sustainable through the changing seasons. Sometimes they're called stonecrops. Most green roofs have them."

"And these Latin names?"

"Well, *Phlox paniculata 'David'* does very well on green roofs." Ramsey speaks like he and the phlox are old friends. "It was actually named the 2002 Perennial of the Year. It's an erect perennial, grows to about three feet tall. Has fragrant white blossoms in its blooming season, which is quite long."

"Sounds pretty."

"It's a nice shrub."

I point to a row of *Aster novae-angliae*. "And what are these?"

Ramsey follows my finger with his eyes. "Those are sometimes called 'purple domes.' The blooms are a nice shade of lavender. Asters are rather daisylike in appearance. You'll like them."

For some reason that makes me smile. "And these?" I point to *Perovskia atriplicifolia*.

"Those are rather unique. The foliage is greenish-gray until early to mid summer, when the stems produce delicate purple flowers. They're very aromatic."

I let my gaze wander around the design, following the footpaths with my eyes. I see a little open area with two rectangular shapes. "And what are these?"

Ramsey peers at the drawing and then draws back a little. "Those are your Adirondack chairs."

He says it so softly, tenderly even.

I sneak a look at him and he looks away from me. "I love it," I tell him. "Reuben's going to love it, too."

Ramsey clears his throat. "So we're ready to fax it then?"

"The cost per square foot is somewhere on here, right?"

"Yes. Right there in the lower left-hand corner. I'm estimating about eighteen dollars a square foot. And that includes the growing medium, all the vegetation, a simple drip-irrigation system, and the first six months maintenance. It covers the permits, too."

"Six months maintenance?"

He looks up at me. "That means for the first six months I will stop in once a month to make sure everything is taking root and thriving. If you want to contract me for additional yearly maintenance we can do that. Or I can teach Mario how to take care of it."

"Okay. So how long will it take to complete?" I keep my eyes on the drawing. I'm almost afraid of the answer.

"Once I have the permits, it will take a week, weather permitting."

Just a week.

"And how long will it take to get the permits?" I ask.

"A week or two. Maybe three."

I'm not entirely sure what this means for Father Laurent. For me. In a month's time Father Laurent will just be beginning the radiation treatment for his cancer. *Just* beginning it. And that's assuming he continues to recover well from his heart attack.

"So what does that mean, exactly?" I ask. "For your dad?"

Ramsey leans back in his chair across from my desk. "Well, I can see that my father likes it here. And that you all treat him like family. I appreciate that. But I think it's best we take it one day at a time."

I can't keep a tiny pout from spreading across my face. I'd rather he had said Father Laurent can stay as long as he wants.

"Actually," he continues, "I've been thinking about how the green roof I'll be creating here will help me get my own business off the ground. I can use it as a prototype for promoting my business here in the Twin Cities…if that's okay with you."

I'm not entirely sure what he's asking of me, but if it just means Father Laurent won't have to hurry through his cancer treatments, that's fine with me.

"Of course. I didn't know you were starting your own business." I don't recall Liam or Father Laurent mentioning this.

He pauses, like he's hesitant to share anything about his personal life. "I've been putting together a business plan. It's just a one-man enterprise at the moment. I wanted to put it in place when I got back from Tokyo. I'm not as fond of traveling as I used to be. Consulting had me on the road all the time. I didn't mind so much right after the divorce, but I've missed Liam. And my dad."

"And they've missed you."

It seems to suddenly occur to him that he has just spoken of deeply private matters. A look of alarm passes across his face. "So do you want to fax that?" he says abruptly.

"Oh. Sure." I slip the drawing into my fax machine and press Reuben's speed dial. Ramsey appears restless as he waits for the machine to be finished with his drawing. When at last the sketch appears in the exit tray, he snatches it up. "Okay. So, thanks." He practically bolts for the door.

I wait until I know that Ramsey and Liam have left the building before I head up the stairs to the apartments above Something Blue. It's been several days since I've had any time alone with Father Laurent. And I simply *must* talk with him.

His voice calls me in when I knock. I find him seated at his computer playing computer chess.

"Daisy!"

"Hello, Father Laurent."

"So how are you?"

"Well, isn't that what I should be asking you?"

"I'm doing fine, really." He stands. "Want a cup of tea?"

"Let me make it, Father."

"Nonsense." He and his slippered feet head for the kitchen. I follow.

"So." He grabs a kettle and fills it with tap water. "Tell me how things are with you."

"They're okay, Father."

He places the kettle on his stove and turns a dial. Then he turns to me. "We can just sit in here." He motions to his little kitchen table. We each take a chair.

"I met Shelby's new boyfriend." I fiddle with his saltshaker.

"Oh?"

"He seems like a great guy. And I can see that she really likes him. I don't know that I've ever seen Shelby so happy."

"Well, I'm sure that makes you happy."

"It does."

We are silent for a moment.

"Father, does Ramsey know about Daniel?"

He looks very surprised that I asked. "Do you mean did I tell Ramsey about Daniel?"

"Yes."

He smiles. "What happened between you and Daniel is your story to tell, if you choose to tell it. So, no—I have not spoken to Ramsey about Daniel."

"Can you tell me what you've told him about me?"

Father Laurent looks very amused. I blush and feel that he deserves more. "I just get the impression he thinks I have it all together, Father. Ramsey said he didn't think I was the kind of person who would understand what it's like to want to protect yourself from getting hurt. I find that very funny. If he knew me, he wouldn't have said such a thing."

"I have told him you are a lovely person inside and out, that you care very deeply for the people in your life, that you are very creative, full of ideas, and one of the kindest people I know."

He is smiling the whole time he's saying this. I drop my head into my hands on propped elbows and moan. I'm not used to hearing such nice things said about me. I hate the idea that it sounded like I was fishing for them.

The kettle begins to whine and Father Laurent stands up. I raise my head and watch as he places tea bags in mugs, fills them with steaming water, and brings them to the table. He sets mine down in front of me. I just stare at it.

"Daisy."

I look up.

"I *do* think you're one of the kindest people I know."

For a moment I say nothing. Then I blurt out my latest confession. "I wanted you to remain at The Finland so you could keep giving me advice and blessing my little blue hearts."

He smiles. "You know that's not the only reason."

I feel a tightness in my throat. "Yeah...well, it's one of the big ones."

Father Laurent leans forward. "But surely you know those are also *my* reasons for staying. I love living here. You are all like family to me. It's very reassuring for a retired priest like me to be needed. I belong here. Just like you do."

I don't know how he does it, but Father Laurent always makes me feel worthy of love when I'm around him.

"So you really think I'm creative?" I ask sheepishly.

"Wildly so."

I lift my tea bag in and out of my cup to release its flavor. Another question occurs to me. "So does Ramsey know why I opened Something Blue?"

"I really don't know what Ramsey knows about Something Blue, Daisy. He hasn't asked me about it. And I haven't told him there's a dress down there that's yours, if that's what you mean."

"Oh."

"If I had to guess, I'd say he probably thinks you came up with a very clever idea for marketing secondhand wedding gowns. It was a great idea, you know."

He winks at me.

"Wildly so." I weakly wink back.

The rest of the month of June is passing in an almost tedious fashion. Ramsey can't start on the roof until the permits come through, so he and Liam are spending their days playing Monopoly with Father Laurent, taking him to his doctors' appointments, and dodging me. Okay, that's not entirely true. Father Laurent always seems glad to see me, and Liam gets bored often enough to want to come down to the store now and then for diversion, but I don't think Ramsey likes being around women. He avoids me.

In a way he's worse off than I am. I know I've put off dating other people—even meeting other people—since Daniel dumped me, but I haven't sworn off the entire male population. Ramsey's an attractive man. He could start dating again if he wanted to. It's like he's given up on women completely. And I have to say, he may like it this way, but he sure doesn't look very happy.

I don't want to be like that. The next time Marshall Mitchell comes through the door I'm going to ask him myself if he'd like to go have a cup of coffee. He came by here a few days ago, while I was at an Uptown retailers' meeting. Mom told me he said he'd try back again sometime. She didn't seem too excited that he stopped by, which surprises me. I would've guessed she'd call me in the middle of the meeting to tell me he was there. But she didn't. It's like she's having second thoughts about him, which doesn't make sense at all. It was her idea in the first place that I meet him.

He hasn't come back.

I am trying not to put myself in countdown mode but it seems to be happening anyway. I'm counting down the days until Daniel marries, the days until my thirtieth birthday, the days until Marshall Mitchell decides to pop in again, and the days Ramsey will be on the roof and allowing Father Laurent to stay here at The Finland.

I don't like counting the days.

FORTY-TWO

Dear Harriet,

I have to say that the smartest thing I could've done this weekend, I actually did. You should congratulate me. It was the Fourth of July weekend, Daniel was getting married, and I had an invitation to go to a lake resort with Shelby and Eric and a bunch of their friends and I went. Bettina was off visiting her family in Florida so Max came, too. He entertained us at night with his magic tricks.

There were lots of reasons to stay home, including the fact that Ramsey had finally gotten his permits and was hauling I don't know how many cubic yards of specialized dirt up onto my roof. But I didn't do it. I packed my little bag and immersed myself into a highly socially charged atmosphere. A couple of the guys I met up there were single like me and I made it a point to be friendly—but not flirtatious.

Say what you will about having Max there. It wasn't to have him sit by me at dinner so I wouldn't have to converse with men I didn't know. He had been complaining about having nowhere to spend the holiday, there was room in Shelby's car and in Eric's cabin, so I invited him along and he came. That's all there is to it.

I had a good time. I hardly thought about Daniel at all.

When I got back this afternoon I went up to see Father Laurent, but he and Liam and Ramsey had gone to see the fireworks over Lake Superior the night before and weren't home yet. I guess they stayed at Ramsey's townhouse in Duluth.

Tonight, Mom, L'Raine, and I watched Seven Brides for Seven Brothers. *We invited Maria Andrea and Rosalina to come watch it, too.*

It was so much fun. Just us girls. We all wore our pj's and Mom made fudge.

I'm glad Daniel got married this weekend. I am. Now that he's married, I don't have to worry about him someday wanting me back.

I hope it wasn't too soon to take Father Laurent out on an overnight trip. He's been doing so well. It would be such a shame for him to have a setback. Especially with his radiation treatment coming up.

I heard them come home tonight. The service elevator makes a bit of a racket.

I'm sure everything's fine.

Of course everything's fine! I'm finally free of Daniel, for one thing.

Tomorrow Ramsey's supposed to be planting the first quadrant on the roof garden. I can't wait to see the phlox and those lovely, fragrant white flowers.

Dear Daisy,

Congratulations on hardly thinking about Daniel at all.

Harriet

FORTY-THREE

The July heat is shimmering off Uptown's asphalt and concrete, sending the few customers into Something Blue to cool off more than to shop for wedding dresses. At least that's what it seems like. No one has bought anything the last couple of days. L'Raine says the heat makes people grumpy and unwilling to part with their money.

I think it's simply the month itself. Any girl getting married in July or August has already bought her wedding dress. Autumn brides *should* be shopping for their gowns but they're too busy working on their suntans.

Maria Andrea and Liam were up on the roof earlier, helping Ramsey create my rooftop garden of Eden, but the heat chased them down. They are now upstairs with Father Laurent, keeping him company and teaching him how to play video basketball on an X-Box. Liam brought his gaming unit from home. Actually, the Horn Blower dropped it off a couple days ago. I didn't meet her. She just came into the store, told my mother Liam had called and asked for his X-Box game console, and set it on the counter. Then she turned and left. I was helping a customer in the dressing room and never even saw her.

It took quite a bit of self-discipline not to ask my mother if Kristen Ex-Laurent is pretty.

The sales floor is dead quiet. This is a good time to peek in on Father Laurent. With a wave to Mom and L'Raine, I make my way to the back of the store and the stairs beyond. As I reach the third floor, I can make out the sounds of a cheering crowd, a buzzer, and the slap-slap-slap of a bouncing ball hitting hardwood. The door to Father Laurent's apartment is open, allowing the sounds of a video basketball game to carry into the hallway. I wordlessly poke my head inside the apartment.

Father Laurent is in his chair, head to one side, dozing. Liam and Andrea are seated cross-legged in front of Father's TV set, each holding a game controller. Their fingers are punching buttons in rapid-fire fashion.

"You fouled me!" Andrea declares.

"Ref didn't call it."

"Stupid program."

"There's nothing wrong with the program."

They are quiet for a moment and then Liam says, "You can't make a shot from there."

A second later there is the sound of a cheering crowd.

"Ha!" Andrea sounds triumphant.

"There's no way you could've made it from there. No way!"

"Must be something wrong with the program!" Andrea's tone is gleefully sarcastic.

I turn and leave them. Father Laurent is obviously fine.

The stairs to the roof fall into my line of vision and it occurs to me I haven't seen Ramsey in a while. He must be sweltering up there. He also might want a drink of water. I climb the stairs and then open the door to the roof. The heat and humidity meet me like a wall. Still, I'm amazed at how much progress Ramsey has made in the last two days since I was up here. It's like looking at a tiny cross-section of Central Park. The garden is coming together so beautifully and it's nearly three-quarters done. I head out on the soon-to-be-stone pathway to the far side, where Ramsey is stretching out rubberized edging material. His skin has turned golden these last few days. Sweat and smudges of dirt mark his face. He looks up at me.

"Kind of a hot one, isn't it?" I say.

"You could say that again."

He pulls a bandana out of his back pocket and wipes his fore-head.

"It's looking so beautiful, Ramsey. Really."

He rewards me with a half-smile. "Thanks."

"Can I get you a cold drink?"

Ramsey reaches down to a cooler by his feet and pops the lid. "Actually, that'd be nice. I guess I drank everything I brought up with me."

"Okay. You want water or ice tea or something else?"

"Water's fine."

"All right. I'll be right back."

I start to head back to the stairs.

"Daisy?"

"Yes?"

"Thanks."

"Don't mention it."

I hurry down to my apartment and rummage in my fridge for a bottle of raspberry Fruit 2-O, my favorite flavored water. I see one in the back. Good. That means it will be really cold.

I wonder if Ramsey's hungry. I check my watch. Two-fifteen. Maybe I should make him a sandwich.

No, sandwiches are for lunch. Besides I don't even know what kind of sandwich he likes.

Maybe I should bring him an apple or a banana?

But his hands are covered in dirt. He probably won't want to eat something with his hands.

I shut the fridge door. Okay, so I'll just bring him the water.

I make my way back out of my apartment and take the stairs to the third floor. I hear voices ahead of me. One I recognize as my mother's, the other I cannot place. When I get to the top of the stairs I see my mother's back and that of a blonde woman as they disappear beyond the door that leads to the roof.

Liam and Andrea must've also heard the voices. They are peeking out of Father Laurent's doorway.

"Do you know who that is with my mother?" I ask Liam.

He nods. "That's my mom."

The Horn Blower.

"Oh."

Liam seems neither interested nor concerned that she is here. I guess to him it's no big deal that his mother would want to come talk to his father.

"Do you know why she's here?" I wonder if I sound as juvenile as I feel.

"Nope."

"Oh."

I just stand there looking at the door at the end of the hall. Liam and Andrea disappear from the open doorway to resume their game. A moment later the door to the roof access opens and I stiffen. Mom emerges, alone.

She walks toward me with a look of consternation on her face.

"Did you see who's here?" she whispers, as if the walls are conspirators.

"That's Kristen?"

"She came into the store demanding to speak to Ramsey. Said it couldn't wait. Like the whole world revolves around her!"

"What does she want?" I'm whispering, too. Who knows why.

"Her *way*, I'm sure. Whatever *that* is." Mom moves past me to the stairs. I'm glad she's thinking that L'Raine is manning the sales floor solo at the moment. My thoughts are far from the store.

The sound of my mother's footsteps fall away and I'm still standing here.

But then I look at the bottle of water in my hand and a thought tempts me. Tempts me big-time. I walk toward the door to the roof access. I carefully open the door, slowly so I don't make a sound.

Harriet, mind your own business.

I ease the door shut silently.

I step out onto the first step, which is surrounded on all sides by brick. If I stand on the second or third step I will be able to hear what she is saying. If I stand on the fourth or fifth step, one of them might see me.

I stay on the second step.

"Please, Ramsey?" the Horn Blower is saying. She is close. Ramsey must have moved to a section of the garden closer to the stairs. Or maybe he came to greet her when my mom brought her up.

I feel my heart begin to pound a little, partly from fear of being caught and partly from wondering what it is that the Horn Blower is begging from him.

"We had an agreement, Kristen."

Ramsey's voice sounds controlled, but sad. It's an odd combination.

"I know, Ramsey. I wouldn't be asking if it wasn't really important."

"This wasn't in the plan for this summer."

"I told you Vic just found out about it. We didn't know we were going until just now. It's just such a wonderful opportunity. Liam's never been to Mexico. And I know he'd love this. And I really want him to come with Vic and Allegra and me. It's just for a week. You can have him on Thanksgiving if that will make up for it."

There is silence for a moment.

"I guess it's really up to Liam." Ramsey finally says. "If he wants to go, he can go. But if he doesn't, I'm not going to make him."

The Horn Blower sighs. "All right. Thanks, Ramsey. This means a lot to me."

"Yeah. Sure."

"So. You doing okay?"

"I'm fine."

"You don't sound fine."

"You don't have to be concerned with what I sound like anymore, Kristen."

"I'm just making a point! You don't have to get so defensive."

"I'm fine."

More silence.

"I still care about you, Ramsey. I don't want you living the rest of your life alone. I want you to move on. Meet people. Go places. Do things. All you do is work! Have you even gone on one date?"

Ramsey doesn't answer her.

I sense something percolating inside me. Something is tugging at the bonds of fellowship shared by members of the Lonely Hearts Club. Something wild. I suddenly want to do something that is definitely more provocative than eavesdropping. Something Harriet certainly wouldn't approve of. But Harriet has fled the premises.

So be it.

I reach behind me, open the door, and then let it close, letting it make all the sound it wants. Then I climb the stairs and allow my body to emerge fully. Ramsey is bent down in the dirt with a little trowel in his hand. The Horn Blower is standing on the other side of him. She is wearing sunglasses, so I can't see her eyes, but the rest of her face looks fairly flawless. Clear skin, rosy cheeks, supple lips, diamond earrings. She has on a taupe flared skirt and a creamy sleeveless V-neck. She's a perfect size four.

"Oh, hello." I sweetly color my tone with a dash of surprise. I walk over to Ramsey and bend down with the bottle of water in one hand.

Then I reach out and rest my other hand on his shoulder, just for a second. A tiny caress. Just long enough for the Horn Blower to see it. Just long enough for it to give me an unexpected thrill.

"Here's your water, Ramsey." I extend the water bottle to him. It's an effort to keep my voice as steady and sweet as a veteran airline attendant.

Ramsey looks up at me with the strangest expression on his face. I can't begin to describe it. But as we look at each other, something passes between us that nearly knocks me off my feet. I quickly stand straight and turn to Kristen. I extend my right hand and she slowly takes it.

"I'm Daisy Murien. I own the boutique downstairs. You must be Liam's mom. He's such a great kid. We all just love him."

Kristen slowly shakes my hand. "I'm Kristen Dorris." She is sufficiently stunned, I'd say. Take *that*, Horn Blower.

"Well, nice to meet you." I keep my voice as cordial as you please.

I don't dare look over at Ramsey.

I can feel him looking at me but I don't turn my head the slightest in his direction.

I simply turn my body and head back downstairs like I've another important errand to run.

There is no sound behind me as I open the door to the third floor and disappear through it.

I head back to Something Blue in a daze, wondering what just happened. Wondering what Ramsey must be thinking. What the Horn Blower is thinking. What I *wanted* her to think. And how the sensation of Ramsey's warm skin and muscle beneath my touch surprised the heck out of me.

I begin to fiddle with dresses and veils, distracted and perplexed. Mom and L'Raine watch me from the back but they don't say a thing.

Many minutes later, when I hear the door to the sales floor open followed by the sound of the Horn Blower's voice, I scramble to get behind the front counter. Liam, Kristen, and Ramsey walk toward the front door, presumably to escort Kristen to her car. I pretend to be marking an inventory sheet. I am making a line of M's—that is all I am doing.

"So it's a big cruise ship?" Liam is saying.

"Really big. With a pool on the top deck and everything," Kristen is exuberant. "We'll go snorkeling. And parasailing. It's going to be great."

They arrive at the front door. "We'll pick you up at seven a.m. on Saturday, okay?" Kristen bends down to hug Liam goodbye.

"Okay." Liam sounds excited.

"Thank you, Ramsey," Kristen says as she breaks away from her son.

Ramsey just nods.

The Horn Blower opens the front door, calls out a cheery goodbye, and waves.

Liam turns to me. "I'm going on a cruise to Mexico!"

"Wow. How cool is that?" I attempt to inject a little excitement into the moment.

"Mom says they serve ice cream all the time. Even in the middle of the night."

"Awesome."

Liam nods. "I'm going to tell Grandpa." He turns and heads to the back door.

Ramsey pauses in front of me like he's going to say something. I look down at my M's. He's either very unhappy about what I did up on the roof or just very confused.

He opens his mouth, and I'm certain it's to say, "What just happened between us up there?"

Before he can utter a word the front door opens. We both turn, thinking Kristen has returned with a last-minute instruction for Liam.

But it's not Kristen. It's Marshall Mitchell.

FORTY-FOUR

I wouldn't say this is the first time in my life I've been speechless. There have been other times. Like when I got the lead role in *Oklahoma* my senior year in high school. And when my mother called me from the hospital and told me my father had died. And when Daniel told me with dry eyes he didn't want to marry me.

I've been surprised beyond words before. But somehow this is different.

As Marshall Mitchell walks toward me with a polite smile on his face, it's like someone has pressed the "mute" button for my mouth.

"Hello, Daisy."

I mutter something like, "Ungh."

"I hope I haven't caught you at a bad time."

I force my tongue to wake from its comatose state. "No. Not at all," I mumble.

Marshall looks at Ramsey, who is standing in front of me dirty and sweaty, and wearing holey jeans. Marshall, by the way, is wearing a charcoal-gray suit and a sapphire-blue silk tie. "If you need to finish with your...customer, I can wait."

Before I can answer, my mother comes sailing up to the front, perhaps to rescue me. "Marshall, how are you? How lovely to see you again."

She grabs Marshall's attention and his arm, like he came to see her, not me.

"I'm fine, thank you very much, Mrs. Murien." Marshall's voice is gracious but he seems taken aback by my mother's hearty welcome. He casts a glance to me that says, *Is she always like this?*

Ramsey continues to stand there, just looking at me.

"L'Raine, look who's here!" Mom announces. "It's Marshall."

I'm not even sure L'Raine knows who Marshall is—or if he knows who she is. My head is swimming.

"It's great to see you again," Marshall says to either my mother or L'Raine—I'm not sure which—and then he turns his head to me. "Would you like to go get a cup of coffee, Daisy? Is this a good time?"

"Oh...sure. This is a great time," I lie. "I'll just go get my purse."

I don't look at Ramsey as I head to my office.

This is *not* a great time.

But I grab my purse and walk out with my eyes on my feet, wondering if I dare sneak a look at Ramsey. When I get back to the front of the store, I decide I will, but when I lift my head I see he isn't there. He has left.

"All set?" Marshall is cheerful.

No.

"Yes."

He smiles and opens the door for me, and I walk out of my boutique into the sultry afternoon heat.

"You have a favorite spot for coffee?"

"Well, there's a nice gelateria just up the street. They serve Italian coffee. It's very good."

"Sounds super." He smiles. I try to. We start to walk up the street.

"How have you been, Daisy?"

I've been in an absolute fog.

"Fine. And you?"

"Good. But busy. I'm sorry I didn't come back to see you sooner. I was out of town. Did your mom tell you I came by to see you?"

"Yes. Yes, she did."

"I hope it's okay that I did. Kellen said...Kellen said you told him that would be all right."

"Oh. Yes. Yes, I told him that."

Marshall cocks his head and looks over at me. "But you don't seem like it's all right."

I'm actually glad he's being completely honest with me. Makes it easier for me to be honest with him.

"I'm sorry, Marshall. I've just had a very confusing day. It has nothing to do with you, really."

Well, that's not entirely true. But I doubt I could explain it.

"Oh. I'm sorry to hear that. Want to talk about it?"

I break into a smile I'm sure he mistakes for something akin to appreciation for our budding friendship. I'm smiling because the thought of telling Marshall Mitchell that I just got an intense thrill from touching Ramsey's sweaty shoulder—in front of his ex-wife—is laughable. "I'm sure you don't want to hear about it."

"Sure I do."

No, you don't.

"It's nothing. I'll be okay."

We take a few steps in silence.

"Look, Daisy, I'm sorry if that dinner date thing offended you. When I let Kellen ask if you wanted to join us for dinner, I wasn't trying to play games. I just wanted you to feel comfortable with saying no."

I look over at him. He really does seem like a very nice guy. "I wasn't offended, really. I just…I don't know. I just didn't want people setting me up on dates anymore. It just seems so superficial."

"Been on a lot of miserable blind dates, eh?" he says this like he knows what I'm talking about.

"Not miserable," I answer. "Just empty. Purposeless. I don't know. It's just not how I picture a lifelong relationship beginning."

"Oh. So how do you picture a lifelong relationship beginning?"

I think back to conversations I've had recently with Harriet. "Well, when it begins, you don't actually know it. It happens when you're not expecting it."

When you're in need of a ride to a choir concert.

When you're busy teaching a science class.

Just now, as we're walking, it hits me. Hits me hard. I am nearly knocked to the pavement with the force of the revelation. I'm a planner. I plan things. This is how I live my life. And now I realize why my life seems so difficult right now. What I want most in life is something I know I cannot plan, nor do I want to. And it's driving me crazy. The planner in me wants to plan. And she can't plan this.

"Daisy?"

I've stopped dead in my tracks.

"Daisy, are you all right?"

"I'm…I'm fine. Here. This is it right up here." I walk up to an outdoor table and slide into a chair.

"Can I get you anything?" Marshall is looking down on me, fairly mystified.

"An iced coffee, please?" I say it as kindly as I can.

He goes inside to get our drinks and I just sit there, contemplating my newest revelation and musing on the fact that I'm sitting at the same table where Daniel told me he was getting married.

Marshall comes back a few minutes later with two iced coffees. He seems to have recovered from my odd behavior moments before. He sits across from me and begins to tell me about himself. Not in a self-centered way. I can tell he's just letting me know what he's like as a person.

I listen to him.

But as I listen, I study his face, his hands, his mannerisms. Marshall Mitchell is polite, interested in world affairs and the plight of people in need, and has a nice sense of humor. He goes to a great church, loves God and his parents, plays golf, and doesn't like to waste time. He's wealthy. He's a bit on the heavy side but not unattractive. He's single.

And yet I feel no sense that I'm drawn to him. There is no stirring within me. Not even the tiniest twinge of attraction.

Nothing like what I know I felt minutes ago with Ramsey.

When we walk back to Something Blue, I think Marshall can tell we will never be anything more than casual friends.

He seems a little sad, a little miffed when we say goodbye. He doesn't seem mad at me, though. He seems peeved at Providence—that he met a pleasant, single Christian girl and yet she's not the one who was created to complete him.

Oh, how I can relate.

I walk back into my shop knowing a lot more about myself than I did when I left it.

But knowing less about a lot of other things, including what was running through Ramsey's mind when I touched him.

And what he was going to say to me before Marshall walked through the door.

FORTY-FIVE

Dear Harriet,

I have yet another new maxim for my Rules of Disengagement: There are things that can be planned and can therefore also be unplanned—a wedding, for example. And a party and a vacation and elective surgery. But there are some things that definitely can't be planned, like when and where you will meet the person you really are destined to grow old with, assuming the one you had been engaged to isn't the one. You just can't put that date in your day planner. You can only realize it has happened after it has happened.

Disengaged women—read "jilted brides"—understand this once they've thought about it. We, more than anyone else, know that you can decide the kind of person you want to spend your life with and you can even plan to marry a person like that, but that's where your control stops.

I had encounters with two very different men today. Both times I was under the impression I was in control of the situation. I don't think I was in either case. And yet I feel like I'm now required to take some kind of action, and I'm thoroughly flummoxed. On one hand, we have Marshall. He's wealthy, polite, obviously interested in me, kind to my mother, perceptive, not movie-star handsome but not unpleasant to look at either, and yet I'm simply not attracted to him. Makes no sense. Then on the other hand we have Ramsey. Moody, introspective, detached, tender at times, hurting like me, more attractive than Marshall but not exactly interested in me. And yet thoughts of him rattle me all the livelong day.

When I had my hand on his shoulder today, I could've sworn he was feeling what I was feeling, and don't ask me to define what it was I was feeling because I'm not exactly sure what it was other than simple desire. Which, believe me, surprised me silly.

I wish I knew what he had been going to say to me before Marshall walked into the store.

I should've gone back up to the roof and just asked him. But I couldn't do it. When I got back from having coffee with Marshall, I just puttered around the store the rest of the afternoon, thinking about going back up there but never actually doing it.

I was afraid to. Let's face it—Ramsey was either offended or pleasantly surprised. Do you see how knowing which one it is changes everything?

I am watching Pride and Prejudice, *big screen version, and eating Wheat Thins and raisins by the handful. There are no wedding dresses to critique. There should be, but there aren't.*

Dear Daisy,

I know why you felt compelled to touch Ramsey on the shoulder. I know why you banished me from the rooftop so you could do it.

Your Voice of Reason might have tried to talk you out of it but not for the reasons that come first to mind. You suspect I would have told you to mind your own business, but that is not what I would've said. You intervened not to stun the Horn Blower but to prevent her from hurting Ramsey any further. Your motive wasn't to snub Kristen but to protect Ramsey, not because you pity him but because you are drawn to him. What you did was all about Ramsey, and not a thing about his ex-wife. The sooner you admit that to yourself the better off you'll be. And the more prepared you'll be when you find out what it was Ramsey was going to say.

There aren't wedding dresses in Pride and Prejudice *because it's not a story about weddings but about what it means to truly love someone, what you are willing to do for that person, and what you are willing to sacrifice.*

Harriet

FORTY-SIX

The gown in front of me hangs on the dress form like a wad of feed bags unearthed from a time capsule. I've never seen a wedding dress in such sorry shape. Wrinkled and crushed beyond recognition. Splashes of crumpled lace at the neck and sleeves give mere hints of former elegance, but only if you look close and then shut your eyes and imagine it.

Rosalina is standing next to me in the alterations apartment with her arms across her chest. Maria Andrea is on my other side, mirroring her aunt's pose.

"This is hopeless." I lift part of the wrinkled skirt and let it fall away.

Rosalina shakes her head. "No. Not hopeless. It just won't be easy. We will have to hand steam all these wrinkles out. And the tulle petticoat underneath must be replaced. It is in shreds. That's half the reason the skirt looks so bad."

"When I talked to this woman on the phone she said this dress was heirloom quality," I scoff. "She's probably had this in her garage crammed in a Hefty bag up against her lawn mower."

Again Rosalina shakes her head. "No. It smells like cedar. She had it in a safe place, I think. She just never took it out. She kept putting stuff on top of it, no? We can fix it, Daisy. It looks bad now, but underneath all those wrinkles it's still a beautiful dress. *Verdad, Andrea?*"

Maria Andrea shrugs. "If you say so, *Tía*."

"The hem is in bad shape," Rosalina continues. "But the woman who wore it was tall. We can cut an inch or two off and make a new hem. It will be fine. Andrea, you can take that out while I go to the fabric store. I'm out of tulle here."

Maria Andrea reaches behind us to our worktable and picks up a blue-handled seam ripper. "You are out of bias tape, too, *Tía*. You told me to remind you."

"*Sí, sí. Gracias*. I'll be back soon." Rosalina waves goodbye and heads out the door.

I pull out the form that nonlocal sellers fill out when they sell me a dress online. The woman who sent this dress to me filled it out nicely, a surprise considering how bad the dress looks. I smooth out the page and direct my eyes to the part where it says, *Tell me about this dress.* I begin to read:

This was my grandmother's dress. She was a mail-order bride who left the East Coast at the turn of the last century to marry a logger from Seattle whom she had never met. She had been engaged to marry a wealthy New Jersey businessman but he died of influenza three days before the wedding. This was the dress she had been going to wear. Instead, she wore it three months later when she married my grandfather. They got married in the train station because the church was still being built in the settlement where my grandfather was living.

My grandmother told me she didn't love my grandfather when she married him. But sometime near the end of that first year, she woke up one morning next to Grandpa and she realized she did *love him, deeply. And she didn't even know when her feelings for him had changed.*

I have no children to pass this dress along to and I'm moving into an assisted-care facility. I can't keep it any longer.

But I feel very strongly that someone should have it.

I never saw two people more in love than my grandparents.

I'm so glad I found your website.

Very sincerely,
Margaret Dearwood

P.S. My grandmother's name was Elisabeth Erdahl.

Elisabeth. With an "s."

My mind conjures a picture of my long-ago paper doll and her lampshade wedding dress. I glance at the wrinkled gown on the dress form. Maria Andrea is carefully removing the ancient stitches on the hem.

Already it doesn't look so bad.

I fold the letter and place in on the worktable as Liam pokes his head in. I cannot keep myself from looking past him to see if Ramsey is with him. But he is alone.

"Daisy, my dad wants me to ask you if it's okay if I hang out here today while he takes my grandpa to the hospital."

The hospital?

"What's going on?" I ask. "Is your grandpa okay?"

"They're doing that radiation thing today. He'll be there all day. I don't want to go."

The last I heard, Father Laurent was scheduled for his radiation treatment to begin on Monday, three days from now. "Why today?"

Liam shrugs. "I dunno."

"Of course you can stay here. I'll be right back."

I make my way out of the alterations apartment and up the stairs. Father Laurent is just coming out of his apartment as I reach the third floor. He is telling Ramsey, who is right behind him, that he wants to take the stairs today.

He smiles when he sees me. "Daisy! Hello."

"Good morning, Father."

Ramsey doesn't look at me.

"Liam says you're going in today for your radiation treatment." I pretend I don't notice Ramsey's silence. "The doctors moved it up?"

"My cardiologist gave me the green light and my oncologist doesn't want to wait. He'd like to just get started with it. And we thought with Liam leaving tomorrow, he won't have to see me getting sick, if I do get sick."

"Oh. But it's still just an outpatient procedure, right?"

"Yes. We should be home by this evening." Father Laurent looks behind him to Ramsey. His son has locked the door and is now fiddling with his car keys. Father looks back at me with a puzzled look on his face. He can obviously sense something is up between Ramsey and me. Something unsettling.

Part of me wants to yell, "Yes, it's true! I touched your son on the shoulder and I liked it! And you know what, I think he liked it, too! And that's what he's so mad about!" The other part of me wants to run and hide.

"Ramsey, didn't you want to ask Daisy something?" Father Laurent says.

"What?" Ramsey glances at me and then turns to his dad.

"About Liam?"

Ramsey swivels his head back around to me. "Is it all right if Liam stays here in the building today while Dad and I are at the hospital?" His voice is toneless.

"Of course."

He nods wordlessly and then turns to his father. "We'd better get going, Dad."

Father studies me for a moment then he turns to Ramsey. "You go on down and start the car and get it cooled off. I'll be right down. I want to talk to Daisy a minute."

Ramsey brushes past me and his elbow touches mine. "Excuse me," he says, without meeting my eyes. He heads for the stairs and disappears.

When the sounds of his footsteps have fallen away, Father Laurent turns to me. "Daisy, what's going on?"

"I think he's mad at me for something I did." My eyes feel hot. I refuse to let them be that way.

"What on earth did you do?" Father Laurent clearly can't believe I could offend anyone. The eyes grow hotter.

It takes less than thirty seconds to tell him about the Horn Blower's visit, her patronizing comments, and my spontaneous gesture of solidarity—the one that took my breath away.

"And before I could ask him if he minded that I did that, Marshall

Mitchell came to the store and asked to take me out for coffee!" I lament. "The timing was terrible. I don't even particularly like Marshall. And Ramsey was going to say something to me before Marshall walked in. I don't know what it was. He won't even look at me now."

Father Laurent looks deeply surprised. "You have feelings for Ramsey?"

I'm entirely unprepared for this question. Oh, these mutinous eyes! They begin to spill their contents. "I don't know. Maybe. I'm not sure. Oh, this is such a mess!"

Father touches my arm. "Messes can be cleaned up, Daisy. Listen to me. If Ramsey was surprised by what you did on the roof, perhaps it was because he has no idea that you can empathize with how he feels. You called it an act of solidarity, but he doesn't know you have also loved someone who chose not to love you back. He also doesn't know you heard anything that Kristen said to him on the roof. He doesn't *know* it was an act of solidarity."

This thought never occurred to me! For heaven's sake, what must Ramsey be thinking about me?

I shut my eyes in shame.

"I can talk to him, Daisy."

"No!" I shake my head and my eyes snap open. "No, let me find a way to make this right. I'm the one who made this mess. I have to clean it up. I'll talk to him."

Father Laurent is silent for a moment. "Daisy, may I ask a favor of you?"

"Of course," I blot my eyes with my sleeve.

"Be careful with Ramsey. He's been wounded in the worst possible way. I know you think you understand how he feels, but what happened between you and Daniel is different than what happened between him and Kristen. So please, my dear, be careful. Seek God's path for you. And for him. Can I ask that of you?"

I can only blink and nod.

"That's my girl. I'd better go." He squeezes my arm and walks past me.

I finally find my tongue. "Father!" I call out and he turns. "I'll be praying for you."

He winks, turns, and is gone.

FORTY-SEVEN

After Father Laurent and Ramsey leave, I head straight for the chapel to pray for his healing. I pray the radiation won't make him sick. That it will do the job. That the cancer will be beaten.

And when I am done, I do the other thing he asked of me. Father Laurent told me to seek God's path for myself and for Ramsey. I tell God I am on the lookout.

Show me the way, God. If I've offended Ramsey, help me to make it right. Help me explain to him why I did what I did.

And oh, God, if I am having delusions about what I am feeling for Ramsey, would you please, please, please, make those feelings go away.

Make Ramsey's way as plain as mine.

Help him to let go of his wounds like you are helping me to let go of mine.

And please help me to be the person Father Laurent thinks I am.

In Jesus' name.

Amen.

I don't get up right away. It is completely tranquil here in the chapel. There is only one other place as peaceful and that is my roof.

I pull myself out of the pew and make as discreet an entrance onto the sales floor of Something Blue as I can. L'Raine is helping someone with our selection of mother-of-the-bride dresses. Mom is at the register breaking open a roll of quarters. She sees me.

"Daisy, there you are. Guess who just called?"

I hope it wasn't Marshall. "Who?"

"Reuben. He called to see how the roof garden is coming and when I told him Ramsey is nearly finished, he said he's coming out to see it."

This shouldn't surprise me but it does. I immediately begin to fret over whether I will have to kick Ramsey and Liam out of Reuben's apartment. And whether Father Laurent will be able to tolerate the radiation treatment so he can stay at The Finland no matter where Ramsey and Liam end up.

"Daisy, did you hear what I said?"

"Yes. Yes, I heard you. So, when is he coming? What about Ramsey and Liam?"

"He said not to worry about that. That he'd get a hotel room this time. He's thinking of flying in on Tuesday." Mom glances down at an appointment calendar by the register. "That's the day before your birthday, Daisy! Oh my goodness. I can't believe it will be here so soon. We should do something special."

I walk over to her, shaking my head politely. I really don't want to *do* anything.

"Let's just do what we always do, Mom. Let's just meet Kellen and Laura for dinner at Ping's. We can ask Shelby and Eric to join us. Reuben can come, too, if he wants."

"But Daisy, it's your *thirtieth*."

Ouch, ouch.

"It's just another birthday, Mom. I don't want to do anything special. Really."

Mom produces a pout worthy of comment. "Can't we have a little party or something?"

"Dinner at Ping's *will* be a little party. It will be just right."

"We had a party for Kellen when he turned thirty."

"Yes, but it was a surprise. You never asked him if he wanted that party, Mom. And I really don't want one. I like Ping's. I like keeping it simple. I'll call Shelby and ask her, okay?"

"You shouldn't have to invite your friends to your own birthday party."

It's not a party. "I talk to her all the time anyway, Mom. It won't be any trouble to ask her."

"Well, if that's what you want."

"It is."

She pauses for a moment.

Mothers know, don't they, when their children are troubled. She stares at me for a second and then her eyes widen.

"It's Ramsey, isn't it?" she murmurs and I nearly choke.

"What?"

"I've seen the way he looks at you. I've seen the way you look at him."

"Mom, you're way off."

"No, I'm not. Why do you think I rushed over to welcome Marshall like he was an old family friend yesterday? I *knew* something was up between you two."

My face flames red. "Nothing is 'up'! I don't think Ramsey particularly *likes* me."

Especially not at the moment.

"No, you're mistaken there, I think. He does like you." Mom's expression turns thoughtful. "But for some reason liking you is making him sad. He must think you're still in love with Daniel."

"He doesn't know anything about Daniel."

"He doesn't?"

"No."

"Oh." She purses her lips together, deep in thought as she ponders why liking me would make Ramsey sad.

I've got to get out of this conversation. "I don't want to talk about this anymore. I'm going back up to help Maria Andrea with that new dress. Call me if it gets busy."

"Mmm." She heard me but she's still engrossed in contemplations.

I leave her, wishing I wasn't so likewise occupied.

❧

The rest of the morning crawls by. I spend it hiding in the alterations room with Maria Andrea, Rosalina, and Liam. At noon I offer to make the kids lunch, which they accept, and we spend the next half hour eating corn dogs and tater tots. After lunch, Liam leaves to get his X-Box to set up in my apartment so he and Maria Andrea can play and not be abandoned on the third floor. While he's gone, I can't help but ask Andrea if she likes Liam as more than a friend. She's only twelve, so I'm half-expecting a facial contortion of some sort, but she just hands me her plate and tells me she's too young for a boyfriend.

"So, when you do start dating, what kind of guy do you think you will be attracted to?" I ask as casually as I can. I could really use the perspective of someone who hasn't made any mistakes yet.

Maria Andrea hands me Liam's plate. She doesn't seem the least surprised that I would ask her such a thing. "He has to be a friend first. And kind to people. Not just me, but everybody."

I rinse the dishes, formulating a question in my mind. "Andrea, do you think there's just one person in the world you are meant to fall in love with and marry?"

She leans against the counter and crosses her arms. "Yeah. I think so."

"So how do you find that one person?"

"Well, if you're meant to fall in love and marry him, then you don't have to look for him. It just happens."

Just like that.

Liam tromps through the open door, his arms full of gadgetry.

"Here." Andrea moves toward him and takes the falling controllers out of his hands.

"I'm going back to the alterations room," I tell them.

"Okay," Liam calls out.

"Bye. Thanks for lunch," Andrea echoes.

I leave them to sort through the cables as they prepare to race skateboards across an urban landscape.

I spend the afternoon hand-steaming the wrinkles out of Elisabeth Erdahl's dress and fussing over other little tasks I usually leave to Rosalina. She tells me more than once that I don't have to do any of it, but I need to stay busy. We keep the door to the alterations room open mainly for Liam and Andrea's sake, but I am listening for the sounds of Ramsey and Father Laurent's return.

By four o'clock, they still aren't back.

Max pokes his head in about four-fifteen. "Hey, that weird sound Wendy and Philip have in their apartment? I hear it now, too," he tells me. "It doesn't bother me, but I told Wendy about it and she thinks you need to hear it."

"It always stops when I get there, Max."

"Well, you can hear it now if you want."

"You just heard it?"

"Yep."

I turn to Rosalina. "Is Mario around?"

"No. He's helping a family from church move today."

"All right." I follow Max up the stairs to his apartment.

"I hear it in the bathroom, just like Wendy and Philip do." Max leads the way into his apartment, which is stuffy and bachelor-chaotic.

"You should turn your AC up, Max. It's positively tropical in here."

"Is it?" Max says, hopelessly unaware of conventional things.

We arrive in his bathroom. The countertop is a hodgepodge of shaving items, dental products, and hair gel. Hair gel not in a bottle but on the counter itself.

"Oops." Max reaches for a wad of toilet paper to sop it up.

"It's all right, Max. Where do you hear it?"

"Just stand still a sec and don't say a word." Max flushes his toilet and we stand in silence as it finishes its cycle. When it's done, I hear a slight scrabbling noise inside the walls, like impatient fingernails tapping on a tabletop.

"What do you think it is?" I ask.

"Bats, most likely. But I don't think Wendy's going to like hearing that. You may want to have Mario check the vents and stuff to see if he can tell where they're getting in."

"Great. How do we get them out?"

"Beats me. I guess if you find where they're getting in, you wait until nighttime when they are out flying around and plug up their entrance."

"All right. Thanks, Max." I start to walk out of his bathroom and he follows.

"Daisy?"

"What?"

"What's the matter?"

There's no use pretending around Max. He's like my mother. Like Shelby. He knows me too well. "I'm just a little confused right now." I keep heading for his front door.

"About what?"

"Oh. Everything."

"Everything?"

I stop at the door and then turn to face him. "I had coffee yesterday with Marshall Mitchell."

"I thought his name was Mitchell Marshall."

"No, it's not. It's Marshall Mitchell."

"And?"

"And he's a nice guy who's probably a great catch. But Max, I don't feel like putting out a net. I just don't."

"How come?"

"I don't know."

"You're not holding out for Daniel, are you?"

"Good heavens, no. He got married, remember?"

Max scratches his chin. "Then there must be someone else you're holding out for."

"There's no one else, Max. How are things with you and Bettina?"

Max smiles. "I think she might like me. I think she just might. We're going to a poetry reading tonight. She called and asked *me*."

"Sounds great, Max." I open his front door.

"You want to come?"

Just as I'm about to say, "No, thanks," I turn my head and see that Father Laurent and Ramsey have returned from the hospital. They are standing just outside Father's apartment and Ramsey is putting the key in the lock. He turns at the sound of Max's voice, just as I am walking out of the apartment. Our eyes meet for only a second. He looks away before I do.

"Bye, Max. I'll get Mario to come take a listen, okay?" I try not to sound like I'm making an excuse for why I'm coming out of Max's apartment, but it sure sounds like one. Bravely, I walk over to Father Laurent. "Father, how was it? Are you doing okay?"

"It was a piece of cake." He looks pale and groggy but he smiles anyway. "Thanks for praying, Daisy."

"Here, Dad. Let's get you inside." Ramsey ignores me. He holds the door open wide for his father and steps aside to let him in. Once Father Laurent is in the apartment Ramsey turns to me. "Can you send Liam up when you have a minute?" His eyes are steel gray today.

"Of course. Can I get you anything? Can I order something for you guys for dinner?"

"No. We'll be fine." There is no inflection in his voice.

This is driving me nuts.

"Ramsey, could I talk to you for a minute?"

"Now's not a very good time. I need to look after Dad."

"Well, how about after you get him situated?"

"It's been a long day, Daisy."

"Yes. Of course. I'm sorry. Well, maybe tomorrow, then?"

"Maybe."

I attempt one last peace offering. "Are you sure there's nothing I can do for you?"

He pauses and then shakes his head once. "Just send Liam up when you have a minute."

Ramsey turns and walks inside his father's apartment, closing the door behind him.

FORTY-EIGHT

Dear Harriet,

Do you remember the day when I realized that Skip, the boy I met the summer after eighth grade, had forgotten all about me? When I finally understood I would probably never hear from him again? Surely you must. It was maybe only the third or fourth time I'd written to you.

If I knew where that journal was I'd get it out and read what I wrote. I believe I told you I felt empty inside. Hollow.

Remember when Daniel sat me down and told me he didn't really want to marry me? I was full of anger, resentment, heartache, fear, grief.

But today I feel hollow again. Like I did when I knew Skip was gone.

I keep reminding myself that a couple of years after the Skip episode I thought the whole thing was rather silly.

I think I am falling in love with the wrong man…again.

Dearest Daisy,

I remember when you had to let go of Skip. I remember telling you the smartest thing you could do was move on. Why would you want to hang on to someone who has no desire to hang on to you? Perhaps you felt hollow back then because the feelings you had for that boy hadn't been that deep and when the feelings spilled out, there wasn't much of a puddle.

The feelings you had for Daniel ran deep. When everything spilled out, there was a flood of sorts. That's not so hard to understand.

As to the other thing, please define "wrong."

Harriet

FORTY-NINE

"So what don't you like about him?" Shelby is checking her tan line as we sit on beach chairs on the shore of Lake Calhoun.

"You're getting burned," I tell her.

"No, I'm not."

"Yes, you are."

"Is he, like, all about himself?"

"No." I sigh and turn my gaze back on the utter blueness of the lake in front of us. "Marshall's very polite. Kind. Successful, but definitely not snobbish. I don't know, Shel. I just felt nothing when I was with him. Shouldn't I feel *something* when I meet a guy and I'm wondering if we're meant to be together?"

"I suppose."

"Didn't you sense something special about Eric when you first met him?"

"Well, no, not exactly. We met at a faculty meeting. He stepped on my foot when he was trying to maneuver himself into the chair next to mine."

"So he sat next to you?"

"It was the only chair left."

"And I guess there were no fireworks when he stepped on your foot?"

Shelby laughs. "No. Not really."

"So when did the fireworks show up?"

Shelby is now studying the water, just like I am. "I don't know. It just happened."

We are quiet for a moment.

"I've got to find a way to tell Ramsey what I meant by that touch on his shoulder." I am talking more to myself than to Shelby. "I think it really bothered him."

"Well, it shouldn't have. He should thank you, that's what he should do. He should thank you for putting that—what do you call her?"

"The Horn Blower."

"For putting that Horn Blower in her place." Shelby turns to me. "So what *did* you mean by that touch on his shoulder?"

I sit up in my beach chair. "For heaven's sake, Shel, I didn't *mean* anything. I just didn't want her thinking that she still has some sort of stranglehold on him, and that other women don't naturally find him desirable, and that Ramsey is still pining away after her. I didn't want her thinking those things."

"Oh."

We are quiet for a second or two.

"Why don't you want her thinking he's still pining away after her?" Shelby says, her brow furrowed under her blue-hued sunglasses.

"Because he's not!"

"Oh."

Silence.

"So why do you care what she thinks?" Shelby asks.

I have no idea. "Are you purposely trying to annoy me?"

"Of course not. Just wondering what you're thinking."

"I don't know what I'm thinking."

"I know what *I'm* thinking."

"Hush up, Shelby."

"You like him."

"Be quiet."

"I think it's great that you like him."

"I don't want to talk about this. We're getting burned. We should go." I stand up and yank my beach chair out of the sand. Shelby makes a fuss over the little shower of sand that lands on her arms and legs.

"Sorry."

"There's nothing wrong with liking him, Daisy."

"Well, what's right about it? He won't talk to me."

Shelby stands up, too, and gently pulls her own beach chair out of the sand. "Then *you* talk to *him*."

I get back to The Finland and try to heed Shelby's advice. But Ramsey is gone when I arrive. I find Father Laurent in the care of my mom and L'Raine.

"It's not so bad," he says when I sink into his couch and ask how he is. He's reclining in his big chair. He face is wan. A cup of water is by his side but nothing else.

"So you're feeling crummy?" I ask. Dumb question, but I ask anyway. It's obvious he's not feeling particularly perky.

"I'm not going to race you down the stairs," he quips. "The doctor said this would take the wind out of my sails. He wasn't kidding."

"Can I get you something to eat?"

He shakes his head.

"We've been trying all afternoon to get him to eat something," L'Raine calls out from the kitchen. "We're making tapioca. Home-made. With real vanilla."

"Tapioca sounds good," I offer.

Father Laurent makes a face. "Nothing sounds good. But I'll try to eat it."

I pat his arm and he looks up at me. "Did you talk to Ramsey?" he whispers.

I shake my head. "He's been avoiding me, I think."

"He's been worried about me. And Liam left this morning for Mexico. He's had a lot on his mind."

"Sure. Of course he has."

"Don't give up on him, Daisy," he says, in a still softer voice.

This request catches me off guard completely. I wonder if Father Laurent knows who has given up on whom. I don't feel like the one who has written someone off. It feels like quite the opposite.

"Daisy?"

"I think he may have given up on *me,* Father."

"Don't let him."

"Father, I don't know that I…" but I don't finish. L'Raine appears from the kitchen with a little bowl and a spoon in her hands. My mother is following her.

"Warm tapioca, Father Laurent. The best kind of comfort food."

"You ladies are too good to me." He catches my eye and grins.

"Daisy." My mother is looking at my unsleeved arms. "You're sunburned."

I glance down at my shoulders. "Just a little."

"You should go put something on it or you'll blister."

I stand. "Goodbye, Father Laurent."

"See you later?"

"Sure."

His eyes follow me out the door.

Ramsey returns just before twilight but heads straight for his dad's apartment.

I consider walking up to the door, knocking, and asking him when he opens it if I can speak to him.

But I picture him saying no and it's easy to talk myself out of it.

Asking to speak to a man and then having him turn you down is a tad too much like being snubbed and I'm just not in the mood for it.

Instead, I invite Maria Andrea over to watch *Thirteen Going on Thirty.* We have a good laugh over the irony of it. I'm going on thirty, she's going on thirteen.

There's a tiny bit of a wedding in that movie. It's toward the end, when Jennifer Garner's character realizes she can't be with the man she really loves because she waited too long to get her act together and he's about to marry someone else. It's a scene to make you cry.

So we do.

When Andrea leaves to go back to her aunt and uncle's, I have an itching desire to sneak up to the roof and look at it in the moonlight. But there's the slight possibility that I will meet Ramsey in the third-floor hallway. And I'm in my pj's. I chicken out.

For the first time in many months, Rosalina and Mario aren't having Sunday dinner at their apartment. They are attending another niece's *quinceañera* in Apple Valley.

It's Sunday afternoon and I don't know what I'm going to do with myself. Mom and L'Raine are at a friend's house playing bridge. Max is with Bettina. Wendy and Philip are on vacation in the Boundary Waters. Solomon is gone, too. I've no idea where. The Finland is empty except for me, Father Laurent, and Ramsey.

I spend the better part of the day working up the courage to speak to Ramsey.

I'm not entirely sure what I'm going to say. Something like, "Ramsey, about me touching you on the shoulder like that. I just want you to know it was because I was eavesdropping and I heard Kristen..." No. "I just want you to know I wasn't trying to come on to you..." No, no, no. "I just wanted her to feel sorry she had treated you so bad because I got dumped once, too..."

A thousand times no.

There's really nothing I can say except that I'm sorry.

And then wait to see if he tells me there's no need to say that.

At a little after eight, just before sundown, I timidly head to the third floor. When I reach the top step, I see Ramsey disappearing through the doorway to the roof access.

Good. At least now I won't have to *ask* to speak to him. I can go out on the roof, pretend I came to see how the work is progressing, and oh, by the way, Ramsey, about the other day…

I head toward the door to the roof. When I am just in front of it, with my hand on the knob, it flies open. I step backward to avoid getting hit and nearly fall over. Ramsey's eyes are wide as he reaches out to steady me. In his other hand he has a pair of sunglasses—the reason, I am guessing, he was on the roof for less than a minute.

"Daisy. I didn't see you!"

His hand is on my elbow, holding me steady as I get my balance back. His touch is gentle but secure.

"I'm all right," I mutter.

He pulls his hand away. "Were you going out onto the roof?"

"No. Yes. I mean—yes I wanted to see how you're coming along."

"Right now? It's almost dark."

"Well, I just…I…" It's no good. I can't lie to him. "Actually, Ramsey, I was coming to apologize to you."

He just stares at me for a moment. "Apologize?"

"If I offended you on the roof the other day when the…when Kristen was here, I apologize. It wasn't my intention."

"Your intention."

"I…" I stop and look at him. What exactly does he mean by echoing me like that? "I'm sorry if I offended you."

"Yes. You said that."

Oh, Lord, help, help, help. What am I doing wrong here?

"*Did* I offend you?" I try to keep my voice steady, but I don't think I'm successful.

"You surprised me."

"Look, Ramsey. I heard what Kristen said. I shouldn't have listened to your conversation with her, but I did. Something in me just snapped. I just felt like showing her that you are just fine without her. I should've minded my own business, but honestly I kind of know how you feel. That's why I did it. I'm sorry."

I can't read anything in his expression. It's like he hasn't heard a word I've said.

"Don't worry about it," Ramsey turns and starts to walk away from me.

I stand there by the door to the roof watching him.

He stops after a few steps, turns, and nods towards the roof. "I'll be finished tomorrow." Then he resumes his march to Father Laurent's door.

"I said I was sorry!" I call out.

He turns. "And I said don't worry about it."

Ramsey opens Father's door, steps inside, and it closes behind him. The Finland suddenly seems as still as a tomb.

FIFTY

Rosalina is proud of our joint effort, I can tell. She is beaming as she looks at Elisabeth Erdahl's dress. The crushed fabric and lace have been reborn. The wrinkles are gone. The tulle petticoat has been replaced. A crisp hem lines the bottom. The gown looked sallow and lifeless before our hard work. Now it breathes creamy-white elegance.

"You were right," I tell her.

"Of course I was."

"It's a beautiful dress.'

"*Sí.*"

I toy with the little blue heart in my fingers, wondering if it's too brash of me to go up to Father Laurent's and ask the ailing man to bless it so Rosalina can sew it into Elisabeth's dress.

I'm not unaware there's a little blue heart just like it in my pants pocket. The one Father Laurent blessed just for me last month. I feel like pulling it out when I go upstairs and asking him to up his blessing to an extra-strength dose.

I don't feel particularly favored at the moment.

I tell Rosalina I'll be right back.

I walk out of the alterations apartment and head up the stairs. The third-floor hallway is quiet. Max is working at his parents' studio. Solomon is giving violin lessons at a parochial school like he does every Monday. Wendy and Philip are still on vacation.

I inhale and exhale before knocking on Father Laurent's door.

When it opens I plaster a polite smile on my face in case Ramsey is there to greet me.

But it's L'Raine on the other side of the door.

"Hello, Daisy. Come to visit the patient?"

"L'Raine. What are you doing here?"

She steps aside and lets me in. "I'm Florence Nightingale today. Ramsey is finishing the roof and I told him I'd keep an eye on his dad and tidy up a bit. You know how bachelors are."

L'Raine closes the door behind me. "He's in the living room." She disappears into the kitchen. I step into the main room. Father Laurent is on the couch today, reading the newspaper. He looks tired.

"Good morning, Daisy."

"Good morning, Father. How are you feeling today?"

"A little tired, a little dull. The doctor said to expect it. It's not unbearable. How are you?"

I sink into the chair next to him, the chair he usually sits in. "All right."

"No, you're not." His tone is gentle.

I don't say anything as I lift and lower my shoulders.

"Did you talk to him?"

"Kind of."

"Kind of?"

"I tried to apologize but he just said not to worry about it. Like it was no big deal."

Father Laurent rubs his chin with his hand. He is thinking. "Do you believe it was no big deal?"

"I didn't mean for it to be a big deal. But I think it was. I think it was a big deal. To both of us."

"Let me talk to him, Daisy."

"Please don't, Father. He'll know I've been talking to you about him. I don't think that would go over very well. Please, don't."

He says nothing for a moment. "I hear Reuben's coming out to see the garden."

"Yes. Tomorrow. But Ramsey doesn't have to move out. Reuben said he'd get a hotel room."

"Yes. Your mother mentioned that. But Ramsey doesn't like the idea. I think he's planning on leaving later today, Daisy."

If Father Laurent is trying to give me advice, I'm not sure what it is.

"What should I do?" I whisper.

"Everything your heart tells you," he whispers back.

"But I don't know what it's saying."

"Yes, you do."

I hear L'Raine opening and closing cupboards in the kitchen. She is humming.

For a moment we are both quiet. Then I show him the little blue heart in my hand.

"Miss your day job?" I ask.

"As a matter of fact, I do." His smile is wide and genuine. "Want to tell me about this one?"

"There is a hundred-year-old dress downstairs that belonged to a mail-order bride. She didn't know the man she married, but she woke up one morning many months after her wedding and realized she was deeply in love with him and had been for quite some time. And she wasn't even aware of when she had fallen for him. Her granddaughter wrote me and told me she never saw two people more in love than her grandparents."

Father Laurent smiles. "That's a lovely story." He takes the heart from me in one hand and covers it with another. Then he begins to whisper a prayer of consecration. I don't catch every word. I hear little snippets.

Love.

Affection.

Devotion.

Trust.

Blessing.

Father Laurent smiles and hands the little heart back to me.

L'Raine sails into the living room. "Tea, Daisy?"

"No, thanks. I've got things to take care of." I stand, lean over Father Laurent, and kiss his forehead. "Take it easy."

"See you later, Daisy."

I leave as L'Raine bustles about the living room, straightening the sections of the newspaper and chattering to Father Laurent about an article she read in *Reader's Digest*.

I tuck Elisabeth's heart in my back pocket. Mine is in my front pocket.

I head for the roof.

I've been stealing looks at the roof all along, so it's not like I'm surprised by what I see when I take the stairs to the top of The Finland and gaze out over all that Ramsey has done.

Perhaps it's my knowing the garden is finished that makes me step back in awe. Or that it's so beautiful and peaceful. Or that it was Ramsey who created it.

I walk the stone pathway that circles the roof like the infinity sign, finding my Adirondack chairs at the intersection of the loops. Ramsey has an open toolbox on one of them. I don't see him at first. All I see are the colors of Eden. Green, lavender, white, yellow, pink, pale blue. It's hard to think of this masterpiece as being merely a utility to keep storm water from overflowing the gutters and storm sewers.

I step around the circling shrubs and I finally see Ramsey kneeling at the far end of the roof, pulling off a dead branch.

I approach quietly. He doesn't hear me.

"Hello, Ramsey." I hope I don't startle him.

He snaps his head around. "Oh. Hi."

He stands and brushes his hands against his jeans. "I was just about to come down and get you."

"Really?"

"Yes. I'm done. I wanted you to see it before I head back to Duluth."

"You're going back?"

"The owner is coming, I hear. He'll be needing his apartment. And Dad seems to be tolerating his radiation treatment. I can check in with him by phone. So, does it meet with your approval?"

I know he's talking about the garden. But I want to shout that no, this does not meet with my approval.

"The garden is absolutely beautiful, Ramsey." My throat feels sticky.

"I'm glad you like it." His voice has taken on an impersonal, professional tone. "I've gone over the general maintenance with Mario. He's all set to manage the plantings. But I'll be back once a month to check on things, as I said in my proposal. And I might bring a prospective client by to see it from time to time, if that's all right."

"Of course it's all right."

"Great. Well, then. I'll get my things together and get out of your way."

He starts to walk past me and I reach out to touch him. "Ramsey, you're not in my way."

Ramsey looks down at my hand on his arm. I let it fall away.

"The project is finished. Dad's doing all right. It's time for me to go home." He continues on his way. I follow him.

"Ramsey, I don't want you to leave like this."

"Like what?" He keeps walking.

"You're mad at me!"

"I'm not mad at you." He doesn't turn around.

We are now at the intersection of the loops. Right by my Adirondack chairs.

"Will you please at least tell me what it is that I've done? Please? What is it that I have done that has so offended you?"

He turns then, just his head and torso. "You've done nothing to *me*."

Before I can mentally process this, Ramsey continues on his way, past the chairs, to the other end of the roof where the stair access is. He disappears down the stairwell. I hear the door open and shut.

Stunned is a pretty good word for what I'm feeling right now.

Why in the world would I be attracted to a man who clearly dislikes me? It defies explanation.

All I did was touch his shoulder.

Yes, it was in front of his ex-wife. But it was just a touch.

How could that have been so repulsive to him?

I can't recall ever disappointing anyone as much as I've apparently disappointed Ramsey Laurent.

I should be insulted. I should be mad at him. I should just write him off.

But I can't. I want his forgiveness.

The air around me is moist, and a light, humid breeze is tugging at the little branches of my new shrubs. A bird has landed on a bush next to me. She chirps now as if to thank me for giving her such a nice place to hang out.

Oh, to be a bird without a care in the world.

I glance down and notice Ramsey's toolbox on the chair next to me. He will be back for it before he leaves.

A thought occurs to me as I sit there staring at it.

I reach into my front pocket and pull out the little heart Father Laurent blessed for me. The one he had been keeping in his own pocket for Ramsey.

I hold it between my fingers. "I'm sorry, I'm sorry," I whisper over it. Just saying the words makes my eyes sting. I'm not even sure what it is I have done. But Father Laurent told me to follow my heart's leading. In my heart I know I have somehow deeply offended Ramsey. And I hate it that I have.

I lean over to the other chair and tuck the little heart inside the toolbox. I close it shut and place my hand over the top of it.

What else can I do, Lord. What else can I do?

FIFTY-ONE

Dear Harriet,

I've never really thought of myself as an unlikable person. I know I'm not perfect. I've got flaws just like everyone else. But I've never had anyone truly dislike me for no apparent reason. At least no reason that I can see.

Yes, there were those mean girls in junior high who made fun of the fact that my parents were as old as their grandparents. But that never felt very personal. I was embarrassed and a little peeved, but I didn't take it as an insult against my person.

But this thing with Ramsey. It makes my head spin.

Can you honestly still question me about whether or not I'm falling for the wrong man?

You want me to define "wrong"?

Okay, I will.

"Wrong" means I am drawn to a guy who doesn't like being in the same room with me, doesn't like talking to me, won't be honest with me, and can't wait to get away from me. Falling in love with a guy like that is falling in love with the wrong guy. I should be falling in love with the guy who does like talking to me, who does want to be in the same room with me, and who doesn't keep things from me. That's the kind of man to fall in love with.

What on earth did Ramsey mean by, "You did nothing to me?"

Who did I offend if it wasn't him?

I can't believe having his forgiveness means so much to me.

I'm watching Father of the Bride, *but I'm going to turn it off.*

I miss my dad.

Dear Daisy,

There is no way to know what Ramsey meant by what he said unless you ask him. I doubt that it means whatever you did doesn't matter to him personally. It's hard to be mad at someone whose actions mean nothing to you.

I know you miss your dad.

Harriet

FIFTY-TWO

Reuben arrived a little before eleven in a rented black Lexus. He's looking well. His first order of business was to say hello to my mother.

They embraced like two long-lost friends. He told her how beautiful she looks. She told him he needs bifocals. They laughed.

Then he turned to me. "Daisy, I caught a glance of the roof from the street and I can't wait to see it. Where's the architect?"

I had to tell Reuben that the architect went home to Duluth.

"What for? Didn't you tell him I'd be getting a hotel room?"

"Yes, Reuben. I told him."

"Well, call him up. Tell him to come back down here. I want to meet him. I've got some buildings on the East Coast I want to talk to him about. See if he can come back tomorrow afternoon. I've got some business to take care of in the morning."

"Sure, Reuben, I'll call him."

I took Reuben up to see the rooftop first, though, and he was genuinely amazed. Mom and L'Raine came up with us. Father Laurent wanted to join us, too but was feeling woozy. He asked me to stop by later.

I know what he'll want to talk about.

After being completely wowed by the roof, Reuben invited my mom, L'Raine, and me out to lunch.

L'Raine declined and I don't have much of an appetite.

So my mom and Reuben left. That was fifteen minutes ago. I am sitting now at my desk contemplating the phone call I must make. L'Raine has gone up to check on Father Laurent and make him lunch. The sales floor is quiet.

I pick up the phone.

I wonder if Ramsey has found the little blue heart in his toolbox.

I press the numbers to his cell phone.

It rings and I tell myself to breathe normally.

When I'm connected to his voice mail, I'm alternately relieved and disappointed. I clear my throat to leave a message:

"Hello, Ramsey. It's Daisy. Reuben Tarter, the owner of the building, is here and he wants to meet you. He really likes the garden and he wants to talk with you about some buildings he owns on the East Coast. He wants to know if you can come by tomorrow afternoon. Hope that works okay for you. You can stay here overnight if you want. Reuben's got a hotel room downtown. Well. Bye."

Click.

That's that.

I stand up and head back out onto the sales floor. My eyes are drawn to the display window, where my wedding dress hangs on a headless mannequin.

On impulse, I walk over to it and touch the billowing skirt. It makes a tiny shushing sound. The woman who made this dress died three months after I was supposed to get married. It was the last dress she made. She was seventy-eight. She told me once that she had made more than a hundred-fifty wedding dresses in her years as a dress-maker and that mine had been her favorite.

Her favorite.

The little bell attached to the front door rings and I turn away from the dress I know I will never wear.

⌒∞⌒

Ramsey never returns my call. I guess I'm not surprised. Reuben assumes that since he hasn't called back by the end of the business day to say he can't come, that means he will.

"Let's go Italian for dinner, shall we?" Reuben announces just as I'm closing the store.

"I'm up for it," Mom answers. "How about you, L'Raine?"

"Well, should we leave Miles alone?" L'Raine asks.

I really don't want to go out. I offer to make something for Father Laurent's supper.

"We won't be gone long," Mom assures me as they head out the front door. I lock it behind them and turn out the lights.

I had been up earlier in the day to see Father Laurent but he had been sleeping. I know he wants to know how I left things with Ramsey. I feel sad that I have so little to tell him.

I tap lightly on his front door and wait for him to call me in. He's at his computer, which is a good sign.

"Feeling better?" I ask.

"Oh, not too bad. As long as I don't move around too much, I'm okay, I think."

"Well, I'm your dinner date tonight, Father. Mom and L'Raine went out to eat with Reuben."

"I'm not terribly hungry, Daisy." He sits back in his computer chair.

"How about just some pancakes, then?"

"Sure," he says with a shrug.

As I busy myself with Bisquick and a griddle, Father Laurent makes his way slowly into the kitchen and sits down at the table. He doesn't ask about Ramsey. He asks about me.

"Are you all right, Daisy?"

"Oh, as long as I don't move around too much, I'm okay."

He smiles at my little joke. Then he says, "You know, I have to constantly remind myself that there is a love that is perfect, undying, and that never disappoints."

I whisk the batter with a wooden spoon, churning the lumps of powder into smooth uniformity.

"And where, may I ask, do we find that?" I don't mean to sound cynical. I hope it doesn't sound that way. It's an honest question.

"I've already told you. You already possess it. You've forgotten, Daisy!" Father Laurent leans forward in his chair. "It's the love God gives you to give away. Don't tell me you've lost that little blue heart I gave you?"

I stop my stirring and a little mirthless laugh escapes me.

"I haven't lost it, Father. I just don't have it anymore."

"You don't?" He is adequately surprised.

"No."

"Well, where is it?"

"I snuck it inside Ramsey's toolbox the day he left."

Father Laurent sits back in his chair, wordless.

I awake on the morning of my thirtieth birthday with a slight headache. I try to chase it away with a strong pot of coffee, but it doesn't want to leave.

Max stops by on his way to work to wish me a happy birthday and to give me a present: a hummingbird feeder for the new and improved roof.

When I get downstairs to Something Blue, Mom and L'Raine have decorated my desk with streamers and placed balloon heads on all the headless mannequins. The balloons have all been painted with smiling faces. They all look like they're lottery winners.

Shelby arrives minutes later with a box of Krispy Kreme dough-nuts and an offer I can't refuse: a day out with her at Nicollet Mall, where we can shop and eat and stroll to our heart's content.

It's a nice way to spend my birthday and it gets me out of The Finland and my monotonous life.

We leave a little before ten in the morning and we don't return until after four o'clock. Ramsey has been by already to discuss the green roof and other projects Reuben has in mind.

My mother makes it a point to tell me he seemed like he was looking for me.

I find that a little hard to believe.

She also tells me Ramsey said he has some appointments in Minneapolis but wants to swing by later to check on his dad before he heads back to Duluth.

I will probably miss that appearance, too, since we are all headed to Ping's for my birthday. All of us except for L'Raine. She has offered to stay behind with Father Laurent, though he fussed about this. I'll bring them home all the leftovers.

Dinner is wonderful—the food, that is. So is the company. Reuben can be quite funny. He's been everywhere and has a story to tell about every place he's been. And I think he's finally winning my mother's heart after all these years. I can't say I blame my mother for showing interest in Reuben. Dad has been gone nearly five years. It's actually a treat to see the two of them having so much fun together. For some reason it doesn't grate on me that she is finally yielding to Reuben's affections. I think my father, if he could do so, would approve. I don't think he would want my mother to spend the rest of her earthly days alone. That's the kind of man he was.

We get back to The Finland a little before nine.

Ramsey's car is in the parking lot.

While everyone else heads upstairs or home, I make my way to Something Blue. I won't run into Ramsey there. I can spend the last few hours of my thirtieth birthday in the quiet solitude of my boutique.

It's a tad spooky fiddling around in the store in semi-darkness. I have only a few lights on so as not to attract attention from the street, and my mannequins still have their merry balloon heads taped to their necks. They look a little eerie.

To calm myself, I begin to hum some of my dad's favorite songs. I am straightening gowns on their hangers and am halfway through

"Someone to Watch Over Me" when I hear a noise from behind. I turn around to see Ramsey walking toward me. He stops when he's a few feet from me. He holds out his hand, palm up. A little blue heart rests there.

"Is this yours?"

That niggling headache I had earlier rushes to the front of my skull. I stare at the little heart while my pulse does a little dance in my veins. "Not anymore."

"You put it in my toolbox?"

"Yes."

"Why?"

Pounding head, pounding pulse, pounding, pounding.

"Because I wanted you to have it."

Ramsey just stands there with the little heart on his open palm and says nothing.

"I know you told me I did nothing to offend you, but I'm not stupid, Ramsey. I know I've disappointed you in some terrible way. And I wanted you to know I was sorry. I'd like your forgiveness, too, if that's not too much to ask. I really am very, very sorry."

His eyes stay on mine. I try very hard not to look away. "You don't even know what you're apologizing for, do you?"

Now I'm the one just standing here, saying nothing.

"Do you ever *think* about what you're doing, Daisy? Do you ever stop and think about the people who will be affected by what you do? Do you honestly think you can do whatever you want, regardless of how it will affect other people?"

Dazed and confused doesn't begin to describe me. I manage to whisper a single question. "What are you talking about?"

"I'm talking about people who take great risks in loving other people. How can you so easily cheapen what that means?"

Words fail me. All I can say is, "Ramsey, I don't know what you are talking about."

His countenance falls as he looks at me. The angry edge fades away. "No, I don't suppose you do."

Ramsey places the little blue heart on the show table to his right, turns, and walks away.

The door closes softly behind him and I can do nothing but stand there in a sea of wedding dresses, staring at my little blue heart on the table.

FIFTY-THREE

Dear Harriet,

I should be mad.

I should be upset.

I should be indignant.

But I'm not any of those things. Honestly, I am sitting here in my apartment in the middle of the night, awake, unable to sleep, and what I am feeling is longing. I long for Ramsey. I long for him to be at peace.

Am I insane?

Is it completely unreasonable that all I want to do is wrap my arms around him and hold him until it stops? Until the hurt inside him stops?

Tell me I'm not being unreasonable.

He has somehow misunderstood me completely. I've no idea how to make him understand. And his words cut me deep.

And yet I ache for him.

Tell me I'm not crazy.

Dear Daisy,

You are not crazy.

You just love him, warts and all.

And that kind of love is the most reasonable thing there is.

Harriet

FIFTY-FOUR

Wendy and Philip have returned from the Boundary Waters. They came in late last night. I actually heard them on the stairs at two a.m. Not because they were being noisy but because I was still awake.

It's a little after nine now and Wendy is in my office to tell me she hears the noises again in her bathroom. She doesn't look particularly well.

"You're home early. Are you okay?"

"No, I must be coming down with something. I feel rotten. So are you going to come listen to this noise, Daisy? I heard it just now."

"Actually, Max heard it, too, while you were gone. He brought me up to his place for a listen. And I did hear it in his bathroom. We think it might be bats in between the walls."

"Bats! I hate bats!"

"Yes, but they're in between the walls. They're not exactly inside your apartment."

"Well, they might as well be!"

"Mario is looking into it, okay? He's trying to find out where they're getting in. When he does, he'll plug it up."

"How long will that take?"

"I really don't know, Wendy. I'm sure it won't take long."

"All right, I guess."

"You should go take a peek at the garden on the roof, Wendy. Ramsey finished it. It's just lovely."

"Maybe later. I don't feel that great."

She turns and heads out of my office. Just the mention of the garden fills me with a yearning to head to the roof and absorb its beauty into my weary body.

Mom is ready to open the store, when I tell her I am going to get another cup of coffee from my apartment and a few rays of sunshine from my roof.

She waves at me.

A few minutes later, cup in hand, I head to the third floor. Ramsey stayed here last night at Reuben's request. Mom told me this morning that Reuben is taking Ramsey to meet some friends of his here in the Twin Cities who own downtown property. He's got several business acquaintances who are interested in Ramsey's green roofs. It could turn out to be a very profitable few days for Ramsey. I'm happy for him, of course.

I'm surprisingly not afraid to go to the third floor. I'm not afraid of running into Ramsey, but I hope I don't. I have no idea what I will say to him if I do. It seems like whenever I open my mouth, I say the wrong thing. When I pass the door to the apartment where he's staying, I run my hand across the door in a silent prayer for him.

The morning sun on the roof is exuberant and my Adirondack chairs are warm to the touch. I ease down into one and drink in the splendor around me. The little blue heart is back in my pocket, where I guess it belongs.

A bird chirps nearby. The fragrance of soft blooms scents the air. I can nearly smell the color green. This will be the one lovely moment of my day.

At least there will be this.

It's not easy to stay focused on wedding dresses today. Not easy by a long shot. Ramsey and Reuben are gone most of the morning and into the afternoon. I don't actually see either one of them. Ramsey, I'm sure, won't step into Something Blue unless he absolutely has to. And Reuben isn't exactly staying at The Finland. Sometime before five, L'Raine comes back down to the store after checking on Father Laurent and tells me Ramsey has returned and Mom has left to go have dinner with Reuben. L'Raine gives me a concerned look.

"Daisy, you look so tired. Let me close up the store, dear. You look absolutely bushed."

"Do I?"

"Yes, you do. Go."

She shoos me away and I don't argue with her. I head up the stairs with not much spring in my step.

I put a kettle on when I get to my apartment and change into a pink cotton sundress that makes me feel feminine and lovely when I wear it.

I want to keep a positive attitude about the ways things have transpired but I can feel the loneliness creeping in. Max has Bettina. Shelby has Eric. Wendy has Philip. Mario has Rosalina. I'm beginning to think Mom has Reuben.

I turn the kettle off. I don't want tea. I don't know what I want.

God, speak to me. Speak to me.

I lean against the wall to my kitchen and close my eyes, waiting for my Deliverer. Seconds later I hear the sound of music. Violin and piano. I recognize the tune at once and it fills me with longing. An aria from Handel's *Messiah*. "He Shall Feed His Flock Like a Shepherd." Dad loved this piece. It was always his favorite part of the entire oratorio, so it was always mine, too. The mere sound of these notes traveling through my head and heart fill me with memories both tender and bittersweet. It's almost like the sound of an answered prayer.

I open my front door and the music weaves its way in. I step out and follow its source to the third floor. Solomon's door is open and the music is flowing out of it. I tiptoe in as if under a spell. Wendy and Philip are sitting on Solomon's couch, drawn from next door by the beauty of the music. Father Laurent is there, too.

Ramsey is at the piano. Solomon is standing next to him, his violin playing the soprano solo line. It's so beautiful…

Father Laurent sees me come in but I'm barely aware he has noticed. I lean back against the wall of Solomon's living room and let the music fall across me. I hear the words that no one is singing. Such beautiful words…

Come unto Him all ye that labour
Come unto Him, that are heavy laden
And He will give you rest.
Take His yoke upon you, and learn of Him
For He is meek and lowly of heart
And ye shall find rest,
And ye shall find rest unto your souls.

I've never really noticed how much this song sounds like a love song. The melody, the lilting meter, the faultless choice of key—all of it is a love song heralding the love of all loves. Perfect and endless and too beautiful for words. It pours into my empty heart and I can barely stand it. This is what Father Laurent was trying to remind me of. This is that love he spoke of, the love that completes me and gives rest unto my soul. It's the love that says I am precious, chosen, and worth dying for. The love that all little girls dream of having.

I'm not aware when I start to weep. I only know that suddenly the room is quiet, the piece is over, I am crying, and all eyes are on me. Wendy, Philip, Solomon—they all look at me like I've gone mad. Father Laurent's expression is one of absolute concern. Ramsey is staring at me, too. I cannot describe his expression other than to say it is annoyed amazement.

I run from the room.

❦

There is only one place to run to.

The chapel.

The store is closed when I burst inside it. L'Raine has gone upstairs, thank goodness. I dash for the chapel door, yank it open, and slam it shut. I lean my back against the door and wait for the sounds of pursuit. But only one person in that apartment would think to find me here.

And Father Laurent does not come.

I hold my breath and wait but I hear nothing.

No one is coming.

I stumble toward the altar and let myself collapse upon it. The tears keep coming. They seem to be coming from everywhere. From every hurting place I've ever known.

They probably sound like tears of despair but this is not what they feel like. They feel like tears of release. Painful, but not unbearable. Agonizing but not entirely unwelcome. And I just let them come. Half of me aches over loving a man who does not love me. Again.

The other half is in renewed awe at being the beloved of God himself. Again and again and again.

When at last my sobs have quieted, I just lay there in the peaceful quiet of that lovely, holy room.

Alone, but not alone.

FIFTY-FIVE

In my dream, my father is standing over me. I am seated at his piano and he is right behind me. I place my fingers over the keys and press them down, but there is no sound. I press harder. Nothing.

"I can't get it to play, Dad!"

He touches me on the shoulder. "Daisy?"

I bang my fingers on the keys. There is no sound.

"It won't play!"

"Daisy?"

Daisy.

My eyes fly open. There is no piano. My father vanishes. Ramsey is kneeling beside me on the altar. It is his hand on my shoulder, not my dad's. He was the one saying my name.

I sit up in one swift movement, every fiber in me at alert. I had been asleep. Why am I in the chapel? What's going on?

Then I remember.

I turn to Ramsey and his eyes no longer resemble cold metal. They have grown soft. He looks as though he may have been crying, too. I reach out my hand to touch his face. And he meets my hand with his.

Am I still dreaming?

"Daisy, I've been looking for you everywhere."

Am I awake? I look at my watch on my other hand to get my bearings. I had only been asleep for twenty minutes. It seems like so much longer.

"I'm so sorry," Ramsey says.

I know what he has said. I understand those three words. But my mind seems fuzzy with remnants of sleep. I don't know why he is apologizing. "What?" I whisper.

"I'm so sorry."

I pull my hand out of his to brush hair away from my face. Confusion is settling over me like a too-thick blanket. I feel less awake, not more.

"Daisy, I didn't know."

His face is bent close to mine; his eyes are searching for mine. I let my eyes meet his.

"What? What didn't you know?" I ask.

He closes his eyes and sighs like he's disgusted with himself. "Anything. I didn't know anything." He opens them again. "I assumed all the wrong things."

"About what?"

"About you."

"I don't understand." Truer words were never spoken. I'm absolutely clueless.

He exhales. "I thought you were seeing Max."

Max?

Max?

"I thought he was your boyfriend. Liam made it seem like he was and I—"

"Liam?"

"Yes, Liam. He made it seem like Max was your boyfriend. And I saw you two going places together. You were together at the hospital with Dad. He went with you and your friend to the lake over the Fourth. And sometimes you'd be at his apartment. I just assumed you were his girlfriend."

"But Max is like a brother to me. He *has* a girlfriend."

"I know, I know. But that's what I *thought*. When you touched me, when Kristen was there on the roof and you reached out and touched me, I...my first thought was, I liked it. I wanted you to touch me like that. I had been wanting it. I wanted it when I first saw you in the airport helping that woman with her bags, and then again when I saw how you cared for my father, and then again when you were singing to yourself on the roof. But you were Max's girlfriend. And I was thinking you shouldn't touch a man like that if you were seeing someone else. And then when that other guy showed up to take you out for coffee, all I could think of was, Max doesn't deserve for you to treat him like that. To flirt with me and then to go have coffee with another man. I had it totally wrong."

My mouth is open and no words are coming out. His words are buzzing around in my head, pinging like they are electrically charged: *I wanted you to touch me like that. I wanted you to touch me like that.*

"Daisy, I didn't know that other guy was some blind date your mom was trying to set you up with. I didn't know Max was just a childhood friend. I didn't know you had been hurt like I had been hurt. That you knew how hard it has been for me to get my life back."

"Your father told you about Daniel."

"Yes, he told me. After you ran from Solomon's apartment, he asked me what it was I had done. I told him he should be asking *you* that. He got angry and told me to come back to his apartment. So I followed him over and started telling him what you were doing to Max. I told him I hadn't said anything to him before because he thought so highly of you and I didn't want him to know what you were doing. That's when he told me how wrong I was. About everything."

I feel my face growing warm. The heat of embarrassment can take the chill right out of air-conditioned air. "He told you everything?"

Again I sense Ramsey searching to make eye contact but I can't look at him. "He told me you were engaged last year. That your fiancé broke off your engagement ten days before your wedding. That you opened this store to try and sell your wedding dress. And that you still have it."

Yep, that would be about everything.

"I know why you did what you did on the roof." His face is still very close to mine. "You knew what I had been through."

My eyes are growing misty again. I raise them to meet Ramsey's gaze. His eyes look glassy, too. "I didn't want her to think she still had power over you," I whisper. "I didn't want *you* to think she still had power over you."

Ramsey takes my hand again. "And that's exactly what happened, Daisy. When you touched me and I looked up at you, I knew she didn't anymore. That's when I knew."

Something magical *had* passed between us. "That's when I knew it, too," I murmur. "That I didn't love Daniel anymore."

"But I thought you belonged to Max and it about drove me crazy that I was still attracted to you. I kept telling myself it wasn't right to feel that way about you. Of all people, I *knew* that. And when I saw in your eyes that you felt something for me, too, I just got angry. I started thinking of Kristen and how she let herself get swept away. I'm so sorry, Daisy. I had it all wrong."

I finally begin to understand. "The moment before Marshall came in the store, you were going to say something to me. What was it?"

Ramsey shakes his head. "I was going to confront you. I was going to ask you what on earth were you doing, flirting with me when you belonged to Max."

"You thought I was being unfaithful to Max."

"Yes."

Ramsey still has his hand wrapped around mine. He looks down at our hands. "Daisy, my father told me you've been confiding in him about all this. That you told him you…you had feelings for me."

I swallow. "Yes. I did tell him that."

"So, is it too late?"

He's stroking my thumb.

"What?" My voice is uneven and childlike. "Too late for what?"

He lifts his head to look at me. Tears are pooling in his eyes. "Is it too late for me? For us?"

All I can do is shake my head. No. No. No.

He looks alarmed, like I am telling him no.

"It's not too late," I whisper.

Ramsey's face wrinkles into something like anguish, but I know it's not the pain of loss that is gripping him. It's the ache of finally having what you thought you never could. A tear spills over onto his cheek. I reach out to catch it and this time he doesn't stop me.

Ramsey turns his head to rest his cheek against my open palm. "When I finally understood, I thought for sure I'd lost you."

"I've been here the whole time."

He pulls my hand away and kisses my fingertips. Then he leans over, touches my face, which is wet like his, and kisses me.

And I finally understand how love can happen to you when you are busy searching for what you think matters most to you.

FIFTY-SIX

Dear Harriet,

I called Vanessa, the beautiful girl who wants my wedding dress.

It was late, a little after eight this evening, but I called her and told her she could have my wedding dress. I explained to her why I was suddenly able to sell it to her. She practically cried when I told her.

She's coming in the morning to pick it up.

Ramsey asked me, while we were still sitting on the floor of the chapel, if I thought it was too soon. He said maybe I needed to give it some time. I told him time is all I've had for the past year.

Time isn't what heals all wounds, Harriet. It's love that heals.

And I know now it wasn't the dress itself that held me prisoner. It was my yearning to be wanted, cherished, and preferred that kept me chained to those simple yards of fabric.

I suppose you're thinking it's too soon for me to know if Ramsey is the only man I will ever love. I've only known him such a short time. I can't believe he isn't, but even if you are right, even if it is too soon to know such a thing, I still can't see the value of hanging onto a dress whose meaning is slipping away like a vapor. Every day since Daniel left me, my wedding dress has represented my longing to go backward in time. That gown belongs to a dream that has been remade. I only have eyes for the future.

Vanessa will look lovely in it.

I cannot sleep. I don't want this day to end and yet I can't wait for tomorrow.

I'm surprised how I feel tonight considering that Ramsey's kisses linger on my lips and the slippery feel of his tears still tingle on my fingertips.

I feel very close to heaven. To a place of unqualified holiness and perfection. Does that make sense?

Dear Daisy,

The Voice of Reason cannot fully know what faith alone reveals, but I have to say I am reminded of that line from the movie Les Misérables. You know, that one you like so much:

> *"To love another person is to see the face of God."*

Enjoy the view.

Harriet

EPILOGUE

Someday I will have to explain to my children why I married their father after knowing him only four months. When they are young, like Liam was when I married Ramsey, they won't care. Months can seem like years to a child. But when they start to wonder about the way of love, when they start to look for that one special person they are meant to be with for all their earthly days, then I will tell them that there is no planning it. Falling in love is not something you organize and measure by the number of times the sun has gone down. Love finds you even when you aren't looking for it. Even if you are looking in the wrong place.

I will tell them that I married their father on a brilliant October day on the rooftop of the old Finland Hotel in Minneapolis, in a garden that he made the summer I met him. There were only a handful of people there, just the people I loved most in the world. Grandma Chloe and Grandpa Reuben, who were married six months after me, and Grandpa Laurent and Aunt L'Raine—whose continuing mutual admiration leads me to hope there may yet be another wedding to be planned before long. Shelby and Eric, and Uncle Max the Mad Magician and Bettina were there. And their real uncle, Kellen, and Aunt Laura and Mia. And Wendy and Philip, who were expecting their first child, and Solomon, and Mario and Rosalina. We all stood in the center of the roof where a path in the shape of an infinity knot meets itself. I'll tell them that their Grandpa Laurent married us and that he could barely get through the ceremony because of the tears that kept blinding him to the words in the little black prayer book he held in his hands. I'll show them the pictures Max took of their Uncle Kellen giving me away and I'll tell them their big brother Liam was their daddy's best man. Solomon played his violin as I walked toward their daddy on the stone pathway.

I'll tell them I wore a beautiful hundred-year-old dress that had belonged to a woman who had been a mail-order bride back when the West was untamed. I'll show them the dress and the little blue heart sewn inside, blessed by their grandpa and carried in my pocket for the many weeks I was learning what it meant to truly love someone.

I'll tell them I carried a bouquet of daisies, my father's favorite flower, and how much I wish they could've known him.

They will ask if we can go see the roof garden where I married their papa, and I will say, "Of course."

And we will drive from our house on the shore of Lake Superior to the busy Uptown street in Minneapolis where the Finland Hotel is and where Uncle Max and his wife, Bettina, still live. I'll show them the beautiful garden where I fell in love with their daddy and where he married me. I'll take them downstairs to the shop I used to own, that Bettina and Aunt L'Raine run now, and that is full of wedding dresses. I'll tell them Bettina sends a box of little blue hearts every month to Grandpa Laurent who lives in a little cabin on our property so he can bless them and send them back. And when they ask why he does that, I'll tell them that a heart is the shape of hope. And that blessings come from God alone. A blessed heart is showered with hope and the favor of God. Who doesn't want that?

Perhaps someday they will ask me when it was that I fell in love with their father. And I will tell them it happened when I really wasn't looking. When I was searching for something else entirely.

I'll tell them how our romance in some ways mirrored the love of God for us all when he plunked his plan of redemption smack-dab in the middle of a world that was only looking to get its census done right.

I'll tell them love wasn't something I fell into—it was something that covered me.

I'll tell them one moment my socks were on my feet and the next I was running barefoot.

And that in that second moment, I suddenly saw Ramsey—their daddy—running barefoot alongside. Barefoot, like me.

ACKNOWLEDGMENTS

I am profoundly grateful to the many people who helped me shape this book. These special ones include Nick Harrison, Kimberly Shumate, and Carolyn McCready at Harvest House Publishers; Don Pape, Donna Lewis, and Beth Jusino at Alive Communications; Kelly Standish at Focus On Fiction; dear writing friends and colleagues Patti Hill, Susie Larson, and Donna Fleisher; and my daughter, Stephanie Meissner.

My mother, Judy Horning, expertly read and proofed the manuscript. Thanks, Mom.

Bethany Holmen unknowingly sparked the idea for this book. On our trip to visit a dear friend in the hospital she told me she had just seen her roommate's wedding dress and it was absolutely lovely. And I in turn said, "Isn't it a shame a beautiful gown like that only gets worn once?" and "What if there was someone who wanted to give used wedding dresses a second chance? What kind of person would do that?" From that little conversation in the backseat of her parents' van, *Blue Heart Blessed* was born.

Rachel Dick loaned me her beautiful birth name, Maria Andrea, as well as her Ecuadorian heritage and the belief that any boy worthy of interest must be first and foremost *kind*—not just to her but to everyone he meets.

Hearing from readers is a tremendous joy. I'd love for you to stop by my website at www.susanlmeissner.com and click on the link to e-mail me. You'll also find discussion questions for this book and my other titles on my website.

Thank you, dear reader, for joining me here in the pages of this book. It's been grand. You are the reason I write.

May you find your heart's deepest longings met within the embrace of the Lover of your soul.

Yours,
Susan Meissner

ABOUT SUSAN MEISSNER

Susan Meissner is an award-winning newspaper columnist, pastor's wife, and author of several previous novels, including *A Seahorse in the Thames, In All Deep Places,* and *A Window to the World* (named one of the top ten Christian novels of 2005 by Booklist magazine). A mother of four, she lives in southwestern California with her husband, Bob.

Visit Susan's website: www.susanlmeissner.com

To learn more about books by Susan Meissner
or to read sample chapters, log on to our Web site:

www.harvesthousepublishers.com

HARVEST HOUSE PUBLISHERS

EUGENE, OREGON

WHY THE SKY IS BLUE

What options does a Christian woman have after she's bru-tally assaulted by a stranger…and becomes pregnant? That's the heartrending situation Claire Holland faces. Happily married and the mother of two when she is attacked, Claire begins an incredible journey on the painful pathway to trusting God "in all things."

When Claire's husband, Dan, confesses he can't be a father to the expected child, Claire's decision to put the baby up for adoption creates a sense of tremendous loss for Claire. Later, unexpected circumstances turn this seeming loss into victory.

This wonderful novel isn't a love story…but a life story, presenting the themes of trusting God in tragic circumstances and reaping the rewards that eventually come with sacrificial loving.

A WINDOW TO THE WORLD

Megan and Jen meet in first grade and quickly become insepa-rable friends. Inseparable, that is, until one of them is snatched away by kidnappers as the other young girl watches helplessly.

The remaining child grows up with the haunting memory of her friend's abduction…and absence from her life. Then, sixteen years later, the stunning truth of the disappearance is revealed. And once again, lives are changed forever.

This wonderful and heartrending novel endears the reader to every character in this intriguing story.

Named by Booklist magazine as one of the "Ten Best Christian Novels of 2005."

THE REMEDY FOR REGRET

Tess Longren is 28, single, and at a crossroads in her life. She finally has a job she enjoys as well as a proposal of marriage from a man she loves, but Tess can't seem to grasp a future filled with promise and hope. Her mother's long-ago death remains a constant, subtle ache that Tess can't seem to move past. When childhood friend Blair Holbrook asks Tess to accompany her to their childhood home to resolve a situation left unsettled 15 years ago, Tess imagines that by helping her friend find peace, she will find contentment for herself.

IN ALL DEEP PLACES

Susan Meissner explores what God does in the deep places of the human spirit in this story about acclaimed mystery writer Luke Foxbourne, who lives a happy life in a century-old manor house in Connecticut. But when his father, Jack, has a stroke, Luke returns to his hometown of Halcyon, Iowa, where he reluctantly takes the reins of his father's newspaper.

Memories of Norah—the neighbor girl who was his first kiss—cause Luke to reflect as he spends night after night alone in his childhood home. Soon he feels an uncontrollable urge to start writing a different story altogether...

A SEAHORSE IN THE THAMES

Alexa Poole's older sister, Rebecca, has lived at the Falkman Residential Center since an accident left her mentally compromised—vulnerable, innocent. Now, 17 years later, she has vanished.

As Alexa searches for Rebecca, disturbing questions surface. Why did the car that Rebecca was riding in swerve off the road killing her college friend, Leanne McNeil? And what about the mysterious check for $50,000 found in Rebecca's room that was signed by her friend's father, Gavin McNeil?

DAYS AND HOURS

A newborn is found alive in a trash bin and a young, single mother insists her baby was abducted. While St. Paul police are skeptical, attorney Rachael Flynn's strange dreams lead her to believe the mother is telling the truth. But who would steal a baby only to leave it for dead?

When the baby disappears again, Rachael agonizes over her decision to allow the baby to be returned to his mother. Did she make a terrible mistake? And where is that missing baby? Who would wish the child harm?